D0853410

History Lesson for Girls

History Lesson for Girls

AURELIE SHEEHAN | *Viking*

VIKING

Published by the Penguin Group

Penguin Group (USA) Inc., 375 Hudson Street, New York, New York 10014, U.S.A • Penguin Group
(Canada), 90 Eglinton Avenue East, Suite 700, Toronto, Ontario, Canada M4P 2Y3 (a division of Pearson
Penguin Canada Inc.) • Penguin Books Ltd, 80 Strand, London WC2R 0RL, England • Penguin
Ireland, 25 St. Stephen's Green, Dublin 2, Ireland (a division of Penguin Books Ltd) • Penguin Books
Australia Ltd, 250 Camberwell Road, Camberwell, Victoria 3124, Australia (a division of Pearson Australia
Group Pty Ltd) • Penguin Books India Pvt Ltd, 11 Community Centre, Panchsheel Park, New Delhi –
110 017, India • Penguin Group (NZ), Cnr Airborne and Rosedale Roads, Albany, Auckland 1310, New
Zealand (a division of Pearson New Zealand Ltd) • Penguin Books (South Africa) (Pty) Ltd, 24 Sturdee
Avenue, Rosebank, Johannesburg 2196, South Africa

Penguin Books Ltd, Registered Offices:
80 Strand, London WC2R 0RL, England

First published in 2006 by Viking Penguin, a member of Penguin Group (USA) Inc.

10   9   8   7   6   5   4   3   2   1

Copyright © Aurelie Sheehan, 2006
All rights reserved

ISBN 0-670-03767-2

Printed in the United States of America
Set in Granjon   Designed by Carla Bolte

For Jenny

History Lesson for Girls

Once upon a time there was a girl who lived in a small shack made from oak and maple trees, quite plentiful in Connecticut. She and her parents toiled all day making dolls out of corncobs and dyeing socks with the juice of pomegranates. They worked hard, tended to go to bed early, and had many nice family talks and nice family traditions.

The lost heroine, for that would become her name later, liked most of all to perambulate about the village—not called Weston back then, in 1776, but something quite like it, Wistin.

Chapter One

ONE DAY I saw them, our dream horses, and on that day I pulled over to the side of the road and cried. There they were, Appaloosas and roans and bays, and I thought I saw, squinting into the last bit of sunlight, a gray. All the horses moved together, a makeshift herd—maybe they'd heard my car, or maybe it was a chill, the first winter breeze, almost imperceptible on a summer day. So many years later and now here they were in front of me. The horses trembled, shifted, and then became calm and separated out again, twelve or twenty of them, more than enough for the Alison and Kate Horse Training Company.

She saved me. That's the first thing you should know about Kate. It was the year we moved to Weston, the year my parents went haywire, the year my back started curving out of control as if it were the life of the party. She was five feet seven and had long brown hair bleached by the sun, and her father was an Egyptian emperor. Was he for real? Real enough for a small suburban dynasty. Real enough to pass on a legacy.

I think of Kate all the time. I think of her like I've got this little silver Egyptian cat in my pocket, a little silver talisman that won't go away. I think of her, and then I think of him, too, Tut Hamilton, sham shaman in suburbia. I can't forget him, any more than I can forget her.

The thing is, she saved me that year, and then it was my turn. That's what friendship is. That's how to make history.

I was thirteen when my parents and I moved to the fancy town of Weston from maligned and honorable Norwalk, two towns over. We were ready for anything, ready for the good things to start happening, and the first thing that went wrong was the blue room.

Mom wanted her studio to be blue, despite the fact that most painters prefer a room absent of color, a blank wall, a clean palette. She'd had a vision, you see, a dream of a blue room.

My father offered to paint the room for her, but she would choose the color, of course. She and I went to the paint store together.

"These men—they're painting the world, creating color wheels, color contrasts, color inspirations—without any real conception, no awareness at all, of what they're doing. They could be artists—but no, *no*—instead of using these glorious choices—all the glory, all the *opportunity,* Alison—they just sit around drinking coffee out of a thermos and painting houses tan, tan, and tan again. How dreary. . . ."

She continued talking as we got out of our Corolla (it also happened to be tan) and walked the short distance from the parking lot to the shopping center. I *did* hope she'd stop, or at least lower her voice, before we got to the store. She had a way of causing a commotion, despite her size. She was a tiny, fragile person, swathed in scarves and perfumes and charms.

Men of uncertain age and weight looked our way as we came in: Scheherazade and the too tall, too bony, too elbowy stalk, in a back brace, beside her.

My mother breezed by their troubling, huntery expressions, and we settled in before the paint chips. I'd just turned thirteen, my back was curved, and my parents were curved, too—bohemians in Connecticut, the Land of Plenty. Either all the colors looked good to me or none of them did. Somehow it seemed that this, like everything else, could go either way.

Mom, however, was confident. She hummed with satisfaction, picking out various small, hopeful cards from the rack, cocking her head, pursing her lips—rejecting one, then the other, until she came to her blue.

Today they've gotten hold of Weston and thrown up these monstrous vault homes, decorated with pillars and neo-this-and-that architectural details, but in 1975 the lovely colonials were what stood out, the historic touch. Some even had plaques near the doorways saying things like PAUL REVERE SLEPT HERE IN 1782 or IN 1801, HERE STOOD WESTON'S FIRST MILL. The split-levels such as ours, built in the aesthetically challenged sixties, were scattered like tawdry cousins among these statelier, storied homes. Still, moving to 12 Ramble Lane was a big step up for us, and my parents had attached hopes to the house, obvious as the taped-up notes left behind by the house's former owners ("Use 5-watt bulb MAX!" "Filter hose needs to be checked 2x year!"). Mom had torn down their notes impatiently the first day we moved in, replacing them with a sign of her own. Purple felt with silver letters, it hung on the door of her soon-to-be-blue room, her first real studio: "Artist at Work." She could turn it to face in or out, indicating whether she was "open" or "closed"—a novel idea in a mother. Dad's office was in the basement (he had another at the university), but most of all he seemed keen on a certain green hillock in the backyard, where he could sit cross-legged and rumble with a middle-aged *Om*.

We were all dressed up now, decked out in zesty Marimekko. And although the first two weeks in Weston passed in a kind of misty, glorious disappointment, most of all we felt lucky to be there, in a town of lilacs and curving roads and studio doors that shut and hillocks and a barn.

Dad stood on the ladder. He'd painted all the edges first, near the ceiling and floors and windows and corners, and then he'd taken out the roller and started in on wide swaths of Prussian Wildflower.

"A bit dark, isn't it?"

"Well, it's what your mother wants. It'll lighten up as it dries, too, Allie Oop."

This cheerfulness was disconcerting. He'd been duped into thinking he could please my mother.

"It looks different from the little card."

"God*dammit,*" Dad said. A slop of paint had fallen to the floor.

The fact of the matter is, both my parents were fish out of water in Weston. Mom with her dreams of being a painter and Dad with his day job and his poetry books, including the award-winning one, all lined up on the mantel. They were attempting to piece together a life with art at its center and also (not that I was fully aware of this at the time) making choices based on what might be good for me, their daughter. Art geeks, adversaries, people who drove old cars: They weren't part of the PTA crowd, and they weren't swingers, either. Mainly they were simply *my parents,* and it was extraordinarily embarrassing, but seemed pretty natural, that they were so weird.

"Look, you can't tell anything from the card," he said. "Take a rag to that spot, would you, please?"

"Why do they have the cards, then?"

"To beguile the willing, Alison."

"Why would they do that? They would never do that."

"You don't think so? Think about the visceral and dark depths of the workingman's resentment, darling, and you might have another idea."

The son of Irish immigrants and bardic descendant of many a workingman, my father looked like he was a half second away from falling off the rickety old ladder—either him or the tray of Prussian Wildflower.

"Do we have any more 7-Up?"

Dad concentrated on his next swab of the roller. His somewhat long and unkempt beard, a poet's beard, bobbed precariously close to the wall.

"Dad?"

He grunted. He smoothed the roller down, then over, making a reverse blue cloud in a white sky. "Try the garage."

I sat at the kitchen table, drinking 7-Up and reading the *Weston Forum.* It featured golf and tennis tournaments, with a handful of asides about "happenings" at the Norfield Grange. I didn't know for sure what a "grange" was, though I thought perhaps it was a place where they stored wheat or made pantaloons in yesteryear. I studied the picture of the winners in doubles at the Aspetuck Country Club Summer's End Mixer, two women in ruffled culottes and their partners, men with thinning hair. Another photo was of four men who'd won the Muscular Dystrophy Benefit Golf Tournament: plaid all around.

I didn't notice the article at first, probably because the accompanying photo was so obscure—a hazy image of boulders, pine trees, and, perhaps, a bit of a stream or river. TEEN DIES IN FALL, read the headline. At first I thought it meant, you know, September, which seemed to bode ill for me specifically as I contemplated my upcoming entrée into public school life, starting with eighth grade.

A sixteen-year-old youth died Saturday night, apparently after a daredevil dive off the rocks at Devil's Glen. The youth, whose name has not been released because of his age, was from out of town. "A tragic act like this, it didn't need to happen. Kids will be kids, but parents need to take action," said Police Chief Riley at the Town Forum on Monday, urging parents to warn kids away from this area, long a hot spot for teenage congregation and tomfoolery.

Tomfoolery? *That* was an annoying word.

Mom appeared on the stairs, carrying groceries. She was wearing purple sunglasses, the frames big and round as apples.

"I found the best store," she said breathlessly. "Zillions of healthy things to eat."

"Oh no," I said. My mother was mounting a campaign against the tried-and-true food of my youth. It had been a sad day when she swept through our cabinets, throwing away yummy things and replacing them with less yummy things. Skippy peanut butter was tossed, for instance, and replaced by an unsalted almond-peanut blend.

"How's the studio coming? Been down there recently?" She extricated herself from her sunglasses, pulled the yellow-and-purple scarf from her hair.

"He's working on it," I said, peering into a bag. Bulk items: the worst. "Didn't you get any Oreos? Or anything to eat?"

"What do you mean? Look at all this!"

She began to pull things out: dried fruit, unsalted almonds, oatmeal, some other cereal with black flecks, a huge bag of brown rice. Her long blond hair whooshed as she moved. She was wearing striped pants and red pointy shoes from Afghanistan. Even in this hippie garb, she stood straight and skinny, betraying years of childhood ballet.

"What about regular food?" I asked.

"What is 'regular,' Alison?" Mom said. "Regular food is for regular people, my darling."

I sat back down and began drawing psychotic spirals on a pad of paper. "I couldn't find anything for lunch."

"Oh, Allie, we've got soup, tuna. Look here—good twelve-grain bread. And loads of cheese."

"Fritos?"

"No. I got some bean sprouts. And kale," she said. "You mean to say you don't like kale?"

"I don't even know what kale *is,* Mom."

"The soul is what's at stake, Allie," she said then, pouring rice into the largest of the plastic canisters with mushroom tops. She gave me a meaningful look. "And your back most of all."

"I just want a nice snack," I said in a monotone.

"Bingo! Carob instead of chocolate! Honey instead of white sugar!" She tossed me a Tiger's Milk bar and trotted down the orange stairs. (Did I mention that the entire house was carpeted in orange, orange as a spilled soda, an emergency flag, a lone life jacket floating on the surface of a lake?)

In a minute I heard what seemed like a cry from below, a bird hitting a window, and then silence and then some other rumblings of what seemed like anger. Then silence again. Next, my mother's Afghan slippers dragged back upstairs, to the living room landing, and then up still farther, toward the bedrooms. Her head was bowed, her shoulders hunched—not at all like a ballerina.

Soon my father appeared. Now he had blue paint on his beard, as if a robin's egg had broken there.

"What's happening?"

"She doesn't like the color," he said, reaching into the refrigerator for a beer.

I went downstairs myself to check out the studio.

The walls were two-thirds done in velvety blue, the remaining white a jagged rectangle of the past. I walked up to the wall, right up to the edge between white and blue. If I squinted, here, where the roller had gone over once, lightly, maybe I could make it the right color. I could settle her down, get her back to the kitchen to eat a plateful of organic apricots. It was only paint, but for Mom the wrongness of the blue was a sign, a constellation that bode ill. The New Age movement was in full swing; hippies and suburban wastrels and visionaries and lost souls were making the transition, copping an allegiance to new foodstuffs and unguents and all manner of alchemy, and some of it was almost divine and some of it was dangerous, far more dangerous than the wrong blue, and we, at the time, couldn't tell one from the other.

That was the day I met Kate Hamilton. She showed up in my driveway, a girl my age, long ponytail. She was on a gray horse. It looked like an Arabian.

"Hello," she said, one hand like a bent sail across her brow, a quizzical expression on her face, like she'd found me trespassing in her town.

I said hello back, uneasy. The bad paint was still drying in the studio, and instead of putting up pictures in the living room, as had been the plan, both my parents were in retreat mode.

"Just moved in?"

"A couple of weeks ago, yeah."

"Where are you from?" she asked, squinting.

"Norwalk." Not as nice as Weston, I already knew that.

"Ah, light-years away."

"Yeah." I liked that expression, "light years."

"I'm Kate. I live on Glenwood—that way, about half a mile."

She pointed past our split-level house, smallest on the block, and her hand in the air reminded me of a signpost. OZ, THIS-A-WAY. NEVER-NEVER LAND, TWO MILES TO GO.

I was hoping she wouldn't notice my father in the backyard,

in inebriated meditation, and I was also hoping my mother wouldn't howl too loudly from upstairs in her bedroom.

"I'm Alison."

"I know," she said. (Had there been some kind of announcement, an article in the *Weston Forum*?) "I noticed you have a horse."

"I do. His name's Jazz." I glanced toward the barn.

"We should go riding sometime. Can you ride in—that?" She didn't look away when she said it, but her voice softened.

"I take it off to ride," I told her.

For a second, everything seemed quiet in the breath of the afternoon.

"Okay," she said, looking nowhere, looking ahead. "Welp, see ya."

Kate watched the tree line, almost with regret. Then she turned the gray horse around.

Like the other children, Sarah Beckingworth went to the little schoolhouse down the lane. Here she wrote her alphabet on a chalkboard and embroidered small yellow suns onto what was called a "sampler." Samplers can be seen today in many museums, but she didn't know that then. And she had no idea at this point that she would become lost, or even a heroine.

Chapter Two

MY PARENTS had thought it would be useful and fun for me to go to the Weston Middle School Get-Along—a four-day camplike experience a week before school, real school, began. I objected strenuously, to no effect. I had a doctor's appointment scheduled at the end of the month, and I'd thought it was possible he'd tell me I could take my brace off, at least for the daytime, and thus I'd be able to start my Weston academic career as a normal person.

I was underwater, doing an enforced Get-Along round of laps, when the thunderous tumult of the pool room, a combination of splashes and echoes and whistles and shouts, changed. I heard a new element. Laughter or something quite like it reached my ears as I did my fifth freestyle lap, my lungs already constricted and bloody feeling from lack of oxygen.

What was going on? Against the rules—Don's rules, he was the swimming coach—I stopped at the end of the pool. Laughter bounced off the walls and mixed with the slap of feet on tile. I popped off my goggles and saw what was happening. I didn't even know which kid it was (they all looked the same: skinny, good-looking, evil), but he was wearing my brace. Wearing my brace over his bare wet skin and walking around by the side of the pool, arms and legs stiff as a tin man's.

I didn't know what to do. "Get that thing off," Don was shouting at the kid now, pointing at the floor. Did Don know that it, *that thing,* was mine? After all, I'd taken it off in the girls' locker room, before I even got close to the pool. How had this kid gotten it? The sense of myself as crooked and ugly flipped around on the wet tile. I didn't know what to do, really, so I just pushed off the wall, slowly, with my feet. Two laps to go. I stretched my arms, lighter than ever. I was a silver fish.

When I had finished my laps, my brace, wet, was perched by the entrance to the girls' locker room, a devoted dog waiting for me at the door. I picked it up and went inside to change.

Some of the girls in the locker room would be my classmates, I felt sure of that, but they all seemed older than me and like they were in a club that I didn't belong to, didn't even know the name of. A blond girl near me was wearing a panties and bra set with little pink hearts sewn onto the fabric, and her legs were tan and smooth. She had on a gold necklace, and she was drying her hair, this side and then that side, purposely not looking my way at all. She had a friend with dark hair, and this girl's hair fell to the small of her back in a long swoop. She looked like some kind of island creature. Her hipbones stuck out, and she had on red toenail polish. She had no problem looking at me. She stared at me sleepily as she talked to the blond girl.

"So I'd never invite her over again. I mean, who does she think she is? What kind of slut would do that with my brother?"

I put on my undershirt. It was a man's undershirt, size small, because we couldn't find any girl's ones long enough to reach past the bottom of the brace. I had two of them, but they still got old and dirty looking even if they'd just come out of the wash because the metal rubbed against the fabric and made it rough and black. The girl with sleepy eyes kept staring at me and talking about something else, and once in a while her blond friend would also toss a look my way from either side of her fluffy towel. There was really no reason for anyone to say anything at all. Who I was had been established.

The morning of the first day of school, I tried putting a scarf around the neck part of the brace, but instead of a frilly little nothing wisping romantically about, it ended up, once I'd adjusted it so none of the metal was showing, looking more like a beach blanket or a bib. I tried one of the new turtlenecks we'd bought at Bloomingdale's. It was okay, but when I looked at myself from the side, I realized it was tight enough that you could make out the full length of the bars running down my back, and the ones in front, too—the big one down the middle, flat like a sword, and the awful, small one over my breast. After that, I tried my overalls. They were good at hiding the brace, loose as a garbage bag, but a little informal, a little too *barnyard,* for my first day of school. There was this really pretty yellow dress I'd coerced my mom into buying me that I loved, but I didn't want to look as if I were on my way to a wedding. Finally I resorted to my striped sailor's shirt—it was loose, too, and it was also my lucky shirt, and even though I would unfortunately be using up all my luck on the very first day, it seemed like the best choice. I also wore jeans, yellow plastic clogs, and another favorite accessory: a bright pink reversible corduroy hat.

Dad's job as an English professor meant he was often around during the day. Apparently poetry itself didn't pay much, so even though he'd published three books of poems, he still had what he called his "day job," like he was an actor in Hollywood or a musician in a jazz band. When feeling unnecessarily surly, he liked to rail against anyone who thought he needed special "time to write" or even a room to write in (never mind my mother and her blue room), invoking instead his heroes, William Carlos Williams (a doctor) and Wallace Stevens (an insurance agent). Except for the days he taught, his status as poet/teacher also meant he could dress casually to the extreme. On our way to school, for instance, he was wearing old jeans, untied tennis sneakers, and the paint-splattered sweatshirt he'd worn to paint the studio. He also had a Cheerio in his beard.

"Now listen," Dad said, squinting over at me in the passenger seat when we got there. "First days are always hard. But you look terrific, and remember, everyone feels like a freak in eighth grade."

Walking up the wide front steps to Weston Middle School, I thought about his words, meant to be encouraging. Though I'd worried about school in various ways, the actual word *freak* had not yet come to mind. Now it echoed in my head as I approached the entrance, walking as normally as I could and ignoring what seemed to be the uniform stares of the small gathered groups of kids on either side of the doorway.

I should have known that my hopes of getting the brace off before the first day of school would be dashed, but I'd maintained my optimism until the orthopedist turned away from the new X-ray and told my mother, "These curves are getting more pronounced, by far." Then he had me lean over again, and he trailed his finger over my spine like a little metal car on a bumpy bridge to nowhere.

I was, as it turned out, late for homeroom. I hadn't been able to find my locker, and then it took me forever, until I was hot as doom, to get it open. When I opened the door to Room 114, Mrs. Balding turned toward me. She looked very much like Big Bird, and she was holding me in place with a querulous stare.

"And you must be Miss . . ."

"Alison Glass," I whispered.

"What? What did you say?" she shouted. She had trouble hearing, I'd find out, so she seemed to think we all did. The entire class was looking my way.

"Did she just call Mrs. Balding an—" one kid said, and a few others cracked up.

I repeated my name, and Mrs. Balding adjusted her glasses and ran her finger up and down her roll book. "Ah . . . Alison. Glass. Yes, Miss Glass. I'm afraid you're tardy today. But I will forgive you this once, first day of school and so forth. Please take a seat, take a seat, dear."

As she spoke, my eyes darted between her imposing

gooselike structure and the twenty-five friendly and helpful faces of my fellow eighth-graders. In the hall, there had been a certain gaiety to the throngs clamoring around me—sometimes fixing me with disinterested stares, but more often than not going about their business. I had set a course, an exquisitely optimistic and faithful course, of forgetting the pool incident, but now, for a moment, I forgot myself—forgot my willpower. Finally I got myself to move again. I spotted an empty seat a row over and a few desks up. I made my way in that direction, tripping once on someone's backpack strap.

At my old school, the Montessori Schoolhouse, everyone had their problems, everyone was unique—to be honest, it was a repository of the feeble, the walleyed, and the maladjusted. We had no grades, no rows of desks, no lectures, and we were all just plain bizarre, an army of happy iconoclasts. But I'd liked conducting genetics experiments with the black and white mice I'd gotten at the pet store, and planting gardens, and constructing homes for caterpillars. I'd liked learning Greek and conducting our own presidential debates and elections in McGovern vs. Nixon (I was the McGovern chairperson—the pinnacle of my political career). And I had been reasonably certain, at the Schoolhouse, that there was a cachet, an appeal, to the word *nonconformist.*

Weston Middle School was different.

It was supposed to be different *good.* My parents had told me, and I'd heard them tell their friends a million times, that the schools in Weston had an excellent reputation, that this was one of the main reasons we'd moved there. The resources were plush: pools, soccer fields, tennis courts. Ninety-eight percent of the high school graduates went on to college, and the rest, no doubt, became accomplished mechanics at foreign automobile dealerships. There was a band, a theater program, and a chess club—all of which, I'd come to find out, were entirely off-limits if you wanted to keep your self-respect intact.

The school was brightly colored, certainly: The concrete walls were painted orange and yellow and purple and blue, depending on which part of the building you were in. I walked around and around that first day, taking in my surroundings, veering toward the purple walls by mistake, finding my way back to orange. More or less avoiding the teachers wearing apple-shaped name tags, HELLO, MAY I HELP YOU? printed on them in worm green.

After pre-algebra and science, I had English. I took a seat smack-dab in the middle of the room, having read somewhere, I felt sure, that the front row was reserved for teacher's pets and the back was for derelicts. The teacher's name, Mr. Snodgrass, was printed on the chalkboard in careful block letters.

Mr. Snodgrass himself stood before us. He was in his early thirties, I'd guess now, though at the time I identified him as solidly middle-aged, an adult, somewhere in that slow, unwieldy moment that seemed to go on forever. He wore wide-wale corduroys (corduroys were *very* 1975), a plaid shirt, a woolen tie, and a pencil behind his ear. He surveyed us from behind his thick glasses with a wide, close-lipped smile, and then he turned sharply toward the door and left the room.

We gaped at the place where a teacher had been, stunned into momentary silence by his surprise exit. Then one kid scrambled to the front, bowed, said, "Nice to meet you, ladies and gentlemen," and slid back into his chair.

The door opened and here came Mr. Snodgrass again, this time wearing teddy-bear ears and oversize sunglasses, the kind you'd buy at a fair.

"Hello, gang," he said, all smiles.

We rumbled a greeting.

"Notice anything different about me?"

"Uh . . . you're wearing ears," said someone I'd know later was Jim, a football player.

"And?"

"And glasses. Funny glasses," piped up a little person (named Nancy).

"Right. Anything else? Anything else, boys and girls?"

We weren't sure what he was getting at.

"Come on, come on, look at me! I'm the same guy as before—right? But with a difference." Mr. Snodgrass whirled about and stood before us again, arms outstretched. "Well? . . . Well?"

"You've become a whirling dervish," I said, breaking the silence. It was my first unnecessary utterance of the day.

"And you were . . . Amanda?" he said, frowning toward me.

"Alison."

"Alison, very possibly I am a whirling dervish. But today I am looking *not* for generalizations, but for *details*. Details! Details, my friends!"

With that, he pulled the tip of a bright blue handkerchief out of his shirt pocket. He waved it in the air, then flung it on his desk. He took off his big glasses and his furry ears. "The English language, my friends, is an *exact science*. We learn

English so that we may provide a very, very clear picture when we speak or, especially, when we write. When you observed me this morning, it didn't take an Einstein to see that I had funny ears and funny glasses, but you neglected to notice I'd also added a blue hankie to my ensemble. This little detail escaped you. Why? Because you had stopped looking. It was more subtle than the rest. Your job, my friends, is to *notice the blue hankie*. Leave *no blue hankie* unnoticed."

He went on to describe the parts of speech, an overview from the year before. I opened my five-subject notebook and wrote the date in the right-hand corner of the page and then, in a careful row, "noun, verb, adjective, adverb, article, conjunction, preposition." I doodled a unicorn mane around the holes of the spiral binding. I hadn't noticed the blue handkerchief, and this was disturbing.

There were two cafeterias, rival country clubs with distinct and prejudicial guidelines for membership, the details of which remained obscure. I sat at an empty table near the entrance of one and took out my lunch. Mom had insisted on making me a "Love Bag"—health food, of course.

"Whirling what the fuck?" I heard behind me.

In my brace, I couldn't turn to look without pivoting my whole body. So that's what I did, turned like a doorknob and faced a table of huge ungainly boys, all in striped rugby shirts.

"Whirling dervish?" I answered.

"What, are you from a different school or something?" one guy asked. He had a crew cut and a red face, as though he'd run around the building a couple of times before lunch.

"Is that, like, *Polish* for stupid jerk?" It was Jim, the football player.

"Maybe she goes to a gimp school or something. Hey, whirling brace girl, you're at the wrong school! You got lost!"

The boys at the table cracked up.

"I'm not from a gimp school. I went to a Montessori school before this."

"Brontosaurus school? What, is that for retards or something?"

"Montessori," I enunciated.

"Whirling idiot," said the red-faced one, no smile on his face.

I turned back to my almond-paste-and-orange-marmalade sandwich on wheat, accompanied by sesame sticks and raisins. The cafeteria noise around me came in waves, like the undulation of a ship. After a minute I put everything back in the bag and got up from the table, throwing my lunch in the trash on the way out.

My afternoon classes were geography and home ec. At two o'clock, I got my stuff from my locker and started down the hall toward the front doors. A group of boys, some I recognized from before, stood near the cafeteria. As I walked past, the red-faced crew-cut one lunged in my direction.

"Whirling *retard!*" he shouted, then spun back toward the safety of his group.

The hall was emptying out by then—maybe that's why it sounded like he was bellowing from a rooftop. Everyone stopped what they were doing, looked over, waited to see what I'd say. I might agree with his statement; I might acquiesce.

Then I heard something new, another voice.

"What the hell's wrong with you, Dave?"

I turned around. It was that girl, Kate.

She stood in the middle of the hall, her hands pushed down into her pockets. She was wearing a man's sweater, and her jeans were faded out, and her hair was pulled back into some kind of messy ponytail. She looked a little mean and a little beautiful, staring at the crew-cut guy.

The people in the hall watched with new interest, not least of all myself. I hadn't talked to anyone all day, and no one was wearing yellow clogs but me. It had been and would be, I felt, a complete disaster, this school, this new life. I was ready to get home and ride, just ride away.

Dave sneered. "What the hell's wrong with *you,* Kate?"

Kate Hamilton raised her eyebrows a millimeter and told him to fuck off. I'd heard the word *fuck,* but it had never been used on my behalf before.

Well, I definitely wanted to say, *Hey, thanks, that was nice, I appreciated that,* but I stood rooted in my spot as Dave turned even redder in the face and then seemed, for a moment, to fade away. A group of kids descended on Kate, and she was explaining and laughing, and they were all laughing, and then everyone was walking away.

On the way to the front door I felt light and strange, not even a physical entity, as if I'd float away if it weren't for my brace, holding me.

One day as the lost heroine was galloping about the land originally known as Uncoway, and then Fairfield, and then Wistin, and even later known as Weston, she saw a group of Indians. Were they Paugussetts or Siwanogs? Or perhaps they were Iroquois or Scaticooks? She didn't know for certain, but she noticed they looked quite ill. She stopped Noble, the eighteen-hand black stallion, a scant distance from them.

"What say you, good men?" asked the lost heroine.

"We are hungry and shall soon die," said the boldest of the suffering and struggling phalanx of Indians.

Sarah Beckingworth rushed home then and gathered up some gruel and berries. She brought the food back to the struggling, ill Indians.

"Go on your way, good and vital members of a community."

The Indians said, "How," and ate the gruel. The lost heroine kicked Noble and continued her perambulations.

Chapter Three

I DIDN'T see Kate right away after that. Or I did see
her, but she was always with other kids. She was actually in
my social studies class, but she always rushed in and out of
the classroom and sat far away from me. I saw that she was
Popular, a fate strange as anything. Yes, I realized, we lived in
separate spheres.

This would change the same day I met the Women of History. It was the second week of school, and I came home one
afternoon and there they were, draped around my living room
like expensively clothed gophers.

I'd heard about them already. Right after we moved in,
they'd come over on a little welcoming mission, giving Mom a
basketful of tangentially Yankee items: bayberry candles, a jar
of homemade apple butter, a dishcloth decorated with acorns
and squirrels, and a few issues of their newsletter, *History!*
Their ongoing mission involved the newsletter and a speaker
series and the welcoming of new ones into the old regime. But
this year was quite different and important, for they were
planning Weston's upcoming bicentennial jubilee.

A bicentennial jubilee? Was this my mother's sort of thing? You wouldn't think so, yet maybe she just wanted to fit in somewhere, suddenly. Maybe she'd been more spooked by the blue-room incident than we knew. Maybe she'd been lured in by the rich-lady largesse, the wealthy kindness, the affluent finesse that, if anything, was like her parents', and then only her father's, circle of friends. It could have been related to that, a countermeasure to the Alternative Lifestyle, made real finally by the studio (now white, after all).

She accepted the apple butter, and then my mother invited the ladies to see her paintings. Their enchantment was enchanting. "It's like being in the arms of one's long-ago mother," said Grete Feneta, gazing at one of the more abstract works— that's what Mom told Dad later. And might she consider a commission? Perhaps something for Mr. Feneta's study? What they did is they *ooh*ed and *aah*ed her into complete submission, and then everyone simultaneously realized it would be enchanting and necessary to have an artist such as herself on the board. It would surely add perspective, add a kind of depth. And she could help with color schemes and garlands and things like that. Would she do it? Would she take time away from her glorious swaths of blue and brown, these visions with names like *Necessity #2* and *Within the Dream*?

Yes, she would, and we would pay for this soon enough.

"Alison, darling," Mom called as I was attempting to glide past the living room and into the kitchen, "come meet my friends."

"Is this your lovely daughter?" said one woman—the strangest and oldest one there. She was now trying to get up from the couch, and as she struggled I took in the fact that she was dressed, head to toe, in red, white, and blue. I'd find out later that for Ruth Hollbrook, Daughter of the Revolution, this was de rigueur. Still, I feasted my eyes on her outfit. Her blue-and-white-striped dress was cinched at the waist with a wide red belt. She wore slim blue moccasins with red buckles and a small silk flag, or scarf, around her neck, secured by a brooch in the shape of a bell (the Liberty Bell, I thought uncertainly). By her side was a purse, also made of what appeared to be flag remnants. Her eyes were bright and amazed, like mine.

"Yes, this is Alison."

My mother looked radiant, I noticed with a fleeting moment of hopeless, perfect admiration. She was in a peach dress with a matching peach sweater—no sequins or fringe anywhere—and a single strand of pearls. It was the kind of outfit she wore to visit her father in the city. "And Alison, this is Mrs. Hollbrook, and Mrs. Bix, Mrs. Livingsworth, and Mrs. Feneta—the Women of History."

"I'm Lucille Bix, but you can call me Lucy," said the fidgety woman on the ottoman with a quick smile, then a look around at the others—apparently unsure if her overture went too far. Gingham-and-espadrille Sally Livingsworth introduced herself, too. She was old money and the least well dressed— economizing on wardrobe to give more to the Episcopal Church or Smith College, Mom would conjecture.

Then there was Grete Feneta, chairwoman of the Women of History. She was staring me down, giving me a look of extraordinary sympathy as I stood there. She was older than my mother, but she seemed to have beaten back the exigencies of age through black magic. She had one arm stretched out on the couch, and with the other she played with her long, dangling scarf—lilac, with darker irises silk-screened on the fabric. She twirled it slowly between her fingers, then drew the liquid fabric to her bright orange lips.

"What an enchanting little person," Mrs. Feneta murmured, as if I were a painting she'd just come across in a museum exhibition.

I backed away from her art patron stare.

"Your mother has put out a delightful platter of doodads, dear," Mrs. Hollbrook said.

"Yes, honey, have a cookie," said Mom. She had bought fancy bakery cookies, nothing whole wheat on the platter.

I was released. I took two raspberry linzer tortes up to my room and closed the door.

Cher was everything, or at least she could be. It helped to have something to immerse myself in after school, to think about a woman such as this: snappy. She was snappier than *MAD* magazine and prettier, too. Her hair swished about in a black ribbon of sharp shine, and on the show she'd look over at that silly Sonny and give him the funniest little smirk ever. She wore outfits, gorgeous sparkly ones, and her stomach was as flat as a chief's hand saying "How," or whatever it was Indian chiefs said to the white ancestors.

I lifted the black plastic cover to my space-age stereo and put on my cherished and only album, *Half Breed*. On the cover, Cher sat astride a furious stallion, looking stalwart to the north. She wore a bikini top festooned with dangling strips of colorful fabric, a deerskin miniskirt, and an immense feather headdress. She was part Cherokee, someone had told me—one-eighth, as I remembered. "Half Breed" was really the best song on the album—I guessed "One-Eighth Breed" didn't sound quite as good—and though I listened to the rest of that side (and sometimes the B side, too), it was only with a sense of duty.

I was halfway into the third song when I heard crunching in the driveway. It took me a minute to realize it was the sound of hooves. I put down my book and looked out the window. It was Kate Hamilton again, on her dapple gray pony.

There had always been horses. They had always been there, and then I had my own, and then, later, the whole thing ruptured and I realized that even horses can get hurt, killed, and now, a few lifetimes later, I try to fix horses for a living. Veterinary practice suits me. I like the wordless part, the part where you're holding the animal's head in your hands as if you're holding the globe. And I like the doughnuts. Yes, vets eat doughnuts: It's not just cops anymore. This is what we're doing in the morning, before our first appointment. It's all about drinking coffee and eating doughnuts with the vet techs and forgetting the death you encountered the day before.

Still, you know, you need to imagine something will survive. You need to imagine that every day.

Before I had Jazz, I'd see a horse on the side of the road as we drove past (on an errand with Mom, say) and I'd shout at the closed window as we sped by. Sometimes I could get her to slow down, even stop. She'd never had her own horse, my mom, but she'd read *The Black Stallion* and seen *National Velvet,* and on Sundays in Central Park she'd ridden the beautiful carousel, around and around. She knew what horses meant to me—what they might have meant to her. First I had lessons, and then, soon after I began wearing the brace, we got Jazz. I put in two hundred dollars I'd saved from selling greeting cards door-to-door and hoarding Christmas money, and my parents put in the rest. It was a couple of months after I was diagnosed with scoliosis, and I think this played into it, the decision to spend money we didn't really have on a horse. They were my parents, and this was what they could do, they could try to even things out for me.

For a year we boarded Jazz, a mostly black pony with one white sock and a stripe, at my riding instructor's place. Then we moved to Weston, and he was just a meandering path away from our house. I fed him every morning and every night, and I changed the shavings in his stall twice a week. I rode him whenever I could, and then I just liked to stand by the fence, too, and tell him things.

Kate and I rode up the middle of the road, past the neighbor's orchard, gnarled trees full of demented little green apples, tight as fists, and a profusion of raspberry bushes, long past their summer prime.

Her arms rested loosely, one on her thigh, one on the saddle's pommel. Her feet were out of the stirrups, but she sat perfectly balanced anyway. Since we'd moved to town, I'd ridden only in the paddock and a little ways down the road. She said she had better places to show me.

Our horses' hooves made slow clucks on the pavement. They were both acting cool for each other: my black-and-white Jazz and Kate's speckled Peach, with a long gray mane, her forelock in tendrils on one side of her face.

"So," Kate said, "how are you enjoying eighth grade so far? Loving it, right?"

"Yes, it's really neat. The people are superfriendly."

"They are. Problems with self-expression, though, as my father would say. Rule number one: Speak your mind. The problem is, Dave Darbis and those guys, they just don't have a mind to speak with in the first place."

She twisted her ponytail into a knot as she spoke, leaving the reins slack and unattended.

"Have you lived here a long time?"

"Since I was eight. Before that we were in L.A. And San Diego. I was born on Long Island, though. My parents like to move around. Mom says she likes a change of *venue*." She glanced my way. "She's always home, so it's more important to her. Dad's gone a lot of the time."

"What does he do?"

"Oh—he's a shaman."

"A shaman? Is that like a priest or something?"

"He's an Egyptian shaman, actually. He wrote this book, *Pyramid Love*? Have you heard of it?"

"No."

She shrugged. "I guess it's kind of famous. He goes around and does these *'playshops'* and people pay him tons of money. He's not really Egyptian, though. He used to be, like, a businessman."

"I like Egyptian things."

"Yeah."

"Cats and mummies and stuff?"

"Yeah. I like the cats," she said, and drifted off. "Here's the turn. C'mon."

We veered from the main road, and she led me up a long driveway lined by trees. Shade and light made a tapestry on the ground. We talked more softly.

"What about your parents?" she asked.

"Well, my mom is an artist and my dad's a poet."

"Really?"

Now it was my turn to shrug.

"So what kinds of paintings does your mother do?"

"I don't know—they're abstract, I guess."

"Abstract—that could be interesting."

"My dad painted her studio and she didn't like the color, and here it is, a new town, but other than that, same as before," I said all of a sudden, then I clammed up again. I ran my hand through Jazz's mane.

"Well, parents . . ." Kate looked into the trees.

"Parents are hard to explain."

"They're easy to *explain*," she said. "Just hard to *entertain*."

"They're easy to entertain, if you're on a getaway train."

She gave me a furrowed brow look. "If you're on a getaway train, they're less of a pain."

I had to agree with that.

"C'mon—Jane." She gathered up the reins from Peach's neck, leaned forward, and pushed her horse into a canter. I followed behind.

We swung around the curve of the driveway, past a green-house with broken windows, and then I saw where we were going: a great old mansion with turrets and gables and an archway in the middle, big enough for cars to drive through. We slowed down the horses in front of the arched tunnel and then urged them in. They spun around, uneasy in the sudden darkness, their hooves clacking loudly against the cement floor. On one wall someone had painted a tree with delicate, fanciful leaves and sweet-looking lemons, two gray doves flying near. Over everything was a long red ribbon banner, the script on it indecipherable.

"Cool," I said.

"It is."

"How did you ever find this place?"

"I don't know. Just riding around. It's been abandoned for ages. Can't you just imagine the way it was, a long time ago?"

"Model-T cars. Guys wearing funny little hats dropping off ladies in white fur coats."

"Hurrying in for an incredible party. Champagne and pet cheetahs and cigarette holders the length of your arm."

"I wonder what the banner said."

"I wonder, too," said Kate. "Something mysterious, I bet. C'mon, I'll show you the rest of the place."

On the patio behind the house, white wrought-iron furniture sat hunched against time, webbed at the edges with rust. A huge garden had been laid out behind that, brick pathways forming an elaborate design. Now everything was crumbling and overgrown. In the center of it all, one stone Cupid stood frozen forever in mid-pee. The whole place reminded me of the Queen's chessboard in *Alice in Wonderland,* where inanimate things come alive.

"Want a cigarette?" Kate said, her eyes skeptical.

"You smoke?"

"Sometimes."

It had been less than a year since I'd launched a campaign against my parents' smoking. I'd spent weeks hiding their cigarettes or sometimes breaking them in half. I'd also showed them, multiple times, the picture in *Cricket* magazine of the black lungs of a smoker. (Had that smoker died? I'd always wondered. How else had they gotten the photograph?) "Didn't you know that smoking makes your lungs into big fat tar pits?" I'd asked, incredulous, as they'd woefully craved their lost cigarettes. The effort had worked with Mom, though my father could still be found hiding out behind buildings sometimes, puffing away on a Carlton.

"Well, okay," I said.

"All right, then."

We tied up our horses, and I stood for a moment, feeling small without my brace. I rotated my shoulders a bit, experimenting. Was my back twisting and sinking, out of control? I was allowed to take off the brace for an hour a day (I used the time for riding, my back exercises, and a shower). An internal clock had been set for me now, and it was hard to tell if it was superstition or fact, the slightly increased ache, the pull of gravity at the end of the designated hour.

Kate walked over to the wall surrounding the courtyard and squatted, lifted up a loose brick, and pulled out a pack of cigarettes and a lighter.

"I see you've done this before."

"It's my little place."

She unfolded the foil at the top of the red-and-white pack, Winstons, and tapped out two cigarettes. Her fingers were long and aristocratic, also a little red and chapped. They were the kind of fingers you'd expect on Joan of Arc or some other capable yet elegant heroine.

The cigarette was light in my hand. Kate flicked the lighter, but the flame was too low, so she made an adjustment and tried again. This time it flared up four inches, unruly. She reeled back and raised her eyebrows and tried it another time.

She lit my cigarette, and I also made an attempt at elegance. The smoke went in my mouth and spilled out again.

"Not too bad," I said.

She laughed. "You look good with a cigarette."

"Kind of fancy, right?"

"Definitely."

I looked around us, at the dying garden.

"Who owns this place? Do they ever come here?"

"I don't think so. It was some old lady, I heard, and then she died and her family owns it but lives somewhere else."

"It's amazing."

I tried another puff. Kate was smoothing out the sleeves of her shirt, refolding a cuff. "It's neat to see you without your brace."

"Oh. Thanks."

"Why do you even have to wear that thing?"

I knew the answer to that question—I had it down like a script. I told her about scoliosis, what I'd learned so far. Eighty-five percent of the cases are what's called idiopathic, which is Latin for who knows what it is or what, even, to do about it.

Both boys and girls get mild curves in equal numbers, but it's in girls, overwhelmingly, that the curves become severe. The spine curves like a leaning tree or, in my case, into an S. A brace can stop it from getting worse; at least that was the intent.

If a parent has scoliosis, your chances for getting it increase quite a lot. (So what do you think, do *you* look like your mother?)

"How long will you have to wear it, do you think?" she asked, releasing smoke from her mouth in an expert curl.

"Not too much longer, I hope. My next doctor's appointment is in October, so I guess I'll find out then how things are." In one of the turret windows, a curtain had been pulled aside: A ghost was watching us. "If the curves get really bad, you have to have an operation, and they put a rod in your back and you have to stay in bed for a year or something like that."

"But you look really straight."

"Thanks."

I looked at my cigarette. It was like some weird foreign smoking object, a tiny gun.

"How much do you weigh?" Kate asked then.

"A hundred and twelve."

"I weigh a hundred and fifteen." She squinted up at the house. "We've got the same bodies, almost."

"You think?" I said, grateful for what seemed like a lie. But why had she, this sassy person with secret cigarettes, befriended me? Later I'd think it might have been very simple: With me, she mattered to somebody. She could help me, and that was a life preserver—for a time, anyway.

"I want to show you something else."

We got back on the horses and trotted down the driveway—like fleeing Russian aristocracy, I imagined, thinking about my solitary Russian aristocracy reference, the *Dr. Zhivago* movie I'd seen on TV.

It must have been this moment when we conceived of her, the both of us. Our heroine, Sarah Beckingworth, riding around, lost and sometimes happy.

She cut between houses, and we followed a crumbling stone wall through a thin forest, over brown wet leaves. We ended up at the bank of a river.

"Now what?"

"We go across," she said.

"But it looks deep."

"So? No problem. Just close your eyes and jump in."

I gaped at the water, amazed and distressed that I was here, and feeling cold, too, like the day was ending in a hurry. Rivers were meant for looking at, for fishing in. I could see a trail winding up through some boulders and trees on the other side, the bank a mash of wrecked fallen leaves and yesterday's skunk cabbage. Rivers were meant for hauling goods to faraway towns. Rivers were meant for boating.

"I don't know."

"But Alison, there's no other way across."

It was twenty feet wide, maybe thirty.

"Well—"

I was going to say something like *Maybe we don't* want *to get across, anyway,* or *Maybe we could follow the river down to some kind of dam or gully or* bridge, *yes, a bridge would be great*—

Kate leaned over and trained her eyes ahead, looking at the spot where she wanted Peach to head. She nudged the horse with her heels and said, "Let's go."

Peach leaned perilously over her front feet, then stepped back like she'd been bitten. "C'mon. Let's go, Peach, let's go."

The horse groaned, you knew she was going to do it then, and she stumbled forward, a loose, drunk step up to her shin, up to her knees. Before I knew it, Kate was holding her boots high in the air above the water. "Jesus!" she cried. "Shit!" They weren't even halfway across, and the horse was up to her stomach.

"Okay," I said low, to myself. "Okay, okay. All right."

Jazz held hesitation in his chest, but then he, too, let go. The water was black and cold and close, and we were going too fast. It was like falling down a rocky slope, tumbling in. I dropped my stirrups and hung on to the saddle, my legs bent up close, the water near the edge of the saddle, and I couldn't believe it was as deep as that. There was this moment, this crazy moment, when Jazz stopped dead in the water: lazy, intoxicated. His ears were up and he looked around, like we were searching for a picnic spot, like he was going to just lie down and call it a day, call it a life. We were in the middle of the damn river, the deepest part, and the current was going to take us, we didn't have a say in anything—but then he woke up again and hauled us out. The momentum changed, and he heaved up with every muscle, and we were standing on the other bank.

The horses got hold of themselves and started acting as if it had never been much of a big deal in the first place. Kate was flicking mud from her jeans.

"Okay, now where?"

"I guess this way." She was peering up through the trees.

I looked at her. "You've been here before, right?"

"No, not really. Damn river always seemed too deep."

She smiled at me.

Mom and Dad were at odds about the Women of History from the beginning.

The night she'd informed us she'd joined up, become a Woman of History herself, we were having dinner, a spinach-and-gluten dish she'd optimistically dubbed "Green Spaghetti."

"They're passionate about what they're doing, and I think it's a terrific opportunity," she said enthusiastically—like a weatherman extolling the virtues of a hurricane. "I can just really *jump* in there and learn something about this town. And at the same time, I can help the community."

Dad looked up from his mashed spinach and Wheaties and stared at the not orange ceiling. "Honey, let's just be practical about this for a minute. We'll start by looking at the language of the thing. You're joining a group of women who are putting on, I believe you said, a *jubilee*? A jubilee? Jubilee? That's a *crazy* word, an ill word. Like a lunatic would use."

"So your resistance is because you don't like the *word*? Well, what if we called it a hoedown, Chris? How would that sound? A Hoedown for History."

"Look, they've already gotten you talking like one of them. First comes *jubilee,* then all of a sudden you're talking about *helping the community.* See what I mean? See the problem? Next thing you know, we'll be joining the Republican Party."

My mother gave a little clenched-teeth smile. Even before Nixon, you wouldn't go *this* far. "Actually, no, I don't see the problem. What could *possibly* be wrong with helping the community?"

"If you really want to help the community, go dole out some soup at the soup kitchen or teach the poor to read. Don't fool yourself into thinking you're doing good works when you're raising money and putting on events with a bunch of rich ladies. But most importantly, most importantly—your studio, Clare, your painting—"

"Just because these women are a little—a little *wealthy,* doesn't mean they're *devil worshippers,* for God's sake. I mean—"

"Why are they called the Women of History, anyway?" I interjected: Divert the stream.

"Because Women from Saks Fifth Avenue doesn't have the right appeal."

"Because they care about their roots, Alison. You know, like the TV show?"

"Only they didn't come over in slave ships, they came over in BMWs."

"Very funny."

Dad had taken to creating small, obsessive squares out of his meal. "*Jubilee? Jubilee?* Why don't they just call it a picnic, or a party, or even a *celebration?* Why must we bowdlerize and obfuscate and create committees, *God,* and boards and meetings?"

"It's just some people putting on a party," I said. "What's the big deal about that?"

"Yes, it's a *party,* " Mom enunciated.

"Well, do what you want with your days, babe. It's a free world. Isn't that what you stand for, anyway?"

I could see it in her face: fragility. But Dad couldn't see that, because *he* was still looking down at his checkerboard of Green Spaghetti. Mom placed her napkin by her plate. "Chris, the thing is, they said they wanted an artist specifically. An artist— like me." She gave him a little smile, like maybe he'd see that she'd already succeeded in this one thing.

This might work, I thought. A little tête-à-tête, a little leveling. But it didn't quite take.

"An artist, Clare? Really? Will they put you in costume, maybe a beret?"

My mother stood up from the table. "You know whom you're *most* like?" she said, her nearly full plate gripped in one hand. "Your mother. You're just like your mother."

She flung her plate into the sink.

Dad looked stunned, as if she'd never said this before. "I am not," he said slowly. "You are."

"No, *you* are." Mom turned and made a dramatic exit out of the room.

I felt hot, my brace pressing into me. The Green Spaghetti sat on my plate in a little lump of ire. My father stood up, pushing his chair hard against the floor. He, too, flung his dish into the sink and left the kitchen.

I got up myself: Dinner seemed to be over. I picked up my plate. Maybe it was a new ritual, flinging plates, like breaking wineglasses at a wedding. To fling or not to fling? I walked across the kitchen and put my plate in the sink, quietly.

I hated when they brought up Grandma. As far as I was concerned, she was just this little old lady who always wore black, a feather in the wind. She'd been born in Ireland, but for most of her adult life she'd lived in Queens. She was always talking about the Troubles. I didn't really know what Troubles she meant, it had something to do with history, but whatever it was kept her shaking her frail little old lady's head years later. Whenever she wrote my dad—which she did frequently, as if phone calls were still billed on a transatlantic basis—she wrote in the return address section, Katherine Glass, Boulevard of Broken Dreams.

*B*esides her schoolmates, there were also, at games of lawn tennis and barn burnings, their parents. And actually the lost heroine was privately convinced that these country-men, who had decided it was necessary to Tryumph over the Hazirduss yet Encour'ging Province and Ransack for the Goode of Gentlefolk the deciduous forest, and who would commonly offer things like Thirteen Coats and the rest in Wampum to the shivering and noble Indians, not to mention trick them with shifty land measurements such as From this Sea Shore a Day's Walke into the Country, were a bit irritating. There was a deep vagueness to them.

Chapter Four

WE ALL come from somewhere; that seemed to be the message.

"You all come from somewhere!" Mr. Bostitch, my social studies teacher, shouted from the front of the room. Behind him hung a set of posters: the American Revolution, the Civil War, World War I, World War II, and Vietnam.

Kate and I looked at each other.

"Where do you *come from? Who are* your *people?"* he now asked in rapid succession.

Mr. Bostitch had a provocative arch to his bushy gray eyebrows. He was a nimble older man, trim and preppy in his pressed Levi's and yellow sweater vest. He had the air of a coach—maybe a church group organizer. He'd been teaching eighth-grade social studies for thirty frisky years.

"What about you, Alison?" he now asked, shocking me—I think it was the first time he'd called on me all month.

"My grandmother is Irish?" I responded—meek since the whirling dervish incident.

"Ah, the Irish," he said, doing an about-face, sending his tasseled loafers into a swirl. He wrote "Irish" on the blackboard and then drew a line under it, fiercely, as if this were the only item truly needed at the corner store.

"Black Irish? Lace curtain? Catholic? Protestant?"

Black Irish—what was that? My father had dark hair. Still, it had an ominous sound—like criminals, or the plague, or a bruise of some impossible kind.

"Lace curtain?" I ventured.

"Traitor! Criminal! Defender of the republic!" he thundered, swinging about, now scratching a hasty question mark at the end of "Irish" and once again underlining the whole, now fearful, concept. My origins, my self, my country—thrown into confusion.

"I'm a hundred percent English," boasted Bruce Johnson, thank God, with dumb donkey pride.

"Have a spot of tea," taunted one of his friends in falsetto.

"One lump or two?" squealed another brawny team player.

Pretty, annoying Priscilla said, "My great-great-great-grandfather came over on, like, the *Mayflower*."

She twirled a lock of hair and smiled, first at Bruce and then at the teacher, who gave her a fatherly grin. "An original," he said in apparent rapture. "An original American."

Kate turned her gaze from Priscilla Shasta to me. Priscilla, an original anything?

Like I mentioned, Kate was popular when we met, friends with nearly everyone. She wasn't entirely *one* of them—she wasn't nearly that dumb—but she'd been granted respect even by the jocks: the reigning majority, keepers of the kingdom. Hanging out with me had already eroded her social standing.

But the girls wanted her back. They weren't going to be upstaged by some bizarro brace wearer.

That day before class, *Mayflower* Priscilla, along with a couple of other girls in matching clothing, had come up to Kate and me and stood, with sweet smiles on their faces, in a questioning row.

"Where are you from?" they'd asked. (Little did I know this question would come at me again, and so quickly.)

"Norwalk," I said.

"Did you live in, like, an apartment?"

"We had a house," I lied. So we had half a house, so what.

"What does your father do?"

"He teaches at Fairfield University."

"I heard he was something weird—a poet, like he writes poetry or something," this girl Lynn Hutchins said, studying me. Her hair was bleached out from playing field hockey or swimming at the country club. She had big breasts already and a pale blue Shetland sweater and dark blue corduroys and blue clogs—an acceptable variation on The Outfit. By now I'd come to realize that every sanctioned human in Weston, every beautiful person, wore the same thing: light blue, navy, or tan corduroys; pink, tan, or light blue sweaters; and little gold lockets hanging cutely between crisp collars. No one else wore a bright pink reversible floral floppy hat the way I did—a Montessori-challenged, happy-dappy person.

Kate pitched in. "Yeah, her dad's a famous poet, that's true. He's got books published and everything."

"Oh, wow," Priscilla said, cosmically unimpressed.

"It's a lot cooler than most parents' jobs," said Kate.

"Your dad's weird, too, Kate," said Lynn. "You're walking on thin ice."

"Hey, my dad makes more money than God," said Kate.

"If your father's such a famous poet, why does he work as a teacher? Doesn't that mean he's, like, not really famous?"

"Maybe he has to make extra money to take care of her—medical—bills," said the third girl, Lisa, in a sickly sympathetic voice. She had ethereal blue eyes and was twirling her necklace, a little diamond horseshoe, with pale fingers. It was Lisa Feneta, daughter of Grete Feneta, the most frightening Woman of History. Lisa rode horses, too, but only ones with bloodlines—Kate had told me about her.

The bell rang before I could respond.

Now, while Mr. Bostitch wrote "True Blue American" on the board, Bruce whispered at the back of Priscilla's neck, "Old gramps was looking for Indian girls."

"We all come from someplace, yes," the teacher said. "Certainly true, certainly true. And what difference could it possibly make, you ask? *Weellll*, let's say you'd just come from Burger King, and you'd had a burger with a nice pickle and ketchup and let's say a slice of onion. You'd smell like—what, my friends? See what I'm saying?"

"You'd smell like your parents?" Kate asked.

"Ah-*hah! Yes!*" Mr. Bostitch said, then did a surprise spin toward a student on the side of the room. "*Name the twenty-eighth president of the United States!*" he shouted, pointing his finger at the boy.

The kid sat straight up like he'd been electrocuted. "Twenty-eighth? Okay, the twenty-eighth." He started pawing his chin in desperate meditation.

"*Who knows? Who knows?*" Mr. Bostitch went on, his pointing hand careening up and down the rows, to no avail. Finally he gave up and went back to his main point. "Today, my friends, we are about to take a step forward. We are about to plunge, nay, cannonball, into—yes—adulthood. Known as maturity, known as *the next great step for mankind!*"

If we weren't worried before, we certainly were then.

"What does 1776 mean to you?" he asked, bending over at the waist and squinting at us as if through a fog. And it was only after we all floundered around *this* question that Mr. Bostitch revealed that Weston, Connecticut—our glorious little town—had been incorporated the *very same year,* the very same summer, in fact, that the Declaration of Independence was signed. We weren't simply *born* in the U.S.A., we *were* the U.S.A. We were a tiny microcosm of our country, of how things could go wrong.

But Mr. Bostitch didn't put it quite that way. He said, "Yes, it's a mighty coincidence. A synergy, you might say, between Weston's proud history and that of our country. *Now,* the question is, where do *you* fit in? This summer, at the Weston Bicentennial Jubilee, every student in this room will experience history *firsthand,* will have the opportunity to create—relevance. Deep, abiding relevance. Yes, I'm offering you the opportunity to write your own story, *to create history.*"

I already knew about the jubilee thanks to the Women of History, but even I wasn't entirely sure what he was talking about at this point. No one did. Bruce Johnson, Englishman, had a look on his face that could only be described as horror. Even the nerds looked uncertain.

Braving the unknown, Jeff Neely raised his hand. "Mr. Bostitch, is this, like, in addition to our regular homework?"

Mr. Bostitch sighed, then went on to explain that in a couple of months we'd do an oral report on some aspect of Connecticut history. In May, we'd showcase our final projects at the jubilee, though we were encouraged to get started on them right away. These could be anything: a diorama, a replica map, a chart of our family's immigration history.

The whole year-long project was called Of Many Nations, into Jubilant Unity. Our first assignment, a list of three ideas for the oral report, was due a week from Friday.

"Here they come again," said Kate in the cafeteria. Lisa, Lynn, and Priscilla were descending on us like the *Niña,* the *Pinta,* and the *Santa María.* They were all carrying trays. The meal of the day was frankfurter on a bun, baked beans, ketchup, a pickle, and milk, and the glittering girls gazed over this prescribed bounty at us. Kate was peeling a tangerine, all in one continuous peel, and I had my Love Bag: celery with peanut butter, roasted sunflower seeds, and a morning glory muffin, whatever that was. ("A full meal in itself!" my mother had said.)

"Hey, Kate," said Lynn. "Junior cheerleader tryouts are this afternoon. You going to try out this time?"

Kate hadn't yet looked up from her tangerine, but now she offered a glance to Lynn, cocked one eyebrow. "Who's doing it this year, do you know? Mrs. Ashcroft again?"

"Yup. She's such a bitch," Priscilla said.

"No pain, no gain," Lynn pointed out, pivoting to look at

her charge. Priscilla hunched slightly into herself and smiled at her frankfurter.

The tangerine peel reached all the way from Kate's hands down to the table now. "Yeah. I don't think so."

The empty seats by us seemed to present themselves then, an unspoken invitation. No one sat down.

"Well, that's a mistake," said Lisa Feneta, blue eyes still, stealthy. I imagined her as a villainess in jodhpurs, crop at the ready, blue ribbons behind her. "Your chances of getting on the real cheerleading squad are much better if you've been a junior cheerleader. Of course, you quit riding lessons, too, so I guess it's a pattern."

Lisa's horse was named Magnus Dynamic IV. His bloodlines went back to 1882: an impressive equine legacy.

"Shit," said Kate—the peel had almost broken, but then she hooked her fingers around and got it all off.

"What are you doing with that stupid thing anyway?" Lynn said.

Kate didn't respond.

Lynn looked at Lisa, incredulous, then said, "Wasting her time—typical." Then she gave Lisa a silent command, something that involved flicking her hair behind one pastel-sweatered shoulder, and the three of them glided away, Priscilla trailing the others.

For the whole exchange, I hadn't said a word. Now I said to Kate, "Welp, I think they're mad at you now."

"So what?" Kate said. "Like that fucking matters in life."

In my head, I tested this concept. The air around us smelled like tangerine.

Instead of joining the junior cheerleaders, Kate invited me over to her house after school. It was a Frank Lloyd Wright–style house, meaning that it was modern and it didn't have, like ours, orange shag carpeting.

It did have her parents, smoking pot in the living room and watching television.

Actually, they weren't just smoking pot. They were in the throes of some kind of ritual of affection, adoration, or subjugation.

Her mom, all in black including black leather pants, was sitting on a red leather couch, and between her knees, sitting on the floor, was a bald man, wearing a white tunic kind of thing. His eyes were closed. Mrs. Hamilton took a long suck from the joint and then started slowly massaging the man's glossy tan cranium.

A small army of dogs raced toward me, skidding and yowling disconcertingly. They were basenjis, I'd be informed later, and they didn't exactly bark, they yodeled. The Hamiltons had named them all after Egyptian gods and goddesses. Not just Anubis, the basenjilike god of the underworld, but also Shu, Geb, Nut, Isis, Osiris, Seth, Hapi, Mut I, Mut II, and Horus. The empire had never been so furry.

"Who's this?" Shana Hamilton said to Kate in a pouting imitation of friendly.

Shana was beautiful in a weary, storklike way. She had short blond hair, starfish sculpted, like Liza Minnelli's. Her lips were bright red, and her fingernails were painted, too, little red dots swirling over the bald husbandly orb.

"This is my friend Alison. She lives off Steep Hill, on Ramble Lane. She's in my grade. I told you about her, remember?"

Kate was leaning on the wall, taking off her shoes.

Her father opened his eyes now and looked my way. He lifted a pipe to his mouth, took a suck from it, and then let out a puff of smoke with a wet gasp. "So you're Alison."

"Yes."

"And there's that brace of yours."

I hesitated. "Yes."

"Honey, you look straight enough to me. What's the problem?" He took another pull, then let go of the pipe stem with a great, puckering smack. "Do you turn into some kind of circus freak if you take off that thing?"

"We're going to get something to eat," said Kate.

"Oh, my God! I forgot the brownies!" screamed Mrs. Hamilton. She leapt up from the couch and stumbled over her husband's legs, and then a wandering brown-and-white hound, as she scampered out of the room.

Tut Hamilton's eyebrows moved now, like caterpillars. He didn't seem entirely shamanlike to me. "You're not a bad-looking little lady, really."

I muttered a "Thank you," then bent to pet the dog running in place on my leg. He knocked his nose into my hand and then stared up at me with mute, eyebrow-bunched intensity.

"Come on, Alison," said Kate.

Giving a polite smile to Mr. Hamilton, I followed Kate to the kitchen, where her mother was standing before the counter, taking a fork to a pan of brownies. I could now see that she was ten feet tall. She blew on a chunk of chocolate, then popped it in her mouth with an *mmm* sound.

"You want some cheese and crackers? Ice cream? Brownies? If Mom doesn't eat them all, that is."

Mrs. Hamilton made a noise to indicate her maltreatment, then kept eating.

"What kind of ice cream?"

Kate opened the door to the huge, sleek refrigerator—it looked as if she were opening up a garage. "Rum raisin, cherry vanilla, butter pecan. I think I'll have butter pecan."

"Me too," I said.

Shana trapped a falling brownie bit with her napkin and then said, "So, Alison, you're in eighth grade, just like my Katie?"

I said I was.

"Isn't that great. And what do your parents do?"

"Well, my father is a poet and my mother is an artist."

"How *wonderful*! We should have them over for dinner. What are they doing tonight?"

"Tonight?"

"Sure. We've got filets in the freezer. From Ruth's Chris Steak House, our *favorite*. Isn't that so, little Shu?"

One of the dogs had leaned up against her leg to receive his share of the treats.

"I've got to clean my room tonight," said Kate.

"Clean your room some other time," her father said from the doorway. "People always come first."

He picked up the phone from the wall and handed it to me. "Call them."

Little curly lines went round and round in his eyes, like a pinwheel.

Happily, my parents were busy that night—or pretended to be—so dinner had to wait for another evening.

Later that week, Kate and I sat together in the Fiction A–L section of the library, books spread on the table. The poster above us read DANGER! LEARNING IN PROGRESS. We'd looked up "Revolution, American" and "History, Connecticut" in the card catalog, and Kate had written "1, 2, 3" on a piece of notebook paper for possible thesis statements, and "Project?" underneath. Now she jangled her silver bangles and tore through pages. She was a faster reader than me, even though Mr. Snodgrass had brought in a special speed-reading teacher for two Fridays in a row. He'd suggested that we read the first and last sentence of every paragraph carefully and skim the rest. This technique upset me—me, lover of *Watership Down, The Hobbit,* and *Slaughterhouse-Five* and daughter of a poet. The poets believed in the middle part, too, I ventured to myself, silent in the middle zone of the classroom.

As far as I could tell, Weston's past seemed to consist entirely of people dividing land into parcels, redividing those parcels, and then forming committees or petitioning committees regarding the ownership of the parcels. Bigger history— American history—had to do with the amount of soldiers sent to the northernmost corner of the easternmost tributary, as compared with the amount of soldiers left to defend the westernmost region of the southernmost territory. Much was made of different kinds of guns and other weaponry, and an inordinate number of messages were delivered "right in time" or "too late" for the Revolutionaries.

"How about these oddities of nature," Kate said. "Ezbon Burr, Samuel Hull, Francis Sturge, George Squire, Phoebe Ogden. They owned the first lots here, before Weston was even a town."

"What weirdos."

"I know."

I went back to *Pioneer!: The Connecticut Experience* but soon turned my gaze out the window, where a sparrow was eating some kind of birdseed. He kept getting hit in the head by drops of water coming from the roof.

In a minute, Kate said, "What is wampum, anyway?"

"Money."

"I know that, but what did it look like? Coins? Beads?"

"Beads. Definitely."

"How much was it worth?"

"I don't know."

"Well, the I-don't-know-how-to-pronounce-this—'*Peek-on-it*'?—Indians sold this land for 'eight fathom of wampum, six coats, ten hatchets, and ten looking glasses.' That doesn't sound like much."

"So did the Indians not have mirrors, maybe?" I envisioned an Indian staring into the glassy surface of a lake.

"I believe they gazed into the eyes of the buffalo, Alison."

"Yeah, I wish I had some wampum," I said. "I'd get those hoop earrings from the Selective Eye."

"I'd get a Snickers bar."

We went back to our books, theoretically. I noticed that

Mrs. Hollbrook—the red, white, and blue lady from the Women of History—was giving some kind of talk to kids on the other side of the library. She was holding a book high in the air, swirling it around as she spoke: Maybe she was talking about airplanes. Children sat cross-legged in front of her, necks craned up, dutiful without complaint to the old lady in patriot frocks.

"Alison," Kate whispered, leaning over the table, "have you ever met a ventriloquist?"

"No, have you?"

"Last night this man came over, a friend of my parents. It was really creepy. He had this doll, and he just sat on the couch, and when I went over there he made me sit down. Then he had the doll say weird things to me."

Kate was leaning across the table and looking at me intently, as if she were reliving what she was remembering. Her cheekbones looked sharp, pink.

"What kinds of weird things?"

"Like what he'd do to me if I wasn't *jail bait.*"

"What's jail bait?"

"A girl who's too young to have sex."

"Oh. Not very nice."

"It was a trick. You can get mad at a *man,* but not a stupid doll saying things."

"And I thought *my* parents had weird friends."

"Yeah," Kate said, looking down at her bracelets. She began to fling one around her wrist, a caught Hula-Hoop. "This whole project sucks."

"Yeah, but it's still due Friday."

We listened to the hum of the library. Finally, that bird flew away.

"Hey, I have an idea," Kate said. "For the final project, we could write a book. A secret history."

Her hands were still now, palms down on the worn wood of the table.

"That sounds cool. What kind of secret history?"

"It could be about a girl, you know? Like us. She could be like a detective and—find out things."

"But what does some girl have to do with history?" I said. "Nothing."

"Well, we could throw in some stuff about the war," Kate said, shrugging.

"We could put in some historical details," I added, getting it now. "And, like, some stuff about trees."

Kate took off one bangle and started winging it around her finger. "This is cool," she said. "So what if Mr. Bostitch doesn't get it? You write some, then I will, then you will and I will, and before you know it we'll have a story."

The bracelet flung off and actually slid under the periodicals shelf, but we had our project idea anyway.

*W*eston—or Wistin—was a town of a thousand souls in 1776, with three public buildings and some two hundred structures that were individually owned, and it was very much as it is today, minus cars, pavement, and telephone poles. Yet these trifling technologies did not matter much to the well-being of the girl who would soon become the lost heroine, for she was joining hands in a quiet circle of toil, love, and tasty gruel with her loving parents. (They'd also had a cat once, but it died.)

One day she heard her father speaking in furtive tones about undisclosed things in the other room. It had something to do, perhaps, with feathers? When the men left they all clapped him on the back in time-honored, manly fashion. Little did she know that this was the day her father, who had once put socks on his ears to amuse her, had revealed his plans to become governor of Connecticut.

Chapter Five

ON THURSDAY, I had to get Jazz clean and saddled up before my riding lesson. I stood at the side of the paddock and watched him first—because there was always this: the remedy of the immediate, the tangible sight of my pony—and then I pulled up the metal hook on the gate and went in the paddock. He kept his head down, finding bits of grass to shear. All around us the trees clicked and whispered the way they do that time of year in Connecticut. The last of the green leaves were curled up and gone, and the red and yellow ones rustled together like coins.

I put a hand on his withers, and he stopped eating and blinked and let me cup his head in the crook of my arm, guide the red halter around his muzzle, latch the strap behind his ear. I let out a stretch of rope, and we walked together to the barn.

First I used the currycomb, scrubbing in slow circles around his neck and chest and belly and buttocks. He leaned into my hand. Then the stiff brush, in swift, regular strokes, along with the growth of the hair, and then a final, gentler smoothing out with the soft brush, and his black body began to shine. I cleaned out his hooves, and then I started on his mane.

Lee pulled up in her blue truck. She lit a cigarette in the cab, then got out and walked toward me. My riding instructor's defining feature—besides her propensity for the rules, the confirmation of horse and rider—was her long blond hair. It was a wig, actually, a four-foot tumble that fell, stiff with spray, from a little nest on top of her head. Her mascara was black, thick, and toxic, and she'd done something strange to her eyebrows: plucked them out and then penciled in new ones, thinner and longer.

"We're going to work a little higher today," Lee said by way of greeting, and opened the gate to the paddock. She stalked out toward the jumps—we'd put up one barrel jump and two with cross ties—and began ratcheting them up, higher and nervous making. We were getting ready for a horse show later in the fall. It was my mom's big idea—last of the hippie dictators. I had pointed out to her that competition wasn't really part of the whole mint-tea gestalt, but she'd said it would be "good for me."

Maybe, but I'd rather ride on trails with Kate, I knew that already.

Lee started us out trotting, hugging the inside of the fence, staring forward. She thought of the horse as a machine, and she treated me the same way. I was an anatomy model gone awry: my knees too loose against the horse's body, my hands too high above the saddle, my heels never deep enough in the stirrups.

Although she never did tell me to straighten my posture. Brace or no brace, I sat rigid as anything.

"Look lively, Alison! Get that horse moving!" she shouted when we got to cantering. "Everyone, wake up out there!"

She lit another cigarette, and then it was time to start jumping.

Jazz was a great jumper—he'd jumped out of our paddock twice, for instance—but you still had to motivate him to give his all. Lee had told me to slap him on the flank with the crop right before we got to a jump.

I held the reins close as we bore in on the cross ties. There was a moment right before he jumped when Jazz seemed to hesitate—when the prospect of obeying reins and people waned—and this was when I was supposed to hit him. I gave him the feeblest little tap.

Still, it worked. He was up, we were up, free, transcending gravity, and I tried to hold the reins loose but quiet, steady—

We were down again, with a thump. Keep going. Straight to the end of the paddock, turn left, come in from the opposite side for the next jump.

I could hear the pummeling of the hard path under our feet. As we barreled forward, then got right in front of the jump, it seemed impossible for him to get over it. Impossible.

"Eyes *forward,* hands down. *Hands down,*" shouted Lee.

We were there, it was up to his head for God's sake, and then—*"Hit that horse!"*—we were over it.

"And again," Lee said, kicking a rock. "Start from the beginning."

There was this moment, right when Jazz was at the top of

his leap, where it seemed we had just possibly tricked gravity: We could keep going.

At the end of the lesson, Lee said, "You've got to practice every day, every other day minimum, Alison, if you want to make any progress at all in the next few weeks. Show the horse who's boss, okay?"

"Okay," I said, cowed by her glamour and authority. That hair was amazing.

"He can jump, but he's lazy," she said. "All right, see you next week."

She gave Jazz a businesslike pat and headed out of the paddock.

I felt like we'd been maligned. I thought, He is not lazy. She didn't know the inside story, the horse and girl story.

It was my pediatrician who had originally discovered the curvature. He'd made me bend forward, and he'd seen it, felt it with his finger: some indication of a curve, like a wind coming from up north and listing a sail down toward the ocean's surface. Then I had my first X-ray at the New York doctor's.

I'd never seen an X-ray before, but there I was, neck to hips, bare as night. My bones peered out at me, hesitant and ghostly. Surely these whispery bones couldn't hold a person together. The ribs were especially mysterious, like streams or rivers, small thin falling creatures.

But it was the stack of vertebrae we scrutinized. Somehow the stack was toppling.

The doctor snapped shut his protractor and made his pronouncement. An S-curve, they call it, and at the time, the

Milwaukee brace was the first treatment as a matter of course. Scoliosis could progress rapidly, he warned us, squeezing or even puncturing the internal organs and leading to pronounced cosmetic disfigurement. Sometimes the brace worked and sometimes it didn't—and then there was the surgery route: Cut the girl open, screw a metal rod onto the spine and jack it straight, and sew her up again.

The doctor winced in our general direction, and then they hustled me back through the corridor in my pale examination gown.

When we got outside, my mom went reeling down the sidewalk, weaving left and then right like a drunk person. I could see only her back, stiff in her gray winter coat, but I could tell from her crazy walk that she was not, to say the least, herself. My father had stopped at the edge of the street, holding the car keys as if he'd entirely forgotten where the car had gotten to in the last, radical hour, when his daughter, just twelve years old, was diagnosed and would be required to suffer what seemed a medieval treatment. I looked from him and his hot grimace to my mother's back, once, then again. He was trembling, about to explode. He would combust, I felt sure, yet when I looked back at my mother, *she* was spinning, literally spinning, there on the sidewalk, looking up at the sky as if at rain, looking up at the pools of salt water in her eyes, blurring her vision of her surroundings, of anything that made sense, of *me,* her daughter.

Hey, wait a minute, I could have said. *Hey, guys—earth to my parents. This is me here, where's my consolation? Which one of you will save me from this day, from what it has become?*

But I didn't say that; I didn't say anything. I stood frozen.

Eventually, the moment passed. My mother quit spinning. She wiped her eyes and came to the car. My father stuttered back to normal life, as if a bolt of lightning had released him, and instead of collapsing he walked over to the driver's side of the car and opened it and got in. He laid the mimeographed sheet of directions to the brace maker on the steering wheel.

"Don't worry, Alison, we'll get out of this," my mother said from the front seat, her face a strained silhouette.

"Get out of it?" Dad said, looking over into the Manhattan traffic before lurching the car into the street, into what came next. "You don't *get out of* something like this."

That was the day things changed. The connection between myself, my unusual invisible self inside, now revealed by X-ray, and the earth-shattering differences (up until then merely charming) in my parents established itself. I became convinced that the road they were on, once straight, was curving off into uncharted territory, and it was no one's fault but my own.

I was wrong about this, of course, yet I wasn't wrong entirely. In the months after the diagnosis, Dad's attitude did lean toward endurance—like you'd sustain on a boat over the Atlantic, holding your fists tight in your lap, hoping for the shore to appear. Yet my mother, with Sarah Bernhardt/ Martha Graham flair, felt that even if you couldn't entirely *get out of* something, some action was in order. Hence the introduction of whole-wheat flour and kelp into our daily diet and the forlorn fate of Snickers bars.

Without a doubt, my back problem and their individual responses caused tension for my parents, but then again it may simply have revealed who they already were. It may have teased out certain proclivities, certain seductions, you might say.

The two men stared at each other like faces on a monument, a new grouping at Mount Rushmore. All the marijuana paraphernalia had been stowed away—would they tell my parents about it later, maybe offer them a joint? The dinner had been a hard enough sell *without* mentioning that the Hamiltons were potheads. Now I worried I should have told them anyway.

"I wouldn't know a creative idea if it jumped up and bit me in the face," Shana Hamilton was saying. "In this household, it's Tut who comes up with the new ideas, then he does some kind of magic in the bathroom, and out come *boatloads* of dollars."

She was swishing her wine around in the glass vigorously, staring into it, her own crystal ball. Little wisps of hair curled onto her forehead and cheeks. They'd been attached to her skin with glue, I felt certain, crescent-shaped echoes of her eyelashes, which were long and fake and beautiful.

"Oh, Shana," said my mother, who had on her serene-as-jade public persona, "we're all creative. Look at these young people surrounding us—just raising them is an act of creation. Remember childbirth?"

"Oh, do I!" Kate's mom said.

Tut Hamilton had moved on from a stalwart assessment of my father and was now giving Mom his caterpillars-on-a-beach-ball stare. The overhead fan was on, and a shadow kept swooping over the tan bright baldness of his head. Smudge, then none. Smudge, then none.

"I've always thought . . . well, I've always thought that my best creative work is not on the canvas at all," Mom continued with a loving look in my direction. "Not that I have anything to do with who she's becoming."

"Nature versus nurture, right?" said Shana. "I gave up on Mick and Kate long ago. I mean, I didn't *give up* on them—I just gave up believing I could make them into my image. Or anything."

She looked over at her husband then, as if for encouragement.

Kate was sitting with her hands folded in her lap.

"You're a wonderful mother, when you're sober, anyhow," Mr. Hamilton said, patting Shana's knee.

Shana Hamilton looked too young to have a couple of kids. I hadn't met Mick, Kate's older brother, though we'd almost run into him earlier that evening. A van full of dark, hoodlumlike shapes was pulling out of the drive when we drove in. Now Shana looked younger than ever, taking in the comment of her husband.

My father cleared his throat. "Tell us more about your business, Tut—now, that can't be your real name, can it?—we've heard rumors. It sounds like interesting stuff."

"Like the Hopis and the Navajos, like so many aborigines, I chose my own name at some point—or really, it chose me. But in any case, my parents—bless their British bottoms—had nothing to do with it. *Anyhoo,* yes, Chris, my business. It's my life. I've had a good run now, for some time. It's been a confluence of certain things. Time, society, me. I'm just a conduit, actually."

A confluence of conduits, I said to myself, noticing that Kate hadn't eaten anything. Would this dinner end in the next century? Maybe we could sneak into her room and smoke Winstons soon.

My mother trailed her finger against the rim of her wineglass. "Tell us."

Tut considered her for a long moment, then smiled and looked back at my father. "Chris, we've gotten so far away from what makes us real, don't you think? We drive our expensive cars, watch our foreign movies. Yet something inside is missing. Yes, we feel empty—we're drawn to drink, to smoke, to have sex with other people's wives—because we don't know how to *fill* that emptiness, to get *rid of* that empty feeling. Does this sound right? Am I making sense yet?"

"I'm following you," my father said neutrally.

"There's a need we have. There's not enough *inner action*. That's the heart of my philosophy, you see. That we need to take *inner action,* and the rest will follow. We need to return to the inner action of the masters, for from that wellspring comes *outer* peace, *outer* tranquillity, and, in case you're wondering, outer riches and outer beauty. Look at my beautiful wife. Look at my beautiful house. You want to know where this comes from? Inner action, my good friend. Just like the Egyptians."

"And how's that?" Dad asked.

My mother was listening attentively.

Mr. Hamilton looked over at his wife, as if to say, *She's so sexy,* which was good, because ever since the "while sober" comment, Mrs. Hamilton had been looking as if she were slowly losing air, emptying out like a balloon. She perked up a little now, before deflating back down.

"Well, if you really want to know, cough up two grand and come to my Empire of the Sun Playshop next month."

"Yes, do," said Shana.

"I want to know, but maybe not quite that badly."

"How about a little teaser?" my mother said.

Dad looked over at her, irritated.

Tut said, "Well, dear Clare, you said it yourself earlier. We're all creative people. We create our lives, you see. There are three steps to building a pyramid, I always say."

"One, get yourself some slaves," said my father.

"One," Tut said with a nod in Dad's direction, "learn control. Learn to channel your energy—very much like getting a bucketful of slaves, Chris. Very much indeed like that—only the onus is on you, not on anyone else."

"And the other two steps?" my mother asked.

Tut winked at her. "Now, let's not get ahead of ourselves."

I felt that perhaps my dad's inner energy was confluencing into a conduit at that point. He reached for the wine by the stack of steaks and poured himself a half glass, hesitated, then poured to the top.

Mom's eyes glittered. She was back to bohemian wear that evening, a wraparound sea green sweater, clasped at the bosom with a silver moon. Now she said, "I bet you need to build the next two steps yourself. I bet that's what you have to do. You have to build the next thousand or two thousand steps yourself, until you hit the sky."

"Hah," said Tut. He looked up at the ceiling and squirreled

his eyebrows around. "Hah-hah. Glorious, Clare. I like that. Well said."

He pulled himself up to the table's edge and looked at my father. "She's got it, you know? Your wife has really got it."

"She certainly does have it, Tut Hamilton."

"Got what?" my mother said with a little smile.

Tut laughed heartily. "Brilliant. Brilliant!"

"May we be excused?" asked Kate. "Please?"

We looked hopefully at the group of four. Mother #1 was perched in her chair like a peanut on the nose of an elephant. Mother #2 looked as though she'd just now discovered there was no Santa Claus. Father #1 was about to start meditating on the physics of exploding devices, and Father #2 was rubbing his stomach, without regard for any of them.

Who's to say shamans don't have manners—he walked us to the door, didn't he? And on the front porch, my father and Tut even shook hands. Then Dad stared out into the night— only to turn back when Mom said, "And Tut, I just had the best idea. Would you like to speak at the Women of History fund-raiser next month? We're raising money for the May jubilee. You know these kinds of affairs—we could use a little something, a little jazz, I think."

She smiled then, looking from Tut to my father to Tut again.

He said he'd be glad to do it. "Only relax, Clare," he added. "Your shoulders—see how they're all tensed up? No artist needs to be that rigid. Let it flow, baby, let it flow."

They waited until they were out of the driveway, as if the Hamiltons maybe had extraordinary powers of hearing.

"Well, Clare. You certainly caught me by surprise. I had no idea that pyramid power or whatever he calls it is relevant to an organization that, theoretically, promotes history."

"Pyramid *love*," she said.

"Pyramid love, pyramid love." He was doing some faux ruminating. "So what do you think he'll call his talk? 'The Pioneer Within the Mercedes'? 'Making Money the Mesopotamian Way'?" Dad glanced at me in the backseat.

Mom wasn't taking the bait; she didn't seem even to be listening. "Tut's interesting. He's got charisma, don't you think?"

"Do I think that man has *charisma*? Is that what you just asked me?"

"I want you to read for us, too, of course. What do you think?" She looked over at him. "Ready to read a little poetry?"

Dad lowered himself in his seat, as if he could maybe pull his beard up over his face and disappear entirely. In a muffled voice he said, "I'm sorry, I think I'm busy that night. I've got a union meeting. The Brotherhood of Man, suburban chapter."

"See, Chris? See what I have to contend with?"

"Sorry about that, though. Send my regrets."

"C'mon, honey—really."

Dad emitted a strange sound, a bit like the trapped bark of the Hamiltons' basenjis. "Clare, you know these people don't care about poetry."

"Of course they do," Mom said as if she were at Disney World. "And that man, Tut Hamilton—what a firecracker. He has a way with people. He makes you feel . . . how would you put it? Vulnerable."

From my station in the backseat, the spectators' gallery, I saw Dad's expression: first thunderstruck, then depressed. He began mumbling something about having heard it all and/or the follies of the New Age.

When we got home both of them hopped out of the car like it was on fire.

I did my back exercises up in my room. They were the most futile-feeling exercises on the planet. I put on my nightgown and crawled under my nice rose quilt. With the brace, you needed to lie on your side and prop up your head on the pillow the right way; otherwise the neck section would throttle you to a sad, gagging death.

I thought more about quitting my horse lessons with Lee, just saying no to the horse show, but I didn't want to disappoint my mother.

The lost heroine traversed along the Paleozoic rock, for that was what Wistin was founded upon. Paleozoic rock includes mica and quartzite. It is old and firm and sometimes shiny. Sarah walked around and around, sometimes on her horse, sometimes on foot, as if she were trying to underscore something.

When it came to figuring things out, most of the girls her age who lived in Wistin weren't very helpful, and neither was religion.

Chapter Six

IN THE waiting room, all of us girls with braces had taken seats as far away from one another as possible. We didn't even look at one another. Four girls in braces, like giraffes in boxes, our heads gawkily sticking out on top, hair knotty in the back where the strands got stuck in the screws, eyes extraordinarily lofty, as if we didn't actually see anything in the room. We were above it all, even as we were sucked down into the corporeal world.

The bimonthly checkups came like the cycles of some horrible moon. Every time I was filled with hope as hopeful as hope itself. I was the optimism poster child. I was Pollyanna Redux Turbo.

I took off my sweater, shirt, and pants in the little dressing room. I unscrewed the top of the brace, undid the buckle on the bottom, extricated myself. For a shivery moment, I tried to lean the brace on the bench, freezing in my Italian-guy T-shirt and underpants and red socks. Pretty soon a nurse yanked open the curtain and said, "Follow me, please."

I stood before the wide tan plate and stared at the camera.

Around me, machinery whirred, little red lights blinked furtively. My socks didn't keep out the cold of the linoleum. I swayed back, my shoulder blade hitting the plate behind me, as if I were in a swoon, so passive that I couldn't even stand upright.

I willed my back straight. *Straight back, please, straight back please, straight back straight back straight straight straight. Please.*

The radioactive camera beeped.

Dr. Cordon came into the examination room and shook my father's hand and then my mother's, but not mine. It's surprising I'd even go near medicine, human or animal, after his kind—or maybe it's not so surprising. Still, at the beginning of the visit, as always, he looked like my savior: I could see an aura around his head. A halo. A crown. Everything depended on the curves and what he said about them.

He snapped the X-ray onto the light box. My parents were tense as could be, and so was I. It was a small family of hope and tension, waiting for the measurements. The doctor pulled out his protractor and faced the film like a mad scientist, maneuvering this way and that, drawing crosshatches of sharp red lines. We couldn't see anything but his white coat and gray head, working.

All our differences were eradicated at that moment. On the way here, we'd gotten lost—my parents never seemed to quite get hold of how to get from Weston to New York City—and they had fought about this, and then the argument had turned to the Women of History and then—for comic relief—to my father's mother, an hour-and-a-half-long series of recriminations and counterrecriminations, until we finally found ourselves at Sixty-third Street and Third Avenue.

But all that was nothing now. I could feel my parents' desire, keen as mine, keener than a laser beam, as we focused together. *C'mon, c'mon, c'mon. Let the game tilt our way.*

The doctor stepped away from the light box. There was my spine, a mermaid or a strange dinosaur inside me. There it was, curling in on itself like a snake taking a nap on a hot day.

The numbers were 38, 42. They'd gone up dramatically.

"Well, folks, this isn't quite what we'd hoped for. The lumbar curve has increased by a full six degrees, and the thoracic, in compensation probably, has increased five. The most dangerous sign is the spinal rotation, which perhaps you can see." He tapped his red pencil on the film. "We've got to be careful—here. See what is happening to the rib cage? This is where the heart is, this is where the lungs are."

The doctor paused and pursed his lips in a gesture of sympathy. The three of us were silent.

"She's been wearing the brace for sixteen, eighteen months now? Well, obviously it isn't working."

"What's the alternative?" my father blurted out.

"I recommend surgery."

"Now wait a minute," my mother cried. I thought she was going to stand up and punch him in the face. "What do you mean? We can't do that. We've been wearing the brace this whole time. She's been wearing it twenty-three hours a day!"

"What the hell kind of surgery?"

My mom gave Dad a desperate look. "You know what kind of surgery!"

Yes, we did know what kind of surgery. We'd heard about it from the beginning. It was the whip that kept us in compliance with the brace regimen.

Still, the doctor described it for us again that day. He described the Harrington rod, the one they screwed onto the vertebrae. He described the way they affixed the rod to the bone and cranked it straight—not totally straight, but a little straighter, anyway—and then sewed the patient back up. He described how the patient—that would be me—would be in traction for a month after the surgery and in a cast for three months after that. For the balance of the year, I'd be at home, basically bedridden. Afterward I could resume most normal activities, although perhaps not horseback riding, he mentioned casually.

"Just look at Joe Namath," Dr. Cordon said, waxing philosophical as he registered the horror in our faces. "He recovered miraculously from that knee operation."

Likewise, this surgery could work out really well for us—that is, if things went smoothly. Sometimes there was an infection or a broken bolt. Then they'd have to go back in and fetch it. And as for the surgery itself, there was also a slight—*very* slight, he emphasized—chance of paralysis or death.

I held my hands in my lap while he talked and while my parents, after they'd more or less got hold of themselves, asked some questions. He said we should think about it and get back to him as soon as possible. In the meantime, I was to keep wearing my brace and doing my floor exercises.

He made my parents sign something.

"Do you have any questions, Alison?" he asked me at the end.

All the adults turned my way.

I loved my brace; my brace was the good news. Could we give it more time? Could I wear it to the grave, please?

"Can I still ride in the meantime?"

The doctor said I could, as if bestowing a gift to a sad little orphan girl, and then he left. For a moment we all just sat there, dumb in the sterile room.

I saddled up Jazz when we got home.

His coat was already thickening and fluffing out from the cooler weather, and as we walked up the road, I spread my fingers against his neck, letting the hairs rush against my skin. First place we went was the mansion. The trees were half-bare by then, and I could see the greenhouse from a distance. It looked stark and more abandoned than ever, exposed to the cold. We trotted past it and through the tunnel with the wispy lemon tree and the unreadable banner. Jazz always hustled through that place; something about it made him nervous. I tied him up to a tree and dug out Kate's cigarettes from behind the brick in the patio wall.

I was getting better at smoking. I could inhale, for instance. I tried letting the smoke become me. It didn't work all that well, but I still had the smell of cigarettes on my hand. This was a distraction, a different kind of danger. I got back on Jazz, and we took Lord's Highway down toward Route 53. The sun was going down and it was cold, but I didn't want to go home. I saw the start of a dirt road across the river from Cobb's Mill Inn, and I'd found what I was looking for.

We started off at a trot. The trees whipped by like pencil scribbles, skeletons. I don't know whose idea it was, mine or his, but in a minute I was leaning over Jazz's neck and we were running like crazy down the road, right in the middle, the wind whistling in my ears, cold, making my eyes fill with tears. We ran and we ran and we ran—a half mile or maybe a million miles, but it wasn't long enough, not by a long shot. I saw in the gray we were coming up to an intersection, a paved road and a stop sign. I pulled him back to a trot, then a walk. Jazz was sweaty by then, breathing hard.

We walked home in the new dark, two shadows on the road.

Mrs. Balding paced back and forth, dropping her chalk twice, before she took roll. Her tiny bird head was mussed, as if she'd walked through a storm on her way to class. Her dress was wrinkled, her practical shoes dusty.

She was a mess today, my homeroom teacher—though not any more than me. I hadn't slept much at all the night before.

"Class, class," Mrs. Balding said in her typical shrill voice.

No one paid any attention. Laura Sleigh, who wore a new outfit every day and had hair like Farrah Fawcett's, was rummaging around in her jean-patch purse.

"I need you to quiet down," Mrs. Balding continued, peering down at us from Big Bird heights. "Class . . . I need you to be quiet. . . . Laura? Rich? . . . There you go. . . . Rich? . . . Thank you."

When the class had more or less settled down, Mrs. Balding

put her hands behind her back and looked out at us for a moment before speaking.

"I'm afraid I've got some bad news."

The quiet in the room became absolute, admirable.

"I don't know if any of you have already heard, but we've lost one of our own, Bob Perkins. Last night, he and his brother were in a car crash. He was taken to Norwalk Hospital. Early this morning, he let go."

In the diffused light of morning, confusion sifted into the room.

Mrs. Balding struggled to fix what she had done. "His brother, Reggie, was driving, and he's in intensive care still. They say he'll be all right."

Someone put up a hand. "Mrs. Balding, did he—did he suffer?"

"No, he did not," she said firmly.

We were glad to hear this, even if she was lying. I didn't know Bob Perkins, but I felt that I should have known him. The others all did, it seemed to me.

There was going to be a school assembly at eight-thirty, and we were dismissed from class until then. Mrs. Balding opened the door and stood there, helpless as a penguin, giving us little pats as we walked out the door.

We filed out into the halls—free, like we'd always wanted to be. We had fifteen whole minutes. The unexpected reprieve settled on us uneasily.

The basenjis came at us like an ambush unit. I shuffled through the mute terrorizing pack, some black and white, others tan and white, Isis, Osiris, and I wasn't sure who-all.

Dad and Mom Followyourbliss were on the red couch, luxuriating over a fat fresh doobie. The smell reminded me of church, the incense they use at Christmas—was it frankincense and myrrh?

Shana Hamilton was leaning into Tut, one leg dangling over his, as they read an uproarious article in the *Weston Forum*.

"One need not step far into the glorious history of this town to know that the future does not lie here, with us, but in the footfalls of our forebears," intoned Mr. Hamilton.

"Four bears? I didn't even know we had one bear," screeched Shana, falling headfirst into Tut's lap.

"Baby pie, it seems that we do."

Shana rose up, like the Sphinx. "And footfalls? Footfalls? Hello. It sounds like—"

She fell back onto her husband in a fit of silent and uncontrolled hilarity. In a few seconds up she bounced, and the laughter came out good and strong, like a honk, and then it was gone again.

Kate was looking through the little pile of mail by the stereo, and I was standing next to her politely.

"Honey!" Mr. Hamilton said. "How was school today?" He gave a wide, Egyptian emperor smile.

"Fine. Only one fatality," said Kate, putting down the L. L. Bean catalog and heading down the hall.

"What the hell are you doing?" Kate said at the door to her room.

"*Unkh,*" responded the figure lying facedown on her messed-up bed.

"You've got your own room, Mick, why don't you go use it?"

He didn't say anything. I was interested. I hadn't met her brother yet.

Kate picked up a pillow from the floor and hit him on the head. "Get out! Get out, Mick!"

She hit him on the leg then, and his foot flipped up, allowing one ragged sock, half-on, to fly off.

"Gross!" said Kate. "Gross!"

Ultimately Mick turned over. His face was red and wrinkled. His flannel shirt had lifted up, exposing his belly. I looked away; it was a lean, boy's stomach. You could see the ridge of his rib cage, and you could see a little spiral of hair working its way up.

"Who's this?"

"This is Alison. Good-bye, Mick."

"What's wrong with you? What are you wearing that for?" He scowled at me.

"I've got scoliosis," I said, words like a hateful confession.

"Jesus, where'd you learn your manners? Nowhere?"

Mick rubbed his face and made that *unkh* sound again. "Do you have any cigarettes?"

"No. Get out, please?" Kate held the door and made an elaborate hand gesture in its direction.

"Goddammit, can hardly get any peace around here," he finally said, stumbling out of the room.

Kate slammed the door after him. "Geesh."

"How old is he again?"

"Sixteen. Old enough to move out if he wanted. Which I wish he'd do."

Kate fluffed up a couple of pillows and smoothed the bedspread. She had a double bed with a brass headboard, which reminded me of a Bob Dylan song I'd heard on the radio. "There we go. Halfway normal."

She opened her nightstand drawer and pulled out an ashtray, a pack of Winstons, and a lighter. I sat on the window side of the bed, one leg folded underneath me, the other hanging off the side (the brace made it impossible to lean back without choking myself). Kate carefully unfolded the top silver square on the pack. She was always careful with her belongings. She folded clothes neatly, and her jewelry box was filled with rings in a row and necklaces spiraled in on themselves, knot-free.

"Crappy day, huh?" she asked.

"I guess," I said. I hadn't told her about the doctor yet. Well, I'd told her it hadn't gone well—that was at school—but I'd said I'd tell her the details later. It felt like that later had come, but I didn't want to get into it.

She shrugged. "It was nice to get all that time off after assembly."

A throbbing beat came from through the wall, as much a physical sensation as a sound.

"Shit."

In a minute, a cacophony of instruments and vocals.

"Led Zeppelin," she said. "All right, I'll be right back."

Kate left the room and stomped down the hall. I heard her banging on the door to Mick's room. *Bang bang. Bang bang.* Nothing. Then she must have opened the door, because the music intensified abruptly, and I heard shouting, something like "Turn that shit down!" and "Where do you get off?"—and the music stopped. The door slammed. A moment of silence, and then the stereo came back on—perhaps an infinitesimal fraction softer this time.

"He's leaving soon anyway," Kate said when she got back. She picked up her cigarette from the ashtray and took a troubled drag.

Kate's room was strange, but I liked it. She had no really frilly things, no leftover toys or clues from a girlhood. There was a lacquered, deep red chest with bamboo handles and Chinese lettering on the top. In one corner loomed a crazily tall stuffed leather giraffe, the head tilted from a crease in the neck. A big plant was in a basket on the floor, and on her bookshelf, she had a grown-up stereo (as opposed to my space age teen unit), a few books, and one framed photograph: her and Mick on some amusement park ride, smiling maniacally into the future.

If you didn't know better, you might think it was a guest room.

Kate took another pull from the cigarette, her eyelids fluttering. She said, "I knew him, you know."

"Who?"

"Bob."

"It seems like everyone knew him."

"Yeah, but not everyone kissed him."

"You kissed him?"

"Yes."

"I didn't know—I didn't know you'd kissed him." I wanted to say, *I didn't know you'd kissed anyone*. I certainly had not. My crushes so far were pretty limited: I'd weirdly liked Willy

Wonka (from the Chocolate Factory—Gene Wilder, that is), and I had, more recently, gazed from a distance at the green eyes of this kid in my biology class, Frank, quiet and smart and disarming, and neither a Jock nor a Freak nor a Brain nor a Play Gay: the Weston categories of human.

But with my brace, what did it matter, any of that?

"It was at Jenna Grossman's birthday party. She had this pool party, with girls and boys. Her parents weren't around, only her big sister and a couple of her friends. They were supposedly taking care of us. Anyway, some of us drank a little beer and played a little hoochie-koochie."

"What the hell's hoochie-koochie?"

"You don't know what hoochie-koochie is?"

"Oh, I know," I hastened to say. But I wasn't *entirely* sure what she meant—how involved did hoochie-koochie get?

Kate looked past me out the big window. You could see the circular driveway from there and one of her parents' Mercedeses. The license plate read DNSTY 18.

She said, "One day someone's playing floor hockey in gym class, and the next day he's dead. Well, what are you going to do, right? No more Bob Perkins."

Kate's knees peeked out the holes in her jeans. A lot of guys at school probably had crushes on Kate. Of course they did: You could tell by the way they looked at her, smiled when she said something.

"It's really sad," I said. Was she thinking of him now, up close: his face, his chin, his lips? I tried to imagine it, but the picture was hazy.

"I'd like to get out of here," she said, looking at me sud-

denly. Her face had gone red in little blotches on her cheekbones. "When we grow up, let's go in together on a horse farm
in Wyoming or Montana, a place with mountains and beautiful sunsets, and we'll raise horses, and train them. It'll be a
gorgeous place. A red barn, and we'll have mares and foals
and horses of all kinds. And the horses will be happy and
beautiful, and we'll sit around in cowboy outfits."

I laughed.

"Well?"

"Sounds good. Okay, let's do it."

"Promise?"

Now it was my turn to flush. I did promise. It was a good
place to be, this fast, gentle future.

"Right now, though, I've got some problems," I said. I
didn't want to cry about it.

"The back doctor, right?"

"They want me to get this operation where they put a rod
up your spine. Then after the surgery, you wear a cast and get
traction and stuff, and then you have to stay in bed for like a
year. And . . ."

And what? All your dreams are shattered permanently?

"And what, Alison? What is it?"

"I might not be able to ride afterward."

Kate leaned toward me. "Alison, of course you can always
ride. How stupid. They can't take *that* away."

"Well—or I could just die in surgery. That's the other possibility."

Her eyes went dark. "Die in surgery? What are you talking
about?"

"It's a really small chance, but they have to open up your whole back, and the spinal column is a dangerous place. Lots of nerves and things."

"God, Alison. We're going to have to run away sooner than I thought."

"Yeah," I said, giving up a little smile. I was still hot with the confession, and her comment felt like a cool breeze. "I wish I *could* run away. I hate that doctor so much."

The afternoon was changing around us. The light outside, which had started out as just blank sunny, went golden first, for about ten fat minutes, and now there was something chilly and silver about it. Mick's friend had come by in a van, honked, and swept away young Mick, and the house was again quiet. The pebbles in the driveway blended together into a white river. The car gleamed, reflecting lights from the house.

We decided on a name: the Alison and Kate Horse Training Company.

"And if you can't ride, so what? I'll do the riding part, and you can train the young ones. You'll work with the yearlings— ground work. It's not like you're going to be bedridden for life. Worst-case scenario, you'll still be able to hold a lead, right?"

"Right. Absolutely," I said. She seemed to know everything.

We heard a noise outside, and it was Mrs. Hamilton, stepping oddly toward the car—like a stork in high-heeled boots or a cat walking through snow. She had on sunglasses even though the sun was down. She was holding a blue plastic wineglass and heading off into the dark.

"Hey," Kate suddenly said, and jumped off the bed. "I've got it."

"What?"

"Have you heard of Donna Summer?"

"No."

"That's right—you only listen to Cher."

"Yeah," I said uncertainly. She'd already given me shit about Cher.

"You've got to check this out. Renee gave it to me—she's my dad's secretary. She's so into it. She's like a disco queen or something. Every night she goes out to dance clubs. You know what else? She wears the same mascara all the time—she never washes it off. She sleeps in it, and the next morning she just loads on a new coat. She only washes it off when she can't get the brush to go through the lashes anymore. Isn't that gross?"

Kate put a tape into the cassette player as she spoke. We waited as the tape wheeled itself around. Then came this breathy river of sound, a thumping beat.

Donna Summer whispered, as if she were revealing some-thing, a broken bone, maybe: "I love to love you baby . . ."

And then pretty quickly she started really losing her focus on things.

"Isn't she . . . sexy?" Kate said in the funniest way. I'd never heard a song like this in my life. This woman was—well, she was really feeling something.

"C'mon, let's dance," Kate said. "First I'll close these so we don't give a show to the neighborhood." She snapped the cord on the window blinds and turned to me. I slid slowly off the bed. Dancing?

"Look at this move," Kate said, doing a kind of hip twirl. "Renee showed me that one. Watch out," she said, and she bumped into me.

"What the hell?"

"It's called the bump, dimwit, and I also know the hustle."

I'd never tried to dance in my brace before. I lifted my legs and swirled my arms a tiny bit. Kate was stepping across the room, spinning, bumping, doing some kind of bump/hustle medley, and I myself did a small twirl. Then I sidled up to Kate and bumped her with my leather girdle and steel hip, and she bumped me back. I tried my own version of the hustle, stomping about by the houseplant. But the music started getting to us, getting to me.

"I—love to love you baby . . . / Do it to me again and again / You put me in such an awful spin / In a spin, ohh ahh . . ."

We were laughing as much as dancing—this woman must be *crazy*—and I started reeling around the room like some kind of Frankenstein tin man disco-dancing machine, and Kate was rolling around on the bed and then jumping up again, moaning. "I—love to love you baby . . ." And then it all seemed clear for a second, the secret message of the song, so I pretended to punch Kate in the stomach on the *"ahh"* part, and she buckled over and then punched me in the stomach, and we were in so much happy pain. Kate staggered to the other side of the room—next time she comes back this way, she's in for it—"Ahh, ohh, I—love to love you baby"—and I lurched around and staggered around, and we were lurching and staggering and laughing in misery as the beat intensified and the disco ball swirled around. When it came to a stop, we stopped, too. And then we rewound the tape and played it again, Donna Summer's two new best fans.

Finally we took a cigarette break.

"Anyway, you're thirteen. You can't die," Kate said, flopping back on her pillow.

We'd forgotten Bob Perkins already. We'd forgotten everything.

*T*hen one terrible night, Sarah Beckingworth's ambling and perambulations came to an end. It was a night of unearthly calm, and she was standing by the window, holding open the gingham curtain she and her mother had made with their own hands. Out there was the clearing made by her father and her father's father, a small clearing on a hill just a stone's throw from Wistin. And out past the clearing, past the little barn where the horse stood, was the forest.

Who lived in the forest? you might ask. It's true that the forest was inhabited by Indians. Indeed, by the Paugussetts, the largest tribe in Connecticut.

Now there was a shift in the shadows. The Paugussetts were approaching, gripping tomahawks made of oak and elk sinew and flinty rock in their hands.

Chapter Seven

I SAW her in the hall, and at first I thought there was something wrong with my vision. I had something in my eye. A fleck of something, a shadow, a problem. But as I got closer, making my way through the hall, delicate as a tiptoe journey through a minefield, like every morning, I saw that it was true: Kate had a black eye. The whole half of her face was swollen.

She had just come out of the bathroom. We usually caught a quick smoke there before first class. It wasn't really about nicotine, it was about having a—what I read about in a book— an *assignation*. Kate and I, and some of the other girls— beautiful Laura Sleigh smoked, and then this girl Karen, who always wore a light blue parka and had watery blond hair and watery blond eyes and a watery blond life of some shy kind. The two or three or four of us would share a cigarette—just a couple of puffs each—and then flush it down the drain. Laura smoked Virginia Slims. Karen preferred Camels. Kate and I, of course, were Winston girls.

But this morning I was a little late, and Kate was already on her way out of the bathroom—Kate with the black eye.

"What happened?" I said, grabbing her arm. "Are you okay?"

This is what was really strange. She looked over in my direction like she didn't know me. Of course, it may have been the discomfort that made it seem that way. Her eyelid was swollen, and there was a sharp purple curve underneath, lovely as the inside of a mussel shell. Some of her eyebrow hairs were sticking up straight.

But the worst part was this slackness in her face: Her usually sharp cheekbone where she kept all her anger and wit was softened, melted down into a dull, puffy person's face.

She leaned in toward me. She held my arm with a gentle fold of her fingers.

"I fell off," she whispered. "I fell off Peach."

"You fell off Peach?"

"*Shh.* I'll tell you more about it later, all right? I've got to get to homeroom, and so do you."

And she walked away.

When I think about that morning, I always imagine it as the moment when I could have, somehow, fixed things—made it all turn out differently. *Look lively! Make him listen! You're the boss!*

Instead I went to homeroom and then to English. More fun with prepositions and conjunctions. Prepositions set things off and conjunctions joined them, but if you thought about it, they seemed like the same thing anyway.

I stared out the window at the playing field—beaten-down grass, some remnants of white lines for soccer or field hockey.

Kate *never* fell off her horse, that was the thing. Lee said you weren't a real rider until you'd fallen a few times, but I had the feeling Kate could ride Peach while sleeping, and she'd still, magically, stay on.

Mr. Snodgrass twirled the tip of his golden mustache, waiting for someone to tell him what "with" meant.

"With" meant Kate. "With" meant friend.

I thought of the little purple place, like spilled ink. Might she have hit a rock? A fence? Why hadn't she called to tell me about it last night? By this time, we were talking on the phone every day, at least once.

I saw her in the hall again after class, this time surrounded by all the jock girls, the bitter glittering evil beautiful ones, Lisa, Lynn, and Priscilla. They had their arms folded across their Shetland sweaters and were looking at Kate intently, listening as she spoke. I assumed she was telling them about falling off the horse. They thought the black eye was a novelty, was what I was thinking as I came storming up.

Kate glanced over at me but kept talking. "It was scary. That thing flew out of nowhere. In the broad daylight."

The other girls glanced at me as if I were responsible, and they all backed up half a step. Why was she telling them about this?

"I'd sell her, if I were you," said Lisa. "A horse like that is bad news."

"Yeah," said Priscilla, always the backup.

"I'll never sell her," Kate said. "Every horse is afraid of bats."

"Bats?" I said, incredulous.

"Peach bucked me off because of a bat. Can you believe that?"

She cast a look in my direction, as if she didn't think I would believe it but she thought she'd say it anyway.

"Damn," I said, trying out a swear word. Also a charlatan.

"What were you doing riding out by the gulch anyway?" said Lisa, best suited herself to riding in circles, under surveillance, swathed in velvet and suede. "That was pretty dumb."

Kate shrugged.

"So here's hoping your eye doesn't look like that for the Evergreen," Lynn pitched in.

"That's for sure," said Priscilla, and the bell rang. The three girls left, and I stood there, next to my friend.

We regarded each other warily for a minute. Second bell came. The halls were clearing.

"So, you fell off Peach."

"I fell off Peach," she said. "Because of a bat."

She squinted at me.

"Kate. She saw a bat?"

Kate turned and started walking. Down the empty hall, past the lockers, her clogs making a racket in the green zone of Weston Middle School. I had math, and I hated math, but that didn't come into play. "Hey!" I shouted, and I followed her. Now she was running.

We ran down past the music classrooms and to the side entrance, and she pushed open the door at the end of the hall, and then we were out, the air still cold with morning.

She balked.

"Come on," I said. "Don't stop now."

I slipped my hand around hers. We walked like invisible

people (I was hoping now, exultant) to the first place I could think of where we could be free and hidden. Between the middle school and the high school, there was a little stretch of woods, a jumble of rocks where the dividing stone wall had been ruined by kids making a path through.

"What do you want?" she said when I finally stopped, letting go of her hand. "Why are you being so incredibly—pushy? And annoying."

"I'm trying to ask you something." She had her arms crossed tightly across her chest. We were exactly the same height, and we had the same hair and hands and ideas and the same everything. "What happened to your eye?"

She sighed and looked up into the heart of the sky, and then she looked down again.

"Okay, Alison. He hit me," she said. "Or really just knocked me down."

"Who?" I said, weak in the lungs.

She was staring at the wall now, the slow way it was toppling. "My dad. He's done it before, Alison. It's usually not so damn *obvious*."

"What the hell, Kate?"

"Well," she said, then stopped. I thought she was going to explain it, let me know about the state of the world, but then she looked confused for a moment. She turned back to me. "Let's not make too big a deal of it, okay?"

The puffs of our breath came and went. Already her face was getting better. No, it was getting worse. The color was really getting worse. I had caught up to her, and we were standing by a broken wall, and I knew this much of what had happened, and I didn't know what to say next.

"We can't just—I can't—" I began.

"It's okay. I mean, I don't want to talk about it right now, okay? Later, though. Maybe."

Kate looked around her, as if she'd just woken up in this place, an old-timey town in Connecticut.

"Looks like we're out of class for second period, huh? Want to hitch down to the Center and get something to eat?"

We bought candy and sodas and ate and drank behind the snowplow garage, down by Weston Center. When we got back to school we slipped into the stream, kids with backpacks and blank faces like all the rest.

My parents were outside when I got home that afternoon, sitting together on my father's meditation hillock. This was quite odd, this togetherness—and in the Zen space, no less. Though it was true that, since the doctor's pronouncement, there'd been a quietness around the house, a lack of criticism at dinner. I watched them from the kitchen window. Their heads were bowed, and they leaned into each other. It was like they were having a picnic with no food.

I went to the living room and took out *A Separate Peace.* If I went up to my room and closed the door, it was guaranteed someone (my mother, probably) would come up and ask, *What's wrong, honey?* I didn't feel like reading, not at all, but if I propped up the book in front of my face, in the congenial living room, I might be able to keep questions and general disturbance at bay.

It didn't work. Before long, Mom came inside, and when she saw I was home she called in Dad, too.

"Hey, Allie," he said, joining her. He gave his beard a once-over and stood awkwardly by the fireplace.

This was worrisome, an unscheduled meeting of three. Had they gotten a call from school?

But it wasn't about skipping class; it was about my back. When Mom announced the topic, I gave her a sinister look— as if the world didn't suck enough without talking about this—but she continued nonetheless.

"Sweetie, we're not going to take this lying down—this surgery business. We're going to look around and see what's out there. We're going to go to the ends of the earth to help you out." She was sitting on the ottoman, leaning toward me.

"We'll get a second opinion, Alison," my father said. He was still standing, his arms folded, like a soldier guarding a country.

"Look, maybe traditional medicine isn't the way to go. Maybe there are options. I have a friend who had *cancer,* for God's sake, and she started on this nutrition program, and what with that and the herbal supplements—"

"And the mercurial nature of the illness—"

A hard glance, Mom to Dad, and then she continued: "She got well. All right? She was cured."

"She's in remission."

Time for my mother to study her hands.

Dad said, "Alison, we'll get a second opinion, and we'll try some things. It can't hurt, right? An herbal supplement can't hurt."

"And body work and prayer and acupuncture and massage. We'll find what helps, and we'll do that."

"Are you going to make me eat tons of tofu?"

"C'mon, Alison. Get serious," my father said sharply.

Mom straightened herself on her seat, letting her hair fall down the length of her ballerina back, a prim angel of wheat and flax.

I closed the door to my room and, after a few minutes, unbuttoned my plaid shirt and took it off, unzipped my pants. I reached my arm around and undid the strap at the small of my back. My belly expanded against the leather girdle and plastic carapace, pushing it open. I twisted the screw at the back of my neck. It popped apart, and I was released from my brace.

The full-length mirror hung behind my door. I took off my undershirt, too, and looked at myself head-on. My breasts were small, but they were bigger than before, and from the right angle, you could see a little weight in them. Indentations from the brace's girdle rose in half-moons over each hip. I turned around. The tip of one of my shoulder blades was rubbed into a petulant black-red forever mark.

It didn't matter what the reason was, whether it was to wait for a second opinion or go see a witch doctor or pile in a few more vitamins. For now, no one was going to cut into my back.

I rubbed my arms, crossed them against my body, held on.

She'd said it was different from being spanked when you were little. She'd said that when you were spanked, when you were little, when you had lunged toward a road, for instance, or stolen jelly beans from your brother, it hurt, it stung, but when your father hit you later—as in now, at thirteen—it didn't feel like a punishment, it felt like a system. "You know? Sort of like a system," she'd said. "Different."

He'd come home, and Peach had gotten out of the barn and trampled the lawn, and it had just rained, and there were huge divots where her hooves had been. So he undid his belt. He was undoing his belt as he came out of the kitchen. You flip the end out of the loop, yank it, break the nail out of the hole, wrench the leather from the loops of your white pants. He was staring at her the whole time, Kate said, like he was having some kind of vision. She was holding a pillow in front of her stomach. She held it until the last minute, and then she bolted. She threw the pillow and lunged off the couch, leapt to the side, making a break for it—but two steps out, two steps toward the hallway, he had her. He wrapped his arms around her stomach from behind and bent her over, and she lost her footing. She fell to the floor, she knocked her eye on the bookshelf, that's what happened to her eye, that's why her eye was purple, Egyptian, and she had a vague awareness of her own shouting, a vague awareness of her mother standing by the kitchen door, watching—*watching?*

The feel of his hand pressing her back into the floor. The feel of the floor, the floorboards, on her cheek and nose, and her one arm wrenched under, and then up with the belt and down and up and down. "Sure, it hurt, Alison," she'd said. "But it's not like he broke my arm. I didn't *bleed,* for God's sake, but it was just . . . just . . ."

Kate, who was so quick with words, couldn't think of a way to describe it.

Did her bedroom door lock? I wasn't sure if it did—I wasn't sure if she even had that, a half-inch bolt, for protection. I had no idea, and my stomach fell and I dressed myself quickly and ran out of the room to call my friend.

*F*ive Indians burst through the roughly hewn door of the small shack on the edge of the clearing. This was long before Health Food, and very few Wistinites were of the mind that these Indians were sacred pals, were anyone's friend. Yes, the Indians were considered in that bleak and faraway time to be the enemy. To be like beasts, scruffy beasts of the forest who wore paint and sang funny songs in deep peculiar voices, and who ate hedgehogs raw.

Trembling, aghast with fear, Sarah Beckingworth slipped behind the gingham curtain and hoped for her life. And she did tend to live, and she would live here. But her parents did not fare so well. They were killed in the darkest, darkest night; they were brutally, viciously slaughtered by the Indians.

Sarah kneeled on the floor, her arms spread and beseeching, to what she did not know. Her eyes held in the terrible sight, and then she closed them. She got up and stumbled toward the door and out to the front porch. "No! No! No!" she cried. "This can't be happening." She went to the barn and found that the men who had done this to her parents had also killed every animal but the eighteen-hand stallion. He was wounded: Perhaps they had tried, but failed, to steal him?

All through the night she cared for Noble, changing his bandages often, rubbing unguents into his skin. Soon it would be morning, and Noble would get better, and the lost heroine would mount her horse again.

Chapter Eight

"SO YOU'RE going to try it once, so what? Since when are you such a prude, Alison? Come on, live a little, try new things," Mom said, hands wrapped tightly around the steering wheel.

We were on our way to a class called Movement for Life. It was certainly possible that my mother was going overboard with her New Age activities, these sad, fitful, hopeful measures. Still, I told myself, I'd eat raw earthworms to avoid surgery.

"Uh," I said to her annoying questions.

It was a gleaming day. All the leaves were gone—gone off the trees and just plain gone—where did they all go? It was as if a great wind had come and cleaned up the town. The car was hot, and I unzipped my jacket. My hair had snagged in the back screws of the brace, and when I'd tried, for the third time, to disentangle it, I got momentarily furious and ripped some out. I could still feel the rip, an evil ache at the bottom of my head. I could survive only if I peered at the passing, wasted Saturday through slit eyes.

Kate had made me swear on a stack of Kurt Vonnegut novels not to tell anyone, *not anyone, not even Jazz,* about her father. I'd thought of this when, after confirming that he would definitely make a presentation at the jubilee fund-raiser (along with my father), Mom said that Tut really did "think out of the box" and that he was sure to "wow all the women there."

Meanwhile, back in my ruined Saturday, I discovered that the Movement for Life class was being held in a church basement, which seemed particularly ignoble.

I ducked into the bathroom, putting my brace in a duffel bag, like I was a hobo at a bus station. But eventually I had to come out and face my fate.

They wore sweatpants and swarmed around the fluorescent-lit room. This was their secret, just discovered habitat. They were a new kind of wildlife. The women, mostly fashion challenged in one significant way or another, were joined by two somewhat woeful men (the young one sported a striped woven cap with a purple tassel on top).

A large, happy woman stepped forward and asked everyone to gather into a circle in the middle of the room. "Gather together, friends. Gather together," she said, reaching her arms to either side in a generous gesture. Her blondish hair shot straight out from her head as if she'd been electrocuted. Her eyes were small, but her smile was wide, and, really, there was nothing wrong with her earthy, earnest persona; it was just a little dull, a hemp Ms. Rogers.

We gathered together, as per her instructions, and then it was time to cling to one another, standing in a circle with our arms around one another's shoulders.

The woman on one side of me, a woolly person, smelled of garlic, and the one on the other side, more of a closet creature, smelled of mothballs. We bowed our heads and breathed, like we were all one, "because we are All One," said the electrocuted leader. Things went downhill from there. We were going to use our bodies to intuit all the separate, but one, parts of the life force.

This had to be more than I'd bargained for with the We Can Make This Right Through Perseverance Plan.

When she said the word *intuit,* I misheard it as *into-it.* The phrase got stuck in my head, and every time she said it I heard it wrong, then repeated it obsessively and derisively to myself whether I wanted to or not.

The first thing we had to simulate was the movement of a tree. We separated out from the circle and stood about, as trees do, in a forest. The latter-day Ms. Rogers clicked on her tape deck, and from its tinny speakers came the sound of one, then many birds—perhaps waking up at dawn's early light. A few women were waving their arms around in treelike equipoise. My mother herself had raised her arms, and she was swinging her my-mother hips slowly from side to side, staring with dreamy concentration at a spot in the brown carpet.

I raised my arms tentatively, just from the elbows—maybe I could be a twiggy little stunted tree. Maybe I could be a stump or a log.

Well, that felt dumb. I raised my arms way up. *You can do this, Alison. All or nothing.*

Soon the blood in my arms rushed down, and my tendons tightened in pain.

Finally I hit on holding my arms out and just slightly

elevated, like the branches of a droopy pine tree. I tried working with my feet. I pushed one foot around a bit—a root of some kind.

The women around me, with gray hair and jungle-colored frocks, with long braids and shirts made by peasants from far away, peasants who didn't know how to hem, apparently, all seemed gloriously pleased to be trees. Even my mother, who had now turned and was facing the other direction and currently was being a *still* tree (for which I was glad), seemed happy.

The leader was simulating, I think, a young tree growing rapidly, over and over again. She kept bending her knees and then standing up again and spreading her arms, then bending and squeezing her arms in again, then jumping up, exuberantly growing, as in time-lapse photography.

The tape switched, filling the room with the sound of rain and wind, and one woman, feeling the change, started a kind of jittery movement with her hands and her head. Rain hitting leaves? Others checked her out and began doing this, too. It became very popular. The women went from shaking their heads and arms to their feet—which didn't make any sense to me, but the tree leader was smiling beatifically.

The tape went to ape sounds and other things, hyenas or hippopotamuses.

Eventually our lead tree/ape/bird of prey glanced at the clock and hopped/swooped over to her tape deck. She slowly turned down the volume until the jungle was no more.

The women and men slowly stopped, knowing instinctively that the transformation back to human form must take place gradually. We came together to breathe again, All One, and then it was time to simulate the movements of a small, fast-moving mammal with a good sense of direction out the door and into the church parking lot.

"That was incredibly horrible," I announced back in the car.

"Oh, it was not, Alison," my mother said, turning into traffic.

"I don't think pretending to be a tree or a darn squirrel is going to help my back. In fact, I think all that swaying and skittering about could be damaging." I looked over at her. "What was wrong with those people? It was like the trees had termites."

"You're being too judgmental," she said. "It's all about channeling the energy of the universe, Alison—you know? Getting into the healing."

"Don't you think that's a little, I don't know, vague?"

She looked like she was going to cling to this Movement for Life business, by God, no matter what.

Her voice was calm: "You're being close-minded, just like your father. How are we ever going to forge a path to the new and the meaningful if you're so narrow in your thinking? Think about it. You were, for a brief moment, a tree."

"I think I'm going to throw up now."

Mom leaned over the steering wheel and accelerated. "Think out of the box," she said. "That's the key."

What did I know about Kate's father? I knew he was a best-selling author, a businessman, a kind of shaman. I knew he

kept a handgun in his bedroom in case of intruders—
"derelicts from Bridgeport," Kate said, to which I'd expressed
shock and horror (never having known anyone who owned a
gun before). I knew he'd been on a football team in college;
there was a picture of him kneeling by his helmet in the hall. I
knew I'd have to see him again sometime, so it might as well
be sooner than later.

Besides, Kate had said—later, after she'd calmed down—
people did weird things when they were drunk; she was simply
planning to go on. Maybe she didn't have a choice on that one.

I fully expected this would be the day I'd meet up with him,
as the black Mercedes with the DNSTY 18 license plate was
parked in the driveway. I opened the door and walked in—
they'd made fun of me for knocking (too polite), so I didn't
knock anymore.

Mick was sitting on the red leather couch, reading *The New
Republic*. The dog population swarmed me. Icons of the underworld god? Underfoot, maybe.

"*Heel, swine!*" Mick shouted. "Hey, Allie."

"Hapi—hi, Hapi. Hi, Anubis, my boy," I said, wading
through. "Is Kate here?"

"She's out with Mom," Mick said, frowning at his magazine. "It's only me."

I fingered the loop of my jacket string. Mom had dropped
me off—*now* what should I do? Might as well act casual. I sat
down and began to leaf through *Dog World*.

Mick's feet were up on the coffee table and he was sprawled
out, the young boy model of his tall mother in an old burgundy
T-shirt and faded jeans. I started an article on the right hair

ornaments for Pekingese and Yorkshire terriers but soon realized it was too dark to read. I glanced over at Mick, entirely engrossed, it seemed—did he have night vision? Was he faking?

I found that I was thirsty, or anyway *could* be thirsty. When I got up to go to the kitchen, Mick didn't seem to notice.

The Hamilton refrigerator was always well stocked with snack food—no health food pretense here. Once I heard Tut Hamilton say, "Transcendence comes from the mind, not the stomach," as he dipped a Slim Jim into a vat of blue cheese dressing. Suddenly unsure whether it would be all right to open a new liter of soda, I went to the sink for water instead.

"So, you want to fool around?" Mick said from behind me. "Could you take off that brace or something?"

I shut off the tap and turned around.

Mick's bangs fell to exactly pupil level, requiring him to look up slightly as he waited for me to respond. *Fool around?* Did he mean kiss? Was this a romantic moment?

"Excuse me?"

"You're kind of cute," he said. "Or you could be, if you took off that brace thing."

The pragmatism of his statement was undeniable. Nonetheless I mumbled, "That probably wouldn't be such a good idea. Because of Kate and everything."

"Oh, Kate wouldn't care," he said. But then he yawned, as if struck by the dullness of our conversation. "Suit yourself." He shrugged and headed back into the living room.

I heard him sit back down. I stood stock-still in the kitchen for a full ten minutes, until Kate and her mother came home.

Shana Hamilton adjusted the mirror. I'd never been in a convertible before, but the roof was up anyway, so it didn't seem free and wonderful, it felt more like driving around in a go-cart—a powder blue Mercedes go-cart, however. When they'd come home, Kate had shouted at me from the front door—did I want to go to Westport? Sure, of course (bye for now, Mick). Now we were whizzing down the wealthy roads. In a sense, money really *could* buy beauty. Maybe other people could drive around here—on their way through, back to Norwalk, say. But it was money that bought the habit of these easy hills, this perfect chilly splendor.

Already some people had decorated their houses or mailboxes or front-yard firs with Christmas lights, but at this time of day they were just a tangle of wires. Everything was trimmed up, mowed, frozen: waiting for the holidays to sweep in and distract us from the bare branches of things, the architecture.

"My God," Shana said. "Did I forget to turn off the oven?"

She was clutching the steering wheel with black-gloved hands. Her tortoiseshell sunglasses had gold Chanel C's on the sides, and her hair looked especially blond, chalky pale against the sleek collar of her black fur coat (what was it—panther? chinchilla?).

"I'm sure you got it, Mom," Kate said with a long-suffering air. "If not, Mick will turn it off. For that matter, it wasn't on in the first place."

"But this morning. This morning I broiled something— Oh my God, I have to turn around. Mick would let the house burn down!" And with that, Mrs. Hamilton slammed on the brakes and peeled off into a driveway.

"I was in the kitchen and everything looked like it was off," I said helpfully from the backseat, my head at a crooked, squished angle between my brace and the roof.

Mrs. Hamilton didn't seem to hear. She threw the car into first and lurched back in the direction of home. When we got there she hopped out, leaving the car idling, and bounded up the front stairs.

Kate turned around and gave me a meaningful look. *Mothers. What are you going to do?*

I shrugged. *Really. Well, just be patient, I guess.*

. In a minute Shana reappeared, leaping giddily down the steps with a white bag in her hand.

"Look!" she said, getting into the car. "I had forgotten this belt I need to return at Ann Taylor!"

"Was the oven on?" Kate asked in a monotone.

"Can you get this?" Shana asked, shoving the bag at me. "I *needed* this belt, so it was obviously meant to be. I had to go back. A little godlet was telling me so."

She let out the emergency brake and spread some gravel on the lawn as she sped out of the driveway. She smelled of pot— maybe she'd taken a little emergency toke while in there.

We had an hour to ourselves while Shana did whatever mothers like her do in Westport. We checked out A Midsummer Night's Dream, the basement shop that sold used jeans, incense, and jewelry; and then we went to Klein's and bought one paperback each, *Cat's Cradle* for me, *Where Are You Going,*

Where Have You Been? for Kate. We also picked out a blue notebook for our project, the 1776 girl adventure. We went to the drugstore and looked at lip gloss, then waited for Shana in the pizzeria.

"So what are you guys doing for Thanksgiving?" I asked Kate.

Kate stared at the soda machine. "Probably buy filets or something."

"Filet of turkey?"

"Filet *mignon,* obviously."

"Like the pilgrims ate?"

"So what kind of Frau Fritters are you having? Tofu burgers?"

"Actually, I think it's going to be tofu with gravy, with some mashed tofu on the side."

"And for dessert?"

"Tofu pie, of course."

Our slices and sodas appeared.

"We need a name for her," Kate said.

"For who?"

"For the heroine girl. Mr. Bostitch, remember? Of Many Nations, into Social Studies?"

"Okay, so? Have any ideas?"

Kate took a sip of her 7-Up. Tut was out of town for a week, it turned out, at a playshop somewhere. There was still the wispiest little purple feather under Kate's eye, but she hadn't spoken about it since that first day.

"Sarah. Sarah Beckingworth."

"Sarah—Beckingworth?"

"Good old Sarah Beckingworth, the youngest daughter of the old Beckingworth clan."

"Oh, them—the old Beckingworths."

"It has a nice ring to it, right?"

"Yeah. It's okay."

"So now we just need the plot."

"Plot? What plot?" I'd mainly envisioned a simple tale involving a girl in a cape on horseback.

"What *happens,* Allie. Something has to happen, doesn't it?"

"Well," I said after some consideration, "she could fall in love with an Indian."

"Or she could get *captured* by Indians and strung up by her toes over a ravine."

"Yeah, she could get captured, but then they're nice Indians after all. After some initial problems."

"First, though, the important part," said Kate, leaning in for a stage whisper. "The terrible tragedy."

"What terrible tragedy?"

"The terrible fate of her parents."

Shana Hamilton burst in the door of the pizzeria. *"Girls! Girls!* I'm double-parked!" she was shouting.

Kate stood up. "We're here," she said under her breath. "Calm down already."

"I've got a great idea, darlings," Shana said after we'd stuffed ourselves into the car. "I'm bringing you out for a little holiday cheer."

She gunned the car onto Main Street, winding up to second, then third gear.

The Longshore Country Club had its own small sailboat fleet, though almost everything was tidied up and battened down that time of year. White sun flashed up through the banks of windows, sharpened by miles of water, the excellent and rarefied view of Long Island Sound stretching out to a lighthouse and beyond. We were the only ones in the dining room. Kate and her mother sat on one side of the table, and I sat on the other. When Mrs. Hamilton's Irish coffee came, she gave a perfunctory little lick to the whipped cream on her spoon and said to the waiter, "This is great. May I have another?"

"Sure," the waiter said uncertainly when she winked at him. She was bobbing one of her legs near his legs. She was so tall she could barely fit under the table. She was in her thirties and he was about eighteen, but that wasn't going to stop her.

"But is there something wrong with—with that one?" he ventured.

"This one's fine," she said, cupping the coffee drink in her hands. "It's just that one is never enough, now, is it, baby? My, it's bright in here—don't you have a darker room somewhere?"

"Um . . . well, the bar is closed until five and—"

"Just some little old room somewhere?" She cocked her head to one side and raised her voice in a singsong.

The young waiter looked confused and perhaps in instantaneous love. "I'll be back in a minute with that coffee," he said, and bolted back to the bar.

Mrs. Hamilton smiled at us, arms folded on the table. "I knew I could get you juvenile delinquents a little drink if I set my mind to it. Easy."

She let a wiry arm find its way down to her black purse. She slipped a cigarette out of the pack, lit it, breathed in with a little *hic* sound, then blew a thick plume of smoke to my side of the table. She'd been at home when her husband knocked over their daughter: a helpmate, a shadowy figure.

"Men are *soooo* easy," Mrs. Hamilton declared.

"How are they easy?" I asked boldly.

"Easy to understand. Hard to understand, but also easy to understand." She furrowed her pretty eyebrows. "Of course I'm talking about Tut here. Eighteen years married—Jesus, that makes me feel old. He robbed me from the cradle, that's for sure. I saw him coming and—boom! End of story."

The sailboats left in the water were huddled together around the pier, as if they were cold out there. The yachts remained calm. One was called *Fox's Luck*. Another was *Miss Adventure*.

"He was killer handsome, Eddie—that's how I first knew him. 'Tut' came later, with *Pyramid Love* and all that. Tut. It seems like his real name now." She stared out the window. "It seems to suit him."

The waiter came back with the second drink.

"Ah, here we go," she said. "Thank you, darling."

The young man grimaced and hustled back to some far corner of the restaurant, there to fold napkins into extraordinary landlocked swans.

"So you married Dad because he was handsome?"

"Oh—not just that." Shana's eyes clouded a little. "He's also smart and so charming. You know how he lights up a room. Now give this a try, girls. You deserve it."

Kate was wearing a turtleneck made of white cashmere. She did look like she had a handsome father, a smart and charming man.

"You first," I said.

She brought the cup to her mouth and got whipped cream on her lip, and we all laughed, and when it was my turn I took a spoon to the green swirl on top.

"Back then, *I* was his pyramid," Shana said vaguely. She took a long drag of the cigarette and then jammed it out.

"What was the first thing he ever said to you?" Kate asked.

"The first thing? The first thing was probably hello."

If you looked hard enough, you could make out Long Island on the other side of the water, or at least you thought it was there.

"He told me . . ." she began again. "He told me I'd make a good mother." She leaned forward on her elbows. "He said I'd make a good mother to someone."

"He was right about that, Mom." Kate squinted. Her words were small and thin, offered on a tray to Shana.

The mother looked at her daughter as if from a great distance. "Well, I never put too much stock in it. I know what mothers can be like."

I didn't know what she meant by that.

"Now drink up, sweethearts, the prize is at the bottom, as they say."

The light was different when we left, ashy, and the club had lit up all their evergreens, a thin, docile forest lining the long stretch of driveway. When I got out of the car in front of my house, I looked back at Kate in the passenger seat and had the distinct impression she mouthed the words *Rescue me.*

We'd made an appointment with a famous orthopedist at the Children's Hospital in Boston, but he wouldn't be able to see me until mid-December—a delay my father had called unconscionable: "Doesn't he realize that young lives are in the balance? Good Lord, the arrogance. And can we wait that long? Can we take the risk?" He then gave me a horrible look I didn't like. My mother, who had been filling out an order form for an audiotape of "healing tones" that would, if you listened for five hundred hours, align your back with God's plan, said something that made him still more furious; a loud discussion ensued, and I stood on the sidelines, tilting in my brace, enumerating in my head all the ways the world would be better if my back were straight.

I stood next to my mother, a sheepish problem, while she explained to our new yoga teacher, whom I'd dubbed Energy Lady, what had happened at the doctor's. Yoga wasn't as bad as Movement for Life in the useless/ridiculous category, though it did make me feel like a fraud and a failure when I tried to bend into contrary, impossible directions, all the while listening to Lebanese chanting and someone urging me to become aware of my body (I was well aware of my body already, that was the problem). Hearing our plight after class, Energy Lady twisted her long thin braid, heavy with sapphire-colored plastic beads, and her eyebrows arched with concern. As she listened to Mom, she leaned over, threw her arm around my shoulder, and started squishing me. There I stood, off balance, half-suffocated, and beloved. It seemed Energy Lady had all kinds of good ideas, not just taking her class—eight a.m. on Saturday mornings!—but ingesting some awful, wizardy thing made out of wormwood and drinking the essences of bucketfuls of weeds.

And there would be more. An acupuncturist. A chiropractor. A woman who taught the Alexander technique—a make-yourself-very-tall type of concept. "She sounds wonderful," Mom had reported after her initial call. "She was a dancer, you know. I have high hopes for this, Allie." It was like she'd looked in the Yellow Pages under "Last Ditch Efforts" and was calling every number.

Mom's bright smile was worrisome as she lined up my new "ligament strengtheners" on the orange kitchen counter. But this was just one of many natural steps for anyone thinking "out of the box," for those of us behaving like trees and doing the Downward Dog in church basements across America.

The morning of the horse show, I got up while it was still dark. Lee was coming with the trailer at six.

I walked out to the barn in my nightgown and parka. The ruffled tops of the pine trees were silhouetted against a deep ocean sky, almost phosphorescent. When I clicked on the light in the barn, Jazz looked up, let out a soft complaint at being bothered so early. I dipped the coffee can into the oats and spilled the slippery stuff into Jazz's trough. I pumped water into the bucket hanging nearby, and he dug with a vengeance into his first meal of the day.

He was in a blanket that morning, red with white trim. We

didn't usually blanket him, except on the coldest winter nights, but I'd bathed and brushed him the night before and wanted him to keep clean. I'd thinned out his mane and braided it, making a little railroad track of knots held together by rubber bands and red ribbons. (Lee had shown me how to thin out the mane: You twisted a small lock of hair in the comb and yanked.)

When Lee arrived, her cigarette shone orange in the gray light as she opened the back of her trailer and laid down the ramp. Mom and Lee and I hustled Jazz in. He balked, his rear legs bending back, close to the ground. Lee looped the lead around his butt, and we pulled. He tried veering left, and Lee lunged toward him. He tried to go right, and it was me in his way that time. Finally he tore up the ramp, the clatter of his hooves on the metal thunderous.

I sat in the front of Lee's truck with her, and my parents followed in our car. On sharp corners, I could feel Jazz stumble, then right himself, back in the trailer.

When we got to Buckner Farms, the rolling hills were already dotted with girls and their horses: little black velvet caps everywhere, like notes on a musical score.

I walked Jazz around on a lead while Lee and my mother talked. Dad set up a lawn chair and was sitting with his legs crossed, a black notebook on his knee. Great circles had been cut out of the pasture surrounding the stable; these would serve as extra rings for the events. Nothing had started yet, but some horses and their riders were already in the rings, walking or trotting in slow circles or just wandering and waiting, as we were.

The sky had lightened into a stark kind of day. The first events were announced on the loudspeakers, but I still had some time. I put a second coat of conditioner on Jazz's hooves, making them black and shiny. I brushed him again with the soft brush, ran my hand under the little rat bottoms of his braided, curled-under mane. He looked beautiful and strange to me, all clean, with his mane and tail done up that way. I wore the number 477, my new identity.

If my stomach didn't already feel marshmallow weak, it got worse when Lisa Feneta slid by on Magnus Dynamic IV— a beautiful bay, maybe eighteen hands tall. The horse glanced at us, extending his long shiny neck to cast us a weary, aristocratic gaze before stepping carefully away, like a ballerina *en pointe,* miraculous and wobbly. Lisa smirked briefly, then looked back ahead, her posture Brit erect, ribbon worthy.

We saddled up. When they announced the event before mine, I got on, and we started walking around in feverish nowhere circles. Mom and Dad started circling, too, holding their Styrofoam cups of coffee, looking cold and bleak as they stood at a slight distance from each other in the morning breeze.

Kate had said she'd come, but she wasn't there.

The intercom called the first rider in my event. I would be third.

"Now listen," Lee said, cigarette clamped between her lips as she checked the girth, then held my boot in both hands and pushed the heel down and in. Her thick denim vest made her look like a bully. "When they call your number, this is what I want you to do. Take a good hold of his reins, like this, and hold him in place. Then give him a few really good whacks with your crop, behind the saddle. And keep him still while you're doing it. This'll get him revved up for the event. He needs to be a powerhouse going in."

"Hit him with the crop?" I repeated. She hadn't said anything about this before.

"Do what I say, and don't go soft on me now, Alison."

She ran her hand down Jazz's chest and then gave him a short slap on the neck.

The second number came over the speakers—disembodied robot instructions coming from telephone poles. I wished they'd shut up. I wished I could go home.

"Okay, get him going," she said. She stood back. "Do it. Go."

I looked at her fast, not seeing anything, and then gathered up my reins and gave Jazz a tap with the crop.

"No! Lay into him!"

I did what she said. I hit him like crazy two, three, four times. Our number was called, 477. We bolted up the hill like something was chasing us.

My event was in the big barn. He *was* a powerhouse, but somewhere along with the adrenaline and the betrayal of the crop, I'd lost control. Jazz charged through the crowd at the front entrance. I shouted, "Excuse me, excuse me!" as we barreled in.

And then we were in the arena and everything slowed down, and the shavings under our feet were a foot deep, thick and soft, and all I could hear was Jazz's huffing breath and my own heartbeat. There was the course in front of us: eight jumps in a figure-eight pattern. The first was a monstrously huge stack of barrels with a double rail about a foot over them. My knees were trembling. We began.

His gait was wrong. I thought his gait was wrong. The jump came right up to us as if it were moving in our direction, too. Jazz started jumping from a greater distance than necessary; we had too much ground to cover. His rear hoof nicked one of the bars on the way down, and it toppled behind us, and we had to keep going.

The horse put his ears back now, as if the bar falling had pissed him off and he was determined to do it right the next time. Before I could take a breath, there it was—and we were sailing, sailing over a barrel jump, high up, in the air for an inordinate amount of time, and then, *boom,* we were down again and off to the next. I had no idea if my legs were in the right place, or my arms, and then we were at the next jump, and I gave him a nudge, and he did this one perfectly, too, the perfect distance away, a beautiful sail up and over, a gentle landing. Five more to go.

Now it was as if my ears cleared up and I could hear Jazz's thundering hooves as we crossed to the other side of the first jump and did the corresponding one in this direction. Beautiful! We were there, we were glorious! Then to the next, and the next. Up! Down, heavier this time, not a stumble, but— and two more to go—a last, double jump. Up-down, step-step, up-down. And then we were gone—racing out of the barn.

It was over. It was done.

And there they were—Mom, Dad, Lee—and Kate. She'd come.

I leaned down and hugged Jazz's neck. He was sweaty, his neck slick and smelly, and he was breathing fast. I whispered to him.

"Not bad," said Lee, smiling.

My parents were nodding and offering congratulations. I looked over at Kate. She was giving me a strange smile. Was she looking into the sun, or had she seen me hit Jazz? We had agreed there would be no hitting at all in the Alison and Kate Horse Training Company.

*F*irst thing in the bitter morning, Sarah rode into town to discuss the murder of her parents with the Town Fathers. The Town Fathers had a large office on the top floor of the tallest building in town. Of course, this was only the second floor, but that was quite tremendous back then, this having taken place in the olden days. When she went in, she found six men sitting on a bench behind a roughly hewn table of some kind. They nodded sagely as she spoke and said they would Do Something.

The lost heroine galloped home.

Chapter Nine

MRS. HOLLBROOK was wearing the American flag again: a festive scribble with red satin patches and blue ribbons. Standing behind her in our dining room, I was struck, most of all, by the way her shoulder blades stuck out against the fabric of her deranged shirt like small stunted wings.

She reeled about, noticing my presence. "Oh, dearie, am I in your way?" she said, then backed up in a shuffling, teetering motion. The cup in her hand tipped to one side. All the ship's passengers listed left.

"Watch out!"

"Oh!" she said, overcompensating. The cup practically fell off the saucer in the other direction.

"I was just going to get a little ham," I said then.

"Me too, me too. Your mother has put out a lovely spread, just lovely."

She extended one trembling, papery hand toward the ham roll-ups and placed one on her saucer, no problem.

"So, dearie," she said, squinting at me, "you're in eighth grade, is that it? And do you have Albert Bostitch?"

"He's my social studies teacher."

"He's my cousin! Isn't that a coincidence?"

I agreed that it was. Mrs. Hollbrook looked incredibly fragile to me, and her lipstick was all wrong.

"And is he leading you astray with all his notions?"

The other Women of History milled closer. I didn't know why Mom was having so many of these meetings at our house—didn't the others have mansions they could go to instead? But everyone was in a complete tizzy because the fundraiser was in two weeks, RSVPs were coming in, and most of the Women of History were, at the same time, getting renovations done on their historic homes. I had hoped to avoid all of them and just snag a quick snack before making my escape to the barn. "Oh, but I'd absolutely *adore* to see St. Petersburg," Grete Feneta was saying to someone, everyone.

Mrs. Hollbrook leaned close, her coffee perilously close to my arm. "Poor man hasn't been the same since that god-awful war. He lost his son, you know. In Vietnam."

"I didn't know that," I said. I had never really imagined any kind of life for Mr. Bostitch outside the classroom.

"The boy was weird to begin with, but you know people love their children more than anything on earth. They go batty, you know, the parents do. Never the same again."

"Shall we get started, then, ladies?" my mother said, clapping her hands.

Before riding, I had to clean Jazz's stall. Guiding the wheelbarrow to the compost pile, I came upon my father, sitting on the steps to the loft, drinking a beer and smoking.

"What are you doing?"

"They're in there. They've taken over."

"The Women of History?"

"Yes. The Daughters of the Mall. The Ladies of the Lost Luxury Liner."

He took a sip of his Budweiser, then stroked his beard. He was wearing a sweater I'd questioned him about several times—apparently it had been his mother's father's. This particular garment looked as if it might have been used by the Vikings as a net for catching salmon.

"One of them is wearing a brooch with rays or talons the length of arms," he said. "She resembles most closely a fierce sun deity in a lost Aztec civilization."

"That must be Grete Feneta. She is kind of strange. But Dad, don't be scared of rich ladies."

"What makes you think I'm scared?"

"Maybe the fact that you're hiding?"

He took a drag of his cigarette and flicked it out into the paddock. "Good point, Alison."

I saddled up Jazz, did a few jumps, and then rode out to the mansion.

There were just so many interesting people to meet and to learn about at the Hamiltons'. The pleasure in this may have been compromised, somewhat, by erratic behavior and too many pistachio shells in the ashtray and far too many dogs for sanity, but every time I visited Kate—and I went to her house a lot more than she came to mine—I felt as though something new might happen, I might meet someone strange or learn something I didn't know before.

That Friday, Tut's secretary, Renee, was taking care of the kids. Shana had joined her husband for a playshop, in Hawaii this time.

I'd met Renee a couple of times before. She wore the tallest platform shoes I'd ever seen—taller even than Laura Sleigh's. She had bleached blond hair in the Stevie Nicks/Farrah Fawcett style, and, as Kate had told me, she never took off her mascara: Her lashes were thick and as solid as the black plastic tabs that closed over the eyes of a sleeping baby doll. Myself, I'd recently read in *Seventeen* that if you put a little Vaseline on your eyelashes, it made them look darker (I'd tried this and found it a bit greasy). I'd also gotten the hair surrounding my face cut into "wings," and every morning I curled these into eager little flips with a curling iron. The look was modified Farrah Fawcett, although regretfully I seemed more to resemble the other Charlie's Angel, the smart one.

Mick was watching TV when I got there. I said hi, and he was on a friendly streak, I guess, because he said hi back. Since our recent encounter in the kitchen, the nonseduction, his detachment had been entire.

Kate and Renee were in the kitchen. The radio was blaring Captain and Tenille: "Love, love will keep us together. / Think of me, babe, whenever . . ."

I sat on the stool next to Kate and watched Renee doctor up a pizza.

"So anyway," Renee shouted, slicing mushrooms with random chaotic anger. "When I read about his sign in Linda Goodman's, I can't *believe* how right we are for each other. His quiet side is so adorable. It's like—vulnerable. He seems so outgoing, so great with people, but then there's this other side, too. John Travolta, get out of town! *Everyone* looks at Ricky. The men want to kick his Italian *ass,* he's so sexy."

Our baby-sitter smiled at the ceiling, holding the butcher knife to her chest like a baby.

"So is he a good kisser?" asked Kate, filing her nail.

"His kiss is like—oh, hand me my purse? I need a cigarette for this."

Kate leaned over and grabbed Renee's gigantic macramé purse from the stool.

"Just light me one, okay, sweetie? The lighter's in there too somewhere. And don't tell me you've never lit a cigarette before," Renee said, slashing away at what was left of a green pepper. Then she about emptied a jar of garlic powder over the pizza.

When she got her cigarette from Kate, Renee said, "Have you ever slept under the stars? Either of you girls?" She took a drag, then held the cigarette meditatively next to her pink frosty pout. "Well, his kiss is like that—like a shower of falling stars."

"Wow," I said.

"So what about—the other?"

"The other? What could you *possibly* mean, Miss Kate?"

"You know what I'm talking about."

"Oh, well, *that's* a story for another time." Renee winked and flung back her hair, revealing a bare shoulder, then maneuvered the pizza into the oven. "Here we go, twenty minutes and voilà! Gourmet Italian."

"Yeah, Kate—what other?" I asked, a little alarmed.

"Okay, girls, time for a beer," said Renee. "What's that cutie-pants brother of yours doing? *Mick! Watch out, here we come!*"

She grabbed four bottles from the refrigerator. Kate didn't answer my question, and we all tramped into the living room to wait for the pizza.

I wished then I'd told Kate about Mick, the little come-on. I wasn't so dumb. I knew what "the other" meant.

A potter came to school, which allowed for this vision: twenty young Republicans unwrapping slabs of clay. "Feel the potential in the lump, my friends—raw potential, and then what happens?" said the teacher, a guest in a poncho with leather sandals and toenails like claws.

Lisa, Lynn, and Priscilla were in this class, and as I sat at the last open potter's wheel and rolled the stool close, spreading my legs wide around the wheel, I could feel them watching me. I leaned forward and craned my neck over the collar of my brace to look down at the clay.

"See the potential in your mind's eye, and then slowly, slowly, something takes shape," the potter lady sang as she swirled around the room, poncho tassels flying.

I tried out the foot lever, but it didn't work. I kept pressing—nothing. I pumped. It started with a lurch, the wheel spun, and my clay flew on to the linoleum.

The jock girls stared down at the lump of clay with long deliberation. They looked back up at me, their eyes wide with disbelief at the high humor quotient in what had just happened.

I got up and picked up the clay. My lump of potential was considerably flatter than it had been.

I pressed it back into the wheel with my fist. *Stay, you bastard.* Finally, I got the wheel to go nice and slow, and the clay between my hands battered my palms and fingers as it went around, slightly smoother with each rub, and then this kid, a Dave Darbis double, came up to me and asked if I was enjoying myself.

"What's it to you?" I asked.

"When you put your hands around it like that, what are you thinking about?"

"What am I thinking about? Um—what I'm going to have for lunch."

I thought this was a mildly amusing reply, but then he said, "Funny, it looked like you were practicing your moves for the boyfriend you'll never have, brace girl."

At this, Lisa, Lynn, and Priscilla gave themselves over to helpless giggles, and I felt myself go red in the face, for I had actually spent much of the night before thinking about what Renee had said about Ricky's kisses: *like stars.* The Evergreen Dance was coming up, and I'd been hopeful that morning, strangely hopeful, that any of the definitely male humans I saw in the halls might suddenly ask me to go. Maybe even Frank, the green-eyed boy from biology.

How stupid of me.

I started up the wheel again and wrapped my palms around the clay gingerly, so gingerly, not making a dent in anything.

To cheer me up after class, Kate suggested skipping gym. We hitchhiked down to Devil's Glen.

Weston is a rocky place, and the glen is one of those veins

where rocks have come to the surface, massive boulders slamming up in friendship for a million years.

First we stood on the bridge, downstream from the big rocks: the cliffs, where kids dared themselves over one precipice in particular, where for one bicycle-pedaling-in-the-air moment, all was suspended, the future uncertain, and then the jumper would slam into the black water forty feet below and disappear—only to reemerge, triumphant.

White light streamed through the pine trees, making them black, a reverse X-ray. The riverbank was crowded with rocks, loose and messed up, like they'd tumbled out of some giant gambler's fist. One silly tall rock stood on top of another one with no discernible means of support, and others lay in defeated crumbles underneath.

The water was breathtaking. In the wispy ghost light, the noise charged at us.

"Man," Kate said.

"Wouldn't want to take a canoe in that."

"Maybe bodysurfing."

"Yeah, sure."

"*Whoosh,*" she said, flying her hand.

"Right—you'd end up like a rubber doll."

"That's the thing: Stay flexible. Did you know that drunk drivers survive really bad accidents because they don't tense up? They hit a tree and just bounce off, whereas the rest of us, our bones would break into a million pieces."

"Another sign that driving drunk is a good idea," I said. I, who had this experience: one juice glass of Manischewitz at a Montessori kid's bar mitzvah, the half an Irish coffee we'd had with Shana, and a Beck's with Renee and Kate and Mick.

"Let's go over there," she said, pointing upriver.

We walked to the end of the bridge and then turned in, stepping off the pavement. We held on to the thinnest of branches, steadied ourselves on unreliable rocks. At the edge of the water, Kate stood on the cusp of sand, her hands in her back pockets, and I stood next to her.

"Hey, who's that?" I said. There was someone on the other side of the river.

Kate shaded her eyes and looked over.

He was squatting on a rock, staring toward the cleft rocks up ahead, holding what appeared to be a camera. He wore big black sunglasses, the kind old people buy at drugstores.

He saw us.

"Shit," Kate whispered.

We were all frozen for a moment, and then Kate waved boldly at him.

"What are you doing?" I hissed.

"Dogs smell fear."

"He's not a dog, he's a weird forest person."

He didn't wave back, whatever he was. He just kept staring, then he jumped up and disappeared into the woods.

"What kind of weirdo is *he,* I wonder," Kate said.

"I don't know."

"The scary woods," she said in a creepy voice.

"Want to keep walking?"

"Let's."

At some point you don't notice the din anymore; the river noise envelops you. We checked a rock with one foot, then took a step and then another, in a rocky meander.

"Look—a lounge area?" Kate asked, pointing to a place in the sun.

"Definitely."

We made our way over there and sat down, leaning on cold rock. Kate opened her purse and pulled out the cigarettes and lighter. I thought I could hear some kids shouting over by the cliffs—small shouts, brief as a stone falling into the water.

"Girls? Girls?" we heard from above.

It was the guy from across the river. He was ten feet away.

"Hello, girls. No fear, no fear. My name is Warren Lipp, Lippacious to my friends. Mind if I ask you a few questions?"

Before we could answer, he had jumped down to our level. He was wearing black jeans and army boots, a trench coat cinched at the waist. His entire outfit looked as though it had come from the Army & Navy Store, but he didn't look like a soldier.

"What kind of questions?" Kate asked.

"Good questions. Now, ladies—ah, don't mind if I do." He sat on the ledge next to us, placing his camera gently by his side. "Nice *ledge,*" he said, emphasizing the second word oddly, as if he'd just made it up or were practicing a foreign language. "So, like I was saying. I'm Warren. Warren. Lipp. Lippacious. The Lippacious Wonder, to be specific. Now, who are you?"

"I'm Kate."

"Alison."

"Are you from Weston, Kate and Alison?"

He pulled up his old-man sunglasses and peered out from under them—and then he just left them there, hung up on his rough blond hair. He was about twenty or twenty-five, I thought.

"Yeah," said Kate.

"And do you go to Weston High?"

"You think we're in high school?" Kate said, perked up by this concept.

"Oh—you're not?" he said with perhaps feigned surprise.

"We're in eighth grade," I told him.

"Ah—eighth grade. My favorite contact sport."

"What?"

"So this is the situation. I'm a follower and a chronicler of events. I see things. I'm a photographer and a journalist. Currently, I'm considering the state of the teenager. Remember the boy who died here this summer?"

"I've seen your pictures," I said, realizing where I'd seen his name before. "In the *Weston Forum.*"

"Yes, yes, yes. My day job. So what is the attraction of Devil's Glen? Is it in the name? Or what is it? I mean, who doesn't love nature, of course, the woods and the rivers and all that crap, don't get me wrong. But why—why do you people *really* come to places like this?"

"*Us* people?" said Kate, lighting up a Winston.

"You little people." He chuckled. "What do you think, girls? Help me solve the crime of the century."

"The kid jumped. Lots of kids jump," said Kate. "So what?"

"Kids can come here and be on their own, without adults," I said.

"Ah, but there's the rub, don't you see? No adults here, right?" He flung an arm out toward the river and then peered past it. "And no adults here." He flung his arm in the other direction. "But surely, surely you wouldn't deny that they *are* here, after all."

He paused and looked at us. Why his sunglasses weren't falling down, I didn't know. They remained suspended on his forehead like a half-closed door.

"They are here. *Here,*" he said, and started tapping his temple. *Tap tap tap*—like a woodpecker. (Still, the glasses stayed.)

"What are you talking about?" asked Kate.

"Honey, may I have a cigarette?"

Kate shrugged and handed him the pack.

"Beautiful. Smoking away with the children of America," said Warren Lipp, knocking one into his palm, then lighting up.

Kate and I looked at each other.

"It's not all about toy dolls and spilled ice cream, is it, girls?" he asked us after a moment. He held his cigarette funny, pinched between two fingers.

"Not quite," said Kate, trying to put a sarcastic spin on it. I scrutinized the rushing water.

"And it's not really about golf, either—or is it about golf? It could, possibly, be all about golf."

The Lippacious Wonder plugged his cigarette between his lips and pulled out a little pad and pen and started scribbling something.

"What's about golf?" I asked.

"The problem."

"What problem?"

"The kid jumping off the cliff."

"Okay, the kid jumping off the cliff," I said.

"The parents—they're all playing golf, I reckon."

"My parents don't play golf," said Kate.

"Neither do mine—not much, anyway."

Warren didn't seem to have heard. He peered up into the world and smoked as Confucius might have smoked. "Golfing parents. They get stuck in the kid's head like a little plastic monkey, clogging the arteries, making everything dark and hazy. The plastic monkey slashes away at the brain matter, slicing here, slicing there, and before you know it—the monkey's taken over! The little golfing monkey jumps up and down *hoo hoo haa haa.* Brain fried, end of story. Little Weston, Connecticut—*place of nightmare!*"

"Are you going to want to take our picture?" Kate asked.

"There's no real monkey, it's more like a dream of a monkey," I said.

"Oh. *Oh,*" said Warren.

"Oh, I get it," Kate said. "A *dream* of a golfing monkey."

"So, girls, what makes Weston tick, do you know? C'mon, you can tell me."

"What makes this place tick is money," said Kate.

"Money? Oh, *money,*" he said, as though he'd never heard of it before. "So do you girls get a little allowance? Do you jump into your fancy cars and go shopping in Westport every Saturday? How does this money business affect you, really? Aren't we all just people underneath?"

"Sure, we're people," I said.

"What do your parents do for a living, Kate and Alison? Tell me, for a moment, about your parents. Hated, maligned figures, correct?"

"My mom's a painter, and my dad's a poet and a college professor."

"My dad's a shaman."

"Oh-ho-*ho*! I've unearthed some lively ones! What, no investment bankers or lawyers?"

"My father used to be a businessman but later decided upon shamanism."

"My mom belongs to a committee—that's pretty conventional. But she's still a painter."

"A committee!"

Warren Lipp took this opportunity to drop his sunglasses back over his eyes and then mess up his hair. It already looked as if he rarely combed it. I found him fascinating and bizarre. Was he a grown-up? He seemed neither here nor there.

"Well, then, what kind of committee, young Alison? I fear to ask what kind of shamanism."

"She's on the Women of History committee—or maybe it's a board. Yes, I think it's a board."

"Board, shmoard," said Kate.

"They're putting on this jubilee."

"Why, *of course,* the jubilant jubilee. I'll be busy that day, taking pictures of goats and beeswax candle makers. Maybe a few stills of red, white, and blue pot holders and some sand art. Wasn't it clever of them to schedule it in May—before the Fourth of July by six weeks or more? What, they were in such a hurry they couldn't wait for the rest of the country? Wanted to hog the show? Well, dears, and what do *you* think of history? Good stuff, isn't it? The Napoleonic Wars, the Industrial Revolution, free enterprise? The rise of capitalism, the descent of man? Everywhere you look, civilization and its discontents, survival of the fittest, the cleverest *Homo erectus* boss men in the land?"

"We don't understand history," announced Kate. "It seems overrated."

"Yes, the important stuff seems to get ignored."

"Ah," said Warren, nodding sagely. "Yet—it's so photogenic at times."

"For instance, we stole all this land from the Indians," I pointed out.

"Those poor, trod-upon indigenous peoples," he said, shaking his head. "Well, shall we forgive dear old golfing monkeyland for its past indiscretions? Mightn't we move on, girls? Let's think about now. Let's think about the present day. Let's look through the *lens* of the *immediate,* shall we?"

"Are you going to take our picture or what?" asked Kate. "Or do you just walk around rivers bumming cigarettes all day?"

He squinted at her and then gave her a little cocking-the-gun hand signal. "Kate, Kate! Patience, my girl. You don't need to say 'cheese.' You don't need to look pretty, see what I mean?"

She looked at him, folded smoke back into her throat.

"Hey, Warren," I said, "do you know anything about making photographs look old? You know, like they were taken a long time ago?"

"Black and white? Is that what you mean? Tintype? Sepia toned?"

"Yes," Kate said, picking up on my meaning. "We're doing this project for social studies—everyone has to come up with something to do with, like, 1776, so Alison and I are writing about a girl who lived back then, you know? We're making it really authentic, with trees and geography and all that. Water pumps, farm equipment. Indians. Maybe even Paul Bunyan."

"Paul Bunyan?" I looked at her.

"Okay, Paul Revere."

I said, "The girl is the heroine, see? She has adventures, and maybe she'll save Weston or something, or solve a mystery. Pictures would be really cool. We could dress up like her— one of us could, anyway."

Warren had lifted his glasses entirely off his head and was now sucking the stem meditatively.

"Yes, you certainly could dress up," he said. "Or even dress down? Never mind. Here's the problem. Just a miniproblem, really. Just a small, almost inconsequential concern."

"What's that?" Kate asked.

"Photography wasn't invented until 1839. In France. The daguerreotype, perhaps you've heard of it? Perhaps not. They didn't start using photographs here until later—Civil War era. Oh, yes. So whether it's Paul Bunyan or Paul Revere is rather inconsequential, my fair maidens of Today. Perhaps— etchings? paintings? cameos in whalebone?"

"Well, that's inconvenient, but maybe not an *impossible* obstacle," said Kate.

"The fact is, we're more interested in the future anyway," I put in.

"Girls. Alison. Kate. The future is just another balm, just another blindfold. Don't be blinded against today. Ideas are not real! They're like shining wee stars, glittering about in the ether."

"Warren," said Kate, "stars *are* real. They're just far away."

"Ah, yes. Well, look at this. Run into a couple of girls on a rock, and you get all the answers you need. My friends," he said, and flicked his cigarette into the river, "this has been illuminating. But I fear I must go. Enough hyperbolizing and hypothesizing—I've become fatigued and perhaps overstayed my welcome." Warren Lipp, photographer extraordinaire and reporter of today, jumped up. "Good luck, my pretties. Ta-ta, America!"

And with that, he leapt from our rock to the next rock and then into the woods, his trench coat ballooning in the air.

Sarah waited for word from the Town Fathers. At night, she tossed and turned on her straw mat, remembering her mother, who told knock-knock jokes, and her father, who might well have been, one day, the governor of Connecticut and who held her close and buried his nose in her long little-girl locks. He also knew some jokes, but he favored the why-did-the-chicken-cross-the-road type. She would have been fine with that kind right now as well, or even limericks.

Where her parents had been felled, the sycamore floorboards of the small and worthy shack were still unnaturally dark.

Chapter Ten

I FELT light and unreal at the Seeds Planted Yesterday, the Fruit of Tomorrow benefit dinner. Somehow I'd gotten both parents to agree I could leave my brace home for the evening: I think they'd been too preoccupied to resist my entreaties. Mom had been roused to a new pinnacle of artist/ socialite tension, and Dad had fallen beard first into a pit of poetic darkness. Me, I just wanted to be different for a night, a strange new person.

Lately I'd been living in a trance state of continuous present, compulsively monitoring my scoliosis in private moments. Did I feel straighter? More crooked? My arm would ache from reaching back and pushing with my fingers at the vertebrae, at the thick muscle surrounding the apex of the curve. A roadblock of muscle had formed to keep the spine from curving farther, like a pile of hard snow at the end of a driveway. I pushed, kneaded, monitored, thought of the words *hunchback, hopeless,* and *death.* And sometimes *miraculous.* Throughout it all, the vertebrae remained fixed in a frozen, chancy S.

Mom had added PowerUpForHealth!, a dreadful quasi-fermented liquid supplement she'd read about in a newsletter, to my nutrition regimen, and though the acupuncturist and chiropractor—not to mention Movement for Life—had turned out to be a bust, we were still going to yoga, and she still continued frantically scanning the horizon for Health. The hokier of the methods she came up with made my father wince, holding his slash-this-metaphor marker in a death grip as he graded student papers. Still, I liked to believe we were together in this. You've heard the notion that a plane stays up in the air because all the people in the cabin believe it can fly? Maybe that was us.

But something else was happening as well. More than once in the past month I'd caught my father giving me wistful looks from the other side of the room, as if he were missing me even though I was right there. As if I were a ghost or he were a ghost. I didn't understand this, but it made me nervous.

At Cobb's Mill Inn (Weston's ancient, quaint, and only restaurant), I wore a black velvet dress my grandfather had mailed me. It had come in a box from Saks Fifth Avenue—an early Christmas present, he'd told Mom. Kate was in a red dress she'd gotten from her mother. The sleeves were a little long, so Kate had folded them up at the wrists. We were both wearing our hair in French braids—the disco secretary had shown us the technique—and we'd hidden emergency cigarettes under our dresses, pressed between L'eggs panty hose and our skin.

Our job was to hand out programs to guests as they came and, at the end of the evening, offer baskets holding jars of apple butter. The restaurant guy had said we could have as much free soda as we wanted, so before the people arrived we went up to the bar. John, the bartender, tumbled ice into our glasses, filled them, and slid them our way.

"Honey," he said to Kate, "when you turn sixteen can we make a family together? I'd like to buy you a house—six bedrooms and about twenty chandeliers."

He was tall and youngish, not bad-looking, but not exactly good-looking, either. He had rippled black hair parted on the side, and he kept running his fingers across the long side, pushing the clump back where it belonged.

Kate looked over at me as if what he'd said were so absurd that she couldn't talk to him directly. "No kids for me," she said, her voice wavering toward derision.

"So much the better," John said, lifting his hand to his hair. "We'll live in a houseboat. What do you say? Wouldja?"

"Can we have cherries in these?" Kate said then, indicating our 7-Ups. "Thank you."

"Yes, of course. Anything for you ladies."

We took our drinks and walked over to our post by the door.

"He must be in his twenties or something," I said, stunned.

"Poor guy won't know where to find me when I'm old enough for him. He has no idea we'll be in Wyoming by then."

She gave me a look—she'd tossed me something.

"That's right," I said. "He'll be too busy fixing his hair."

"I wonder how he knew I wasn't sixteen. Do we look that young?"

"I think you look sixteen," I said. But what about me? I was masquerading as a braceless person, and he hadn't even glanced in my direction. "Anyway, Warren Lipp said we looked like we were in high school."

"He was just buttering us up, Allie, so he could fill in his little report on teen life in Weston."

"I kind of liked him."

"You've got strange taste, Allie cat." Right. I had taste in men, but what difference did it make? It was like having opinions on Martian footwear.

People started coming. The men wore tuxedos, and the women were all in fur coats: black, brown, silver, spotted, striped. It looked as if a menagerie of diverse animals had escaped from the zoo. A restaurant employee took the coats, then the women and their husbands passed us, and we smiled and held out the delicate scrolls tied with blue and red velvet ribbon.

"Hi, Mrs. Hollbrook," I said, handing her a program. She'd checked her blue cashmere coat and was wandering in our direction, a blissful, teary look on her face. As far as her outfit was concerned, she'd outdone herself. It was killer. It brought tears to your eyes. Red, white, and blue, of course, but in an abstract design featuring wavy stripes of red and blue sequins on a shimmering silver background.

"Well, hello, dearie. Don't you look beautiful. And who's your friend?"

I introduced her to Kate, and they shook hands.

"Well, this is lovely, just *lovely*! Here you are, gracing us with your young energy. I'm so thoroughly delighted. Delighted, darlings. Really I am."

"We should talk to her about 1776," I said to Kate when

Mrs. Hollbrook had meandered on. "She's the one who knows so much about the Revolution."

"Really? Glad to know you want to interview the actual *American flag,* Alison."

The guests poured in, glittery and perfumed, and some of the men had red scarves, burgundy cummerbunds. They were briefly stars as they walked up to the restaurant, bathed in light, on a red carpet.

Shana slipped on the path coming in and laughed and laughed, then regained her composure. Tall Tut stood by her side, dressed in trademark hues, this time an ivory suit with a white shirt and tie. He looked relaxed and smooth, his head emitting a muted velvety glow.

"This dress looks *vonderbar* on you, Katie koo," Shana said when she reached us, after a lengthy hug for her daughter. Tut puffed on his pipe and surveyed the territory. I didn't look at him directly: Lately, I hadn't been able to.

Mrs. Feneta glided up, her face made large and frightening with makeup. She whisked by Kate and me on her mission to clasp Shana's hand and explain how very, very honored she was to meet the wife of "such an icon, a marvel, really."

I squinted at the woman as she spoke. She had the same look her daughter had at the horse show: determined, certainly, and animated into some preconceived role I had yet to figure out. (Lisa herself had gotten out of Seeds Planted Yesterday, the Fruit of Tomorrow duty because of some debutante party in New York City. Thank God, Kate and I had agreed.) Now Grete Feneta grabbed each Hamilton by one arm and guided them in.

The room was beautiful, white tablecloths and candles under glass globes and glimmering silverware. A bank of windows lined one wall. You could see the river, a trail of fake gaslights illuminating its shore.

The menu was modified Revolutionary: Boston Tea Party Salad for starters, then Patriot Medallions of Beef with Liberty Mashed Potatoes (although "liberty" and "mashed" didn't seem to go together), corncakes, Pioneer Beet Flambé, and, for dessert, chocolate mousse (in deference to some French folks back during the war).

Mom had said we could eat at any table that wasn't full, but Mrs. Feneta hadn't liked that idea. ("The kids won't have any *fun* that way," she'd said, sounding stressed. "Let them eat alone.") In the end, we sat at the bar, and John the bartender regaled us with stories of his weekend, which was spent drinking in various locales. Sometimes, while he was gazing at Kate, I'd look over to where my parents were sitting. Mom kept getting up and conferring with Mrs. Feneta or Mrs. Bix or another Woman of History, and Dad seemed to be stoically enduring a conversation with one of the fur-coat crowd. That afternoon I'd seen something I'd never seen before: my father meditating *with* a beer. There he was, sitting in our backyard, wrapped in a sleeping bag—and by his side a can of Budweiser.

Kate and I polished off our Patriot Medallions and went outside to smoke flattened cigarettes between some bushes and a silver car.

"Let's go talk to Mrs. Hollbrook," I said between strenuous puffs (the panty hose press hadn't done much for the draw).

"Nah. Let's just sit at the bar," she said.

I looked at her, surprised by this—here we had a chance to get the information we'd been looking for—but she was looking someplace else. She hadn't put on her coat, and she bent her knees now and held on to herself, rocking slightly in the cold.

When we got back in, Grete Feneta was at the podium. She was talking about the glories of Weston and the glories of the assembled guests and the glories, generally, of the past, present, and future. Then it was time for Tut Hamilton to give his speech, and everyone began to applaud. Kate gave an exaggerated pretend yawn, which John misinterpreted and which engendered a wounded/assuaging conversation between them.

Tut walked up to the podium. His white clothing blended in with the tablecloths, as if he were a stealthy table moving out of the room—but no.

He bowed his head for a long moment, perhaps praying to Osiris or giving some kind of thanks to the rest of that god crew. Then he lifted his head in triumphant release, flung his hand into the air. Raised an object to the audience.

"What is this?" he asked in a thundering voice.

From here, it looked like a dollar. I couldn't tell if it was one dollar, a twenty, or what. A murmur passed through the room.

"Oh, this old number," said Kate, then went back to her conversation with the man polishing the tumblers.

"Not enough," said one silver-headed man at a front table, and a bevy of people chuckled.

No one else had any ideas.

"Novus ordo seclorum," said Tut. "A new order of the ages. That's what it says right here, beneath the third eye of Horus. What I have to say to you tonight, ladies and gentlemen, is very simple. It's something you can slip into your wallet. Here." He stepped out from behind the podium and gave the dollar to the silver-headed man. The man lifted it excitedly, as if it were a nugget of gold, and then stuffed it in his pocket to more accompanying laughter.

"Listen. We're here tonight to celebrate history—our history, the history of this town we call home, Weston, Connecticut. We're affluent, lucky people, my friends, to live in such a place. We're lifted up, without even knowing it, by the hands, by the long hard work, of others. Think about those damn pioneers—making applesauce, cutting down trees—right? When was the last time you cut down a tree, boys? They started their own churches, little congregations sitting on *tree stumps*, for crying out loud. They married women who wore *calico* and calico *only*—none of these sexy silky things your beautiful wives are wearing tonight, gentlemen. Look at these beautiful women. We are lucky, again, men—surrounded by such goddesses. Yes, ladies. You keep us going."

He paused, looked around the room, letting his gaze rest appreciatively on one and then another Weston woman.

"My thought for you tonight is, as I said, simple. An image of the Great Pyramid, built of course by the great pharaoh Khufu, second ruler of the Fourth Dynasty, is in your wallet. At least one—I'm hoping, anyway. [Laughter.] It's on every dollar bill. It's on the dollar I just gave this man. It's on the dollar I gave to the kid who parked my Mercedes-Benz 450

SL. It's on each of the eight hundred dollars my wife spent, last week, on a pair of red thigh-high boots from some crazy Italian designer.

"Now, as you may know, there's a Freemason heritage in this country, and they, bless them, were determined Egyptologists. Some thought they were descended from the pharaohs. Ben Franklin thought so. And that cherry tree fellow—what was his name? [More laughter.] Sounds crazy, right? Well, maybe they were on to something, after all. I won't make a case that we here today, sitting in this lovely restaurant, in this lovely town, are descendants from the great pharaohs of Egypt, although it *is* true that my name is Tut, and there— over there, I see her—there's Cleopatra. [Even more laughter.] But what I'm saying is this. We've been trained in this country, in recent years, to feel rather badly about the dollar bill and all it represents. We've been trained—by the media, the politicians, the old fuddy-duds in the churches—to regret the fact that we even *have* a dollar in our Bill Blass wallets. What? Bill Blass? No, I wouldn't know who made my wallet, you say. But this is a lie. You love your Bill Blass wallet. Admit it! And women, you love your Salvadore Chopsticks red boots. You know it's true, ladies. Well, I'm here to say: *No one is going to take them away from you.* I'm here to say: I know the dissonance you feel, the dissonance between wanting— loving—these things and, *and,* at the very same time, being— *knowing* yourself to be—a good, kind, generous, spiritual human being.

"Without going into all the details—you'll need to come to my playshops for that, or buy my book, *Pyramid Love,* available in any decent bookstore—I want you to rest assured that, indeed, there is a *spiritual basis to acquisition*. There is the Eye of Horus. There is the Great Pyramid."

He paused and took a drink from his glass, then went on. The room was swathed in stunned, rapturous silence.

"Our task, ladies and gentlemen, is to humbly accept acquisition as a time-honored, indeed, a *historically sanctioned* mode of self-fulfillment. Ladies and gentlemen, pharaohs and empresses, there is a spiritually fulfilling reason to keep up with the Joneses. The great creative principle is with us when we furnish our homes, when we select a red over a black Maserati. Just as those with fewer pyramids in their pockets lovingly adorn their Pinto's car seat with purple fur seat covers and so on, just as even the poorest miscreants will pay four ninety-nine for a little fucking hood ornament for their piece-of-shit car—the path, the literal and true path, between ourselves and eternity resides—carefully, humbly— in the steady, honest, hot chase—of beauty. *In the form of cash.*"

John was showing Kate a trick involving toothpicks, a bottlecap, and a glass. She elbowed me in the ribs—*Check this out, Allie*—and I missed part of the speech while trying to determine how John was getting the cap to twirl around the glass's rim and then leap off into his hand. When I turned back, Mr. Hamilton was summing up. From what I could tell, Kate hadn't looked up at him since the beginning.

"And so, friends, visionary artists of the dollar bill, humble servants of manna, be grateful, as grateful as I am, for all the good men and good women who have brought us to where we are today. In this last month or two of the tax year, give generously to the Women of History and the upcoming jubilee. It's not just a celebration of the past but also the future. Our future. A place where the separation of money and love can finally be breached, where we can all wear red boots to bed and open our wallets to the beneficence of the universe. Peace, prosperity, good works."

With that, Mr. Hamilton bowed deeply and moved humbly back to his table. Shana was there, waving her arms out to him in a slightly drunken gesture.

It was time for my father to read poetry, but he had to wait for the crescendo of applause to die down.

Which took a while. It looked as though all the sleek people in the room had, indeed, achieved spiritual resolution of some kind. The men's shiny gray hair seemed shinier as they pushed their shoulders back proudly against their tuxedo jackets. The women, Cleopatras and Nefertitis and Shebas, had a new litheness and intoxication to their movements. Even the fur coats were dancing in the coatroom.

Lucille Bix was to do my father's introduction, and she laid her spangled arms, bracelets up to the elbows, on the sides of the podium. "My goodness. My goodness," she began in a dazed sort of way, tapping the microphone until it screeched and thumped. Then she smiled—hugely, absently—at the people sitting around her. "We're doubly lucky this evening, for one of our members, Clare, had the foresight to marry one of today's best poets, Chris Glass, and he's graciously, wonderfully, generously agreed to read for us tonight."

Polite applause.

Mrs. Bix read a list of awards and such. "Now sit back and let the beauty of poetry fill your body. Beauty, poetry—and money—it's all we seem to need."

Dad, who had been studying the intricacies of the tablecloth during his introduction, now got up and walked somberly over to the podium, giving Lucille Bix a quick nod.

I smiled toward him, and then it was my turn to elbow Kate.

"What?" she said.

"Dad's reading."

"Cool," she said, but then went back to her conversation.

My father coughed and extracted two books from the brown sacklike object formerly known as his briefcase. He put them on the podium and started glancing around for water. Not finding any, he indicated this to Mrs. Bix, who ran away, scandalized and appalled, so she could do violence to a busboy.

The room quieted down. My father stroked his beard briefly and then scowled up at us. "Hello," he said. "I've come to read you a few poems."

Now John was doing a shell game with Kate, using coffee cups and peanuts. He was grinning and chewing a swizzle stick and rubbing his hair back with his palm.

To hell with her, I thought rather dramatically. I got up and walked over to the edge of the tables. I could see Mom sitting with Mrs. Feneta. She was smiling. We were all smiling, in our anxiety.

"I don't know how much these have to do with history," my father said. "Weston history, anyway. But they are about *personal* history and, for what it's worth, reflect my own sense of . . . an homage, I suppose—to literary history. To books and words."

He looked up and scrutinized those around him. They were dead silent.

He cleared his throat, put on his reading glasses, and opened one of the books on the podium. Mrs. Bix came scurrying up at the last minute with the glass of water, which meant he had to start the whole ritual over, clearing his throat and flipping through the book and stroking his beard.

"I'll start with one from my first book, *Ash Wednesday*. It's called 'How to Be a Son.'"

Five sizes of galoshes, fallen over, but when
the sun stumbled in and penance began, we became
like new men, dressed for faith again.

I knew this one: Sometimes while washing dishes or folding laundry at home, he'd belt out lines from it as if it were a Baptist revivalist church song.

"Hey, don't leave me alone with him," Kate said, coming up behind me.

"What? I thought you were having fun."

"Yeah, but now he's getting weird on me. Your dad sounds good."

"Thanks," I said. It meant something, coming from Kate. She wrote poetry herself. She'd let me read a couple of her poems, and it was my opinion that she was great and visionary, like Sylvia Plath—the highest compliment I could think of then. I became willing to forget the annoyance of John the bartender.

After all the prayers were done, and we drove back home,
myrrh in our trousers, after wishes had gone and sunk

in holy buckets locked away from us until another time, he'd
spiral and spin out; become, like the priest, an icon. I was
the most accurate of weathermen, and so when she said,
as she did every Sunday, come again, *and gestured toward him,*
I knew I'd echo—I'd echo one of them.

Dad went on to the next poem, and for a moment it was as
though he'd forgotten where he was, didn't care that this was
the Seeds Planted Yesterday, the Fruit of Tomorrow fund-
raiser or that the chocolate mousse had small American flags
in it and that now these flags were fallen, in disarray, smudged
and broken.

Kate and I listened, our arms folded across our velvet and
silk dresses, cold now in the darkened restaurant. I knew a lot
of my father's poems. And if I didn't know them exactly, the
exact words, I heard *him* in them. I knew his voice, knew his
sentences—long and spiraling in on themselves, sometimes
short and broken. I knew that he wrote about his mother and
father and sometimes just about walking in the woods or
working at a gas station when he was a teenager. And I knew
that sometimes he wrote about my mother. And sometimes
about me—from birth onward.

Things were going just fine (he hadn't read any of the embarrassing ones), but then I began to get nervous. Dad had
said that if a reading was going well, you could feel something
in the air, an electricity of some kind, the sound and energy of
people listening. But at Cobb's Mill Inn, I heard waiters stack-
ing plates. I heard John whistling and messing with his hair. I
heard the adults drinking what was left of their after-dinner

drinks, rattling ice cubes. I heard all that, but I wasn't entirely sure I heard listening.

Into an exhibit of trees
Lost as we'd never realized

Dad began to rush, as if someone had pressed a stopwatch and with the ticking sound poetry could no longer transport, transform. He finished this poem and started in on another, plunging right in even though they were still clapping for the last. And when he finished with that one, too, he shut his book, said good night, and walked back to my mother.

Grete Feneta got up and thanked everyone for coming. She beseeched them to stay, enjoy themselves as long as they wanted, but to be sure to pick up their apple butter and tax information forms on their way to the door.

Kate and I hurried back to our station up front, and it was a good thing we did, because people started packing it in right away—as fun as it all was, no need to tarry. We handed out the baskets lined with blue-and-white-checked fabric and topped with red ribbons, and they looked odd, rinky-dink, in the pale hands of the well-dressed women.

I glanced back to the dining room. My father was standing alone, staring out the black window toward the lights by the water. Nearby, a group was clustered around Tut Hamilton. One of them was my mother. I was glad when a lady in a cream-colored gown tapped my dad's shoulder, then clasped her purse to her breast in a Broadway gesture, after he'd turned away from the river toward her and her rapture at—his little poems.

Things weren't exactly joyous on the way home.

"Well, *that* was humiliating, Clare. Perhaps at your next event I could read the Dow Jones."

"Oh, c'mon—it was a wonderful evening. Everyone loved your poems," Mom said, sounding slightly hysterical. The car was still cold; it held the brittle smell of diminished perfume.

"You all are so enamored with Tut Hamilton—I've *never, never* encountered a greater charlatan."

"What do you mean, 'you all'? I'm your wife. So what if he has charm?"

"That's right. You think he's got *charisma*. You think he's got *charm*."

The Corolla's pathetically weak heater fan was on high. Now Mom spun the dial back down. "If you think he's so horrible, why don't you go tell him yourself instead of backbiting in the safety of your own car, hmm?"

He turned to look at her and they locked stares, going thirty miles an hour down the winding country road.

Mom continued in a slightly more appeasing tone: "For God's sake. You take everything so personally. He was successful, you were successful."

I very much wished that she'd look back at the road.

My father broke their gaze first and directed his eyes, instead, at the passing landscape. The Norfield Church had its Christmas candles in all the windows—absolutely picture book, a postcard.

When we got home, Dad stayed in the garage and did

something with an old bird feeder that had been neglected far too long.

My mother was mumbling to herself as she hung her coat in her closet.

"What are you looking at?" she snapped as I stood by her in the hall.

"I'm waiting to hang up my coat, Mom."

She looked at me then as if she hadn't seen me before. "Oh, honey," she said. "I'm sorry. I'm sorry, Alison."

And she looked crestfallen, heartbroken, and ruined, frail as a bird that had slammed into a glass wall, even in her ecstatic new silver gown.

Time passed, and kept passing, and so eventually Sarah Beckingworth returned to see the Town Fathers (a motley crew, to be sure), for they had done nothing at all for her cause. She stormed into the Meeting House and flung a crucifix down on the floor. "This was my father's," she said. Then she flung the knitting needles down. "These were my mother's. Now there is nothing and no one. It had been my understanding that I could count on you. Why have you forsaken me? Why am I, one young girl, alone?"

The Town Fathers nodded sagely and began muttering among one another. They were all wearing strange white wigs, and none of them had showered for aeons. Indeed, they wore the same underclothing day and night until it fell off in tatters around them. The lead Town Father spoke. "We are sorry for your loss, but now you must get on."

"Get on?" Sarah said. "But things have changed. Things will never be the same."

The Town Fathers whispered together at length.

"We must now ask you for the back taxes owed on your shack," they said to Sarah Beckingworth. In point of fact, their wigs were made of yak hair. I may never yet trust a man in yak hair, Sarah thought.

Incredulous, she got back on her horse and galloped off—but to where, she knew not, nor her purpose nor fate—for fate indeed had a hand in this, the true life of the lost heroine.

Chapter Eleven

AFTER THE fund-raiser, my parents floated back into their respective corners, with occasional smoke signals regarding a playshop my mother would be attending in January. (Tut had invited Grete and my mother, a gesture of gratitude for their help in getting the word out about *Pyramid Love*.) Weather had forced my father inside now, sleeping bag or no sleeping bag, and so mostly he was shuttling vast quantities of books and papers down to his basement office and back upstairs, muttering about committee work and the decline of the English language. Mom had started a new series of paintings entitled *Torpor*.

It was raining the day we went to see the Furtherton sisters, and I was surprised, when I saw the Corolla outside school, that my father and mother were in it together. At our last yoga class, Energy Lady had come running up and put her hand on Mom's arm. "Clare, something very, very interesting is happening," she'd said in a hurried, joyous whisper. Then she told us about the profound experience her friend Becky had had recently with these two sisters who'd come in from Oregon, Emma and Mae Furtherton. "Becky couldn't use her hand,

Clare. She couldn't use her right hand at all, it was so riddled with arthritis. Emma and Mae healed her." Energy Lady had tears in her eyes as she handed my mother a piece of paper. "Here's their number."

It was the first time I'd heard the term *faith healer*. As we drove to the church in Westport where the Furthertons held their herbal medicine classes, I considered the options regarding my father. Maybe he was going to make sure no one boiled my head in a pot for dinner. Maybe he was in a trance state, hypnotized by the womyn from afar.

Emma Furtherton came striding up to us and put out a huge lumberjack hand and shook our hands. She was a massive smiling mountain person, unwieldy and powerful, and she was wearing, not exactly lederhosen, but some kind of weird Swiss overalls. Mae Furtherton was much smaller, as though they hadn't come from the same litter. She appeared ill, as if she'd spent most of her time in a closet or fending off tuberculosis in a century prior to ours.

We sat on folding chairs. The first thing Emma Furtherton did was gaze at me with her brown wildlife eyes and then beam, a wide, highly healing smile. She said, "Take heart, my young friend. Before you know it, we'll be able to throw that brace away."

They all seemed to be unbearable optimists, these New Age people, as if there were an unguent or tincture for any conceivable malady, and it was dreary as all get-out down here in another church basement, and it seemed that Mae might simply just die while we sat there, but when Emma said this, so sweetly and wholesomely and plainly, I felt a surge of pleasure, the pleasure of hope.

Then I went back to skeptical. My mother was nearly crying, she was so excited. Dad looked lost, the second most lost person, after only Mae.

Emma Furtherton on the subject of nutrition: "You are what you eat, plain and simple, and if you eat the system of hate and degradation of animals, and the industry of the destruction of workers' souls, and if you eat, more tangibly, the chemicals used to distort vegetables and foodstuffs of all kinds today so that men in power can make more money, well, it will come back to haunt you. So you have to lay off that stuff, all right?"

Tobacco was natural, I was thinking to myself as I said okay.

Emma Furtherton on the subject of exercise: "The exercises the orthopedist gave you can't hurt, and it would behoove you to continue using them. Really, you need to show respect for the doctor—you show *respect,* do you understand—in that act alone there is reprieve. And you will continue with yoga. You should be practicing yoga and meditation every day. I will also show you an exercise for aligning your hips, Alison."

Not that I'd have time for life *itself* if I did all that exercise—and meditation! I smiled and nodded, assuming I could skip a few of these ideas, after all.

Emma Furtherton on the subject of God: "God is with us, and God resides in your back, as straight or curved as it is. That's something to start with. Hard to believe, but really the first step in your path to healing."

Instead of giving me another sunshine-blast smile, now Emma started scrutinizing my face as if I had a small beetle traversing my features. She leaned toward me, her brown-yarn braids falling forward. "A touch of resistance," she said. "But then, didn't we all have that at your age? The thing is, you don't have a choice, Alison. You can't fall before the dark power."

"I'll try not to," I said. What dark power did she mean, exactly?

"Lie down, darling," she said.

Mae, whose eyes had been fixed on a dust mote suspended somewhere above our small circle of folding chairs, now fell to her knees. For a confused moment, I thought lumberjack Emma had meant for her, the sister, to lie down. But no, Mae simply knelt, letting her tranquil gaze shift toward me.

I lay down on the floor. My brace, in its blue duffel bag, waited near my father's chair. Mom gave my foot a little helpful squeeze.

Mae put her hands on me. The first thing she did was fluff the air around my back, as if she were whisking away invisible particles with a feather duster. The effect was somewhat relaxing, little nips of light touching my body. Then she placed her hands on the base of my spine and kept them there for ten, fifteen minutes, maybe more. Her hands were hot, and I was beginning to fall asleep when she suddenly rubbed the place she'd been holding and then sat back up, away from me. "It shifted. We're done for today."

I got up as my father and mother and Emma—the chatty one, the front man—talked about when to meet again, the possibility of giving them a donation. No, they wouldn't take any money, Emma said.

I looked at Dad when I got up. My hair was all ruffled and

staticky, and it felt as though my cheek must be red from the floor. He gave me the most peculiar smile.

I reached around to the small of my back and touched where Mae had touched. The hard muscle on one side, the snowpile muscle knot that kept the scoliosis in check, hunching all along the left side of my spine, was weirdly flat. Flatter than before, anyway.

Emma showed me the hip-aligning exercise, and then everyone shook hands. We put on our coats and went home.

We were all pretty quiet as the slanting rain hit the car.

Despite the fact that they lived less than fifty miles from each other and had us to bind them, my father's mother and my mother's father had met only once or twice, and that, it seemed, had been enough for the both of them. And so no one was surprised when the call came in: Grandma from the Boulevard of Broken Dreams wouldn't be at Thanksgiving dinner. She had been caught in a freezing, pelting, vicious rainstorm, she'd told my father, and had gotten a terrible head cold.

"Of course she's sick. That's wonderful. Why doesn't she just come out and say it, she doesn't want to spend time with my father?" said Mom. She was organizing a huge, unwieldy ball of stuffing, and her arms were dotted with bits of bread and butter.

As usual for a holiday, she was a frantic, insane, pissed-off person. Dad played the moribund miserable one. Somewhere in the middle was happiness, and that was my job: the enjoyment of the cranberry sauce, contemplation of the Horn of Plenty.

Still, underneath their roles trembled love, I knew. I sat at the kitchen table, unhungry before my bowl of unbleached, unsweetened, uncleaned, and uncooked granola. (If things had been bad, culinarily speaking, *before* the Furtherton sisters, now it was really quite dire. This despite the fact that the day after Mae's laying on of hands, my back's thick muscle had again resurfaced, a hump of anger.)

"The woman has a fever. Of course, she *would* have to be crazy to want to spend time with Andrew, but that's another story." Dad took one last look at the front page of the *Times*. "You think Ford plucked that turkey himself, or did he get Scowcroft to do it for him, that cowardly bastard?"

"What did you say about my father?" Mom stood with her hands on her hips.

"Listen, the whole thing will be over in a few hours. Then we can eat leftovers and drink beer."

"Over? *Over?*"

She was prepared to begin an entirely different conversation, but Dad hurried on. "All right, besides cornstarch, what else do you need at the Center?"

"I don't know—a new life?"

"So I'll stop at the pharmacy? Or perhaps the liquor store."

He was down the stairs and out the door.

Mom turned to me. "Have you done the dusting yet, young lady?"

"What? Mom, I'm eating breakfast. I just got up, like, one minute ago."

She stared at me in a way *I* didn't particularly think was at one with the protocol of soy protein, chamomile tea, and TM. What would Emma Furtherton say now?

"Well, you better get on it. I don't want the house smelling like cleansers when they get here. Have you done Jazz's stall?"

I gave her *my* stare—see how she likes that.

"Alison, you're supposed to do the stall twice a week, on the weekend and Wednesday. Here it is, Thursday. Thanksgiving."

She shook her head as if that one word held within it all the important and unhappy information we could possibly need.

"My God, I hope Louise doesn't bring that horrible little yapping poodle," she said to the window over the sink, to Dad's abandoned hillock behind the bird feeder.

"It's a Shih tzu."

"Shit on this, shit on that, but not in my house, Louise," she said. She turned back to the stuffing and plunged her hands in.

The vast white Cadillac rumbled into our driveway tentatively, as if this might be the wrong address. I heard Tender yipping, and my mother must have, too, because she muttered a healthy expletive or two from the kitchen, then glided serenely down the stairs. Dad appeared, freshly showered, wearing a green turtleneck and a khaki sport coat with brown suede patches at the elbows (poet gear).

"Hello hello hello hello!" resounded in the bright orange front hall.

Aunt Louise hugged me, pressing her large squishy breasts into my brace, and then it was Uncle Clem's turn. I felt his boxer's grip, smelled his evergreen aftershave. He looked like the men in plaid who won golf tournaments, the ones Warren Lipp photographed for the *Weston Forum*. He and Mom didn't get along particularly well. It's not that they fought, they simply existed in a kind of harmonious freeze-out, a sibling intimacy that extended the length of three sentences and back: "How've you been?" "What have you been up to?" "Any plans for Christmas?"

And then there was Grandpa—his firm, brief grip, his black coat and white hair. He was the most powerful trembling person I knew. Now that he'd retired as a surgeon, he was busy with all sorts of boards and organizations, and he usually made his presence known to us through the sending of checks or presents rather than actual visits. Yet here he was, a scrap of ice lost in black cashmere.

After a short tour of the house, we settled in the living room. Everyone drifted into his or her respective corners, and Dad took drink orders. ("Scotch for you?" "Sounds fine, Chris." "A little soda in yours, Louise?" "You got it, dear.") Mom brought out a bowl of salted nuts and a plate of carrots, celery, and olives before returning to the kitchen to work on dinner. I sat in my regular chair and smiled out at everyone. Partly politeness, but I was also just glad to see them. I was thirteen, and they were my family, after all.

"So did you get much golf in this year, Chris?" asked Clem. Golf was one of their three conversational gambits—the other two being Nixon and lawn care.

"Not as much as I wanted to, what with the new house and all—"

"You know they let women become members at Triple Gold?" Clem said, easing a shiny lighter out of his pocket and lighting a Benson & Hedges. "There you go. That's the way to ruin a good club."

"Now, now," said Louise, leaning into her husband.

Louise and Clem had met at a real estate convention in Las Vegas. Those Las Vegas administrative assistants—they were very leany and pink. Indeed, Louise was wearing pink from head to foot. Pink pantsuit, pink hair clip, pink shoes. Pink polish on her fingernails, long as flamingo feathers.

"Ah, my better half," Clem said, and gave her three quick pats on the knee.

Grandpa shook his head and stared into his Scotch. "Progress. *Pssh.*"

Silence. Drinking.

Louise leaned over and selected an almond. She popped it in her mouth. "*Mmm, smoky!*"

"Well, what have you been doing with yourself, Chris? Still writing those poems?" asked Grandpa. Sometimes when we went to visit Grandpa in New York City, Dad would come, but most of the time it was just my mother and me who said hello to the doorman with the view of Central Park.

Dad placed his drink on the cocktail table with exaggerated care. "Still at that, Andrew."

"And they buy the books, eh?"

"Not many of them, actually."

"I met a woman at a dinner party the other evening, a benefit for the Harlem Boys Choir. She'd read your poems. I don't even know how you came up, but there it was, a live reader. I thought I should get her autograph for you."

Dad gave a gallows laugh. "Normally it's the other way around," he said, then turned to his brother-in-law. "Clem, how's business with you, buddy?"

"You know what I say, Chris? People never stop buying

houses. Look at you two—moving up in the world, right? Has to be done. The American way. You can talk to me about the recession, you can talk to me about the decline of Western civilization, you can talk to me about gas prices, but no matter what—you need a domicile. Isn't that right, darling?"

"Absolutely, honey."

"Glad to hear things are going well," my father said, nodding at a sideways angle, as if his head weren't straight or there were a ruler under his beard.

"Oh, my God!" Louise shrieked. "I forgot Tender's blanket! Honey, can I have the keys to the car?"

She took the keys and ran downstairs (the little dog's fate was to be leashed to the porch, by the front door).

"Everyone okay in here?" Mom said, looking out from the kitchen with a strained smile on her face.

"Fine, Clare," said her brother.

A moment passed. Three silent men, one sucking on a cigarette. With mugs like this, they ought to be playing shuffleboard or at least a game of marked cards. My Holiday Feeling was fragile in their hands.

"Well, Alison, how's school?" Clem said. "Bet you're driving all the boys crazy."

"Actually . . ." *Actually, Uncle, I'm not driving anyone even remotely crazy. As a matter of fact . . .*

"I suppose you're avoiding your schoolwork like the plague," Grandpa conjectured.

"I do schoolwork," I said, offering him a reassuring, I'm-quite-the-granddaughter smile. "We're doing this project, you know? In social studies. It's called Of Many Nations, into Jubilant Unity, and—"

"Of many *what?*" Grandpa asked.

I repeated the name. He was Of Many Nations, too, of course. He was a Self-Made Man from Romania.

"What's that supposed to mean?"

"Well—"

"Mind if I check the score?" Clem asked no one in particular. He stood up and left the room.

"I don't know *what* they're teaching these days, Alison, but you won't get anywhere if you don't work hard," said my grandfather. Even when I looked straight at him, I could never quite tell what color his eyes were.

Louise showed back up, stomping her pink pumps and rubbing her hands and trembling melodramatically, her little way of showing dissatisfaction with the no-dogs rule of my mother's.

It was time for dinner.

All the traditional foods and then some. All the good china— including crystal water glasses and a matching pitcher. Dad put on Vivaldi's *The Four Seasons,* and then he sat at the head of the table, looking above all of us as if in silent, private prayer. Mom had smoothed her hair and put on some lipstick, but she still looked as if she'd been dropped in by parachute.

"This looks great, Clare," said Clem.

"It looks wonderful—and smells so good, too! Now what are *these* little things?" Louise chimed in, pointing at some healthy supplement to the meal.

Mom told a story about a woman at the grocery store who got on her hands and knees to gather up the cranberries that had spilled on the floor—the last bag had torn, and she was determined. "The desperation, can you believe it? Like it has to be cranberries. Like Thanksgiving is *cranberries* and that's it, nothing else. What about apricots or grapes? Why not? Would it be going overboard?"

"You've got cranberries right here," observed Clem, and then he began to guffaw. We all held our own breath until he regained his composure.

My mother looked as if she were going to say something, but she didn't after all. Grandpa sat silent, too, steadfastly memorizing the measly set of items on his plate: little dabs of everything, like a painter's palette. Back in the old days, he used to make up these medical-life limericks for me. There was one, something about a little girl called Wendy whose knee was quite bendy: "They hacked and they sawed, they called the nurse Maude . . ." I didn't remember the rest, but it had been a long time since I'd heard anything like that from my grandfather.

"Alison, tell us all about school," said Louise, having missed this subject earlier.

"Oh yes," said Mom. "Tell them about the wonderful project you're doing in social studies."

"What kind of project?" Louise pressed with a joyous pink smile.

"Oh, nothing. Just a social studies project."

"Go on, Allie," Mom said.

I hesitated. "Well, like I was explaining to Grandpa and Uncle Clem before, it's this big project on history, called Of Many Nations, into Jubilant Unity. We're doing an oral report and then some other things, like dioramas."

Dioramas, I thought, or perhaps manifestos or exposés. Stories from a lost civilization. The lost, heroic, and unsung.

"Of Many Nations—? Jubilant? Unity?" Grandpa repeated— rather hung up on the name, I thought.

Dad spoke up: "It's a way to learn history, Andrew. Hands-on. Seems as good a way as any."

"But come on, 'Jubilant Unity'?" Clem now said, swishing his wine between swigs. "I've got to agree with Dad on this. That sounds like a bathroom cleanser."

My grandfather cleared his throat. "If she's going to learn history, then let's start with the facts. 'Jubilant Unity' it is not. Never has been."

"Yet we regularly feel jubilation here in Weston," my father said. I could hear it in his voice: the get-in-trouble tone.

"People ought to work harder if there's that much jubilation going around," said Grandpa, stabbing a yam.

"Making a diorama may not be so helpful," I said boldly, "but we do a bunch of research first."

My heart was beating fast from my minispeech, but Grandpa seemed not to have heard.

"Research is always good!" said Louise. *Tender* would have been a better conversationalist.

"It is, and Alison is working hard on it," my mother now declared, looking suddenly more windswept than before. I hadn't been, particularly, but it was nice of her to say so.

"For instance, research can reveal the folly of medicine," said Dad.

Grandpa put down his fork. "Excuse me?"

The room became quiet. Six years before, his wife, my

grandmother, had died on the operating table. Grandpa had been one of two surgeons in the room. As her husband, his participation was against hospital protocol, but he'd insisted, and somehow they'd given way. In this family, we didn't use the words *folly* and *medicine* in the same sentence anymore.

"No one's infallible, are they?" said Dad. His eyes were focused hard on his wife's father, who wasn't answering.

"No, no one's infallible," said Clem, sounding out "infallible" as if it were a word he didn't use often, if at all.

"Not even you, Andrew," Dad continued, just to make sure Grandpa got the message.

Grandpa was this word entirely: *inscrutable.* But Mom certainly looked miserable, as if she were the one linked to something horrible, something amazingly flawed. With her Healing Arts mania, she was indeed guilty of one thing: resisting her father.

Grandpa enunciated his words carefully. "Are you talking about something in particular, Chris?"

But my father had become confused, exhausted. He sat back heavily in his chair. "Well, yes, as a matter of fact. I'm tired of the way everyone tiptoes around you all the time, Andrew. It's getting a little old. Heck, you're just this—"

Dad didn't continue. He picked up his napkin and put it on the table, a crumpled flag of surrender. He looked out the window at the dark yard.

Grandpa folded his own napkin into a straight square, shook it out, and then refolded it again.

"I'm going to try to catch the final score—anyone need anything while I'm up?" Clem said, standing and smiling at all of us. Even if we fell into it facedown, *this* real estate agent wasn't going to admit to a sinkhole in the backyard.

Mom was plainly relieved to get off the subject herself. Did anyone want coffee, dessert? And then, as we forked pumpkin pie into our mouths, she conducted a geometry experiment: Direct your vision at everyone seated around the table except the man you're married to, sitting before you.

When they were leaving, Grandpa gripped my shoulder with a rough hand and leaned in. His scratchy cheek rubbed against mine, and his breath was hot and insistent. I thought he was going to let me in on a secret, bring all conversations to a reasonable conclusion. Instead he said, "Be good, Alison."

In bed later, I heard dishes clanking, cabinet doors opening and shutting in the kitchen, swaths of silence, and then loud words and then silence again. I tried to remember Gram. All I could remember was this one dress of hers—polka-dotted with a swirly skirt. She may have worn it just once, but that was my memory of her. And she made cookies. When we went over there, she'd have cookies in tins, layers of them between waxed paper. Once I found a last cherry cookie at the bottom, hidden between folds, almost forgotten.

We were all happier back then; people spoke and listened and laughed sometimes. After Gram's death, my grandfather held his role in the surgery—though maybe it would have happened anyway, maybe he had nothing to do with it at all—close to his chest, like a hand mirror, and he wasn't going to, he would never again, show what was reflected there to anyone. Just one small, seemingly personal decision, but out of it grew my mother's stubborn determination never to find failure in him.

The lost heroine could not find it in herself to leave what had been her home. Day after day, alone in her bloodstained shack, she ate gruel. Gruel is not as bad as it sounds.

One melancholic afternoon, she was shucking corn out on the porch when she saw something. There was an Indian out by the edge of the field, looking in her direction. No longer afraid of anything, Sarah walked up to him. (It turned out that not all Indians were evil, after all, but this realization was one that, for Sarah Beckingworth, would be long in coming.) He was young, and his horse was spotted, and he had rough heels and seemingly gentle hands. He had emerged from nowhere, and he now said: "I'm sorry about your parents. It was not our intent."

Sarah was certainly, once again, incredulous. "Not your intent? How can I believe that when you Indians came in with tomahawks in the quiet of night and spilled the blood of my good parents?"

"Well, yes. That seems to be a slight problem. Still, let's move on."

"I can't. I can't move on," said Sarah, wringing her now hateful hands. (She had been raised to be kind.)

"Let's work together, shall we, toward a new, beautiful land?" pressed the last, lone Indian.

"We shall not," cried Sarah Beckingworth. "For I shall work alone. For you do not even know my name."

"But I do know your name," said the Indian. "You are the lost heroine."

Chapter Twelve

THIS HIGH school kid, Bo Riley, asked Kate to the Evergreen. I'd never met Bo, but his name sucked, and I didn't like the way Kate didn't tell me about it until two days before, when she'd already bought her dress and known for a week that she was going. When I acted strange about it (a Connecticut variation on anger), she just shrugged her shoulders—of course I didn't know everything, and why should I, when it really came down to it?

The night of the dance, Dad and I watched *Hawaii Five-O.*

Hawaii Five-O, then *Barnaby Jones.* I think we both preferred the mysteriously coiffed Jack Lord to milk-drinking Buddy Ebsen—but it was Saturday night, Mom was painting, and Kate was out with Bo. Neither of us really cared what was on the screen.

Mom's recent paintings included swirling figures, figures that looked like they'd been caught in cyclones, tornadoes, whirlwinds, siroccos, suction tunnels, dizzying spins, flying corkscrews, gusts, drafts, sneezes, undertows, one-way tickets to hell, the Bermuda Triangle, or bad seventies-style marriages.

When the phone rang, Barnaby Jones had yet to discover who was responsible for killing the old woman and making off with her two dachshunds. Dad grunted, then leaped up and went to answer it in the kitchen.

"What?" he shouted into the receiver in his annoyed/concerned voice. "Yes, all right."

He turned and looked at me, lifting the phone in the air. It was almost eleven; I never got calls this late.

"Hello?" I said, taking the phone.

"Allie?"

"Kate? What's wrong?"

"I'm just calling to say I love you." She said it like a maniacal cheerful gallows person.

"Well, I love you, too. You sound weird."

"You're such a, such a nice friend."

"Are you at the dance?"

"Did you know that Bo can write his name with pee in the snow?"

"No, I didn't know that."

"He can. Isn't that sweet?"

"Well—"

"But Alison, *you* can't write your name with pee in the snow, but I love you best."

"That's nice, Kate, but, are you *drunk*?" I whispered this last word, having twisted the phone cord around the doorjamb so I could stand in the living room.

My mother showed up at the bottom of the stairs. She had

on her extra-large THE EARTH IS OUR MOTHER T-shirt (paint splattered), and she was here to investigate the phone call. I turned back into the kitchen and sat at the table, tried to fold myself into privacy.

"I wish I could write my name in the snow," Kate was saying. "K-a-t-e. That would be excellent. And then maybe the snow would freeze and—oh, I guess snow is already frozen, well, okay, so the snow would get double frozen, like a chocolate-dipped cone from Carvel—" And she began to giggle and snort with the intense cleverness of this.

I began to feel double frozen myself, water trickling over my bones. "So where is Bo now, Kate? Where are you?"

She wasn't laughing anymore—was she crying?

"Kate," I said, "talk to me."

"It's okay. Everything will be fine. It really will be."

The phone was silent then. I tried to hear into the dark, away from the orange brick linoleum floor and my parents eavesdropping from two angles.

"Okay, I just wanted to say hi," she said, sounding both more businesslike and uncertain.

"Kate—are you home? Where the hell are you?"

"Home is where the heart is, Alison. Where do you expect me to be?"

"If you're not home, you should go home. What's Bo doing?" Besides peeing in the snow, I thought. I hated Bo.

"I'm not sure Bo really likes me," Kate said as if she were reading a distant street sign: ROAD CLOSED. "But maybe he does. He just gets—angry."

I started formulating words, not speaking, about to speak—

"If he's drunk, say. But then he goes back to normal again. It's like, it's like—" She stopped. "Hey, Bo!" she shouted as if he were on the other side of a golf course.

That's where I pictured her: at a phone booth in a snowstorm in the middle of nothing. I wanted her to go home and bolt the door and hide under her coat and have her mother or a rented mother or *some* mother bring her chicken soup and hot chocolate and take her temperature.

"I like Bo a lot," she said now, changing course again. "He's sexy."

My kitchen was bright, and she was fading out, her voice a black thread in a dark hole. Then she said, sounding suddenly, incomparably bored: "Everyone has two faces. Remember that, Allie. Be careful, okay?"

She hung up the phone, and I was back in my own kitchen with a dial tone and my mother and father staring at me.

I called over to the Hamiltons' at ten the next morning. Mick answered on the third ring.

"She's asleep," he said, his voice gruff but somehow inviting.

"Oh, okay."

"You coming over?"

"I might. What time did she get home last night?"

"The fuck if I know. She was already asleep when I got in, around two or something."

I saddled up Jazz and started down the road. He kept throwing his head, as if the bit were bothering him, even though I'd warmed it in my hand before putting it in his hot, yawning mouth. His furry winter ears were shaped like milk pods, a delicate curve. He snorted in the cold.

It seemed like no one was up, no one was going anywhere, and the day was taking itself too seriously, ominous and austere.

At the Hamiltons', there were no cars in the driveway and the garage was empty, too. Peach stuck her head out of the barn and whinnied, like she'd been waiting for us all morning. She knocked her gray head up over the rail, gave Jazz a once-over, then flung it back to the other side. I looped the reins over a post and went inside. The basenjis charged me.

Kate's door was closed. Mick was lying on the couch in jeans and an Oxford shirt, half-unbuttoned. He was just staring at the ceiling, unusual for him.

"Hi, Mick. Is Kate still asleep?"

"I guess so. Those school dances *can* wear a girl out."

He turned to me, leaning on an elbow and staring, as if he'd just taken off a head bandage and were now testing his vision. There was something urgent in his look, or unseeing.

"My parents are on a bender of some kind," he said in a calm voice. "They drove to Katonah to get more cocaine."

"Oh." I didn't know they did cocaine. Renee called it "snow," and if you did it you were a "snowbird," which sounded pretty. "Why did they need two cars?" I asked, though not sure why this detail mattered. Maybe I'd been watching too many detective shows.

"Renee has Dad's car. She totaled hers last week."

"Oh," I said again. I sat on the chair and looked at the coffee table. Same as always: bowl of pistachios, ashtray filled with shells and cigarette ash and pipe residue and cigarette stubs like broken candles on a broken cake.

I picked up *Town & Country*. After a few minutes, Mick

spoke again, his voice gravelly and raw. "Parents on drugs—it's not a pretty sight, Alison."

"I guess not."

"For one thing, you want to reach your dealer, and they're all tied up trying to score for your dad."

Mick was gazing out toward the backyard.

"Inconvenient," I said.

"You can say that again."

"Inconvenient."

He looked over at me. Because of the way he was twisting his neck, I couldn't tell if he was smiling or not.

"What's inconvenient?" said Kate. She'd appeared at the far end of the living room.

She was listing to one side in her pink-and-white nightgown. She was pale, and her hair and eyes looked dark, like she was a vampire victim.

"Look who made it out of bed," said Mick.

"Frickin' A," she said, and walked over.

"So, Dad and Mom made off for Katonah. They said they'd be back this afternoon. They had to make an illicit purchase of narcotics."

Kate sat down, ignoring the report. "Does anyone have a cigarette?"

I pulled a pack out of my parka and slid it down the table.

"Thanks, Allie. How long have you been here?"

She lit a cigarette and then folded her legs close to her body. She wrapped her arms around her knees.

"Not long," I said. I was scanning Kate for damage.

"So'd you get laid last night, Kate?"

"Shut up, Mick."

No one said anything for a while. Smoke drifted into shadow, clear as a cloud, then disappeared again in a slash of light. Back in shadow. Back in light.

I lit a cigarette for myself.

"What time did you get in last night?"

"I don't know. I didn't look at the clock."

"Was the dance fun?"

"Oh, yeah. The place was really pretty. They had tons of streamers and a strobe light. 'Stairway to Heaven' was the last song, and they let out all this smoke while it was playing. Lisa Feneta had on a long silver gown that made her look like some kind of bathroom plumbing."

"Where were you when you called me?"

She looked up, as if I were trying to pull one over on her. "I didn't call you."

"You don't remember calling me?"

She squinted at me. "Oh, sure—I called you from the party. Yeah, we went to some party up on Valley Forge."

It didn't sound like a party. It was quiet as winter.

I felt ill. I found a spot in the ashtray and stubbed out my cigarette. I must not have really gotten it, because a thin line of pistachio-carcass smoke wavered up.

"Jazz is tied up outside," I said. "C'mon, let's go."

If I used my imagination in a bullying sort of way, if I did that, and it was a little like prayer—then she could look strong again, be strong, and we could race together down the road.

And it worked that time. She loved the road as much as I did. Our horses loved it, too. They both had racehorse blood somewhere in their suburban pony bodies, and when we let them loose, when we leaned forward and urged them on with our legs and arms and will, when we went head-to-head down the hard brown road, a mile long, following the frozen river, glassy with malice in the melting spots, under the skeletons of trees, they ran flat out. They dropped their heads and stretched their necks, and their ears went back in the wind, and every once in a while one would look at the other as if to say, *I can beat you, motherfucker.* And then we'd surge. And we were right there, right down at road level, veering close and then apart, aware of nothing but the wind and galloping hooves and the breathless monarchy of downhill, totally out of control, filled with love and fear and the end of the road nowhere in sight—nowhere except in some distant, very distant future—and then the horses began to breathe heavier, we could hear them. Still no one wanted to slow down: not us, not them. Bare trees whipped by. The river wouldn't stop. Ahead, a grievance of black water was breaking ice, tearing it from rocks and fallen branches, sending it coursing down. Then we were at the end of the road—there was the start of pavement, a real road, and a car passing in the other direction.

We leaned, using our bodies to halt the flow, stop the competition. *Huff. Huff. Huff.* Kate had to pull Peach's head all the way sideways before she'd even consider breaking gait. Jazz and I jumped around her, until he, too, settled down. Their fur was slicked back now, their chests painted with sweat. The warmth rose from Jazz's body and heated up my own.

On the way back, everything was different. Now we could see things again, the tears weren't blinding us, we had to remember things again, remember where we were. We were definitely in Weston, Connecticut, and it was 1975, and we were young—but we had plans—and that was definitely a telephone pole, and that was definitely a dam.

The horses caught their breath, and their fur started to harden up into tips. Kate looked over at me. Another road presented itself. She had no expression in her face at all. Did I know what she was thinking? Did I know what was going to happen next?

"Go!" she shouted, and we went.

The two days later, my parents and I drove to the Children's Hospital in Boston.

I'd never been in a hospital just for children before. We were told to take the elevator up to the fourth floor. When we got there, we followed the purple-painted line to orthopedics. Sick kids were everywhere. They came toward us in slow motion, bearing messages like Dickens's Christmases past, present, and future. First we passed a little girl in a wheelchair. She was probably six or so. Her hair was gone except for a few brown strands, thin as cobwebs, and she had shadows under her eyes. She wore a white nightgown with pink flowers, like Kate's, and held a pink teddy bear. As we passed, she just stared forward, the way you look at a screen before the movie starts. Right after her, an orderly came by wheeling a stretcher. At first I could just see two casts sticking up in a V, a bad victory sign, but when it came closer, I saw a tiny kid under the sheets. He was sleeping, his dark face closed to the world.

My mother's own face was florid, as if anything could happen any minute now, and my father held the map between his arm and his body, and his lips were pressed tightly together.

A kid who looked normal walked by with his parents. What could be wrong with him? I found myself thinking. Was it something invisible? Something small?

The Wizard of Oz was on in the waiting room, the part where the Wicked Witch gets melted by water. In the corner, two children were playing with bright beads on mystifying, garbled wires.

I suddenly decided to give prayer a try: *Get religion, young lady!* A children's ward will do it to you every time. But my entreaty soon became complex and long and fogged with a sense that, comparatively speaking, I had nothing to pray for.

Dear God, please make my back straight, so I can ride horses and look normal and not have an operation. But while you're at it, while I've got your attention—if you're listening at all—please heal everyone at this hospital. I don't know if you've noticed, but there are some children here who may even die. They've got cancer and stuff, God. Can you work this out? Like the girl with the pink teddy bear? Can you keep her and the others and me, too, I guess, if that's all right with you, free from death and suffering and disease—okay, Lord? Thanks, Alison.

Pretty soon I was standing in a bright green gown, staring down the X-ray machine.

"Hold it," said the technician from the other side of the wall. If I held my breath forever, I could keep change from taking place. If I stood on my head, I could fix gravity, fix fate.

"And relax," came the follow-through order, and my parents and I were escorted into the examination room.

"Have a seat," my father said to my mother, indicating the chair.

"No, you," she said.

"No, you," he said.

She gave him an irritated look and perched on the chair's edge, as if going any farther would indicate actual acquiescence. I sat on my special throne: the examination table. Dad stood in the corner, like a coat stand.

After a while, he said, "Allie, did I mention that the aquarium has an amazing sea anemone? Apparently the biggest one in captivity in the world."

"Oh," I said, picturing a large writhing octopus in a jar. To pretend this was a fun trip to Boston, we were going to the New England Aquarium afterward.

Dad pursed his lips and looked at the tongue depressors. Mom was studying her crib sheet, the piece of paper on which she'd written my back's numerical history (the numbers increasing as my spine kept falling) as well as a list of alternative methods we were considering or had considered.

Finally we heard a rustling outside the room: someone looking at my chart. Then the door opened wide and there he was, Dr. Lyon, our golden hope for the future.

"Hello, hello," he said, greeting us all in turn. "I've looked at the X-rays you had sent over. Now let's see what we've got going today."

He snapped the film onto the light box and turned on the light. There I was, good old me, back like a garter snake. Was I straighter or more curved than before? For a fleeting moment my spine looked straighter, positively, but then I blinked and it sank in on itself, coiled up—the nice snake turned angry.

"Let's see," he said. "About the same as your X-ray from October. You were thirty-eight on top, and now you're thirty-nine, and then on the bottom, forty-two last time and forty today. Of course, a degree here or there is of no consequence—it can amount to a measuring error, for that matter."

"Dr. Lyon," my mother began querulously. She had a speech to make, and she was going to get it over with. "As you know, our other doctor has recommended surgery, after Alison has been wearing this brace for over a year and a half. We wonder—we feel strongly—that we'd like to look at all our options here."

I thought about moving like a tree. I thought about the Alexander technique lady and her tight ballerina bun and her bitchy ways. I thought about the Furtherton sisters, one wholesome and giant and chewing a mountain daisy, the other furtive and magic, like a bat or a ghost girl who lives in a well. I thought about vitamins and Tiger's Milk bars and seaweed and Winstons and prayer, last minute and faulty.

He nodded. "After looking at her history, I certainly can see your previous doctor's cause for concern. These are some very high numbers and the scoliosis has worsened considerably in the past year. On the other hand, your daughter has also grown—what is it here?—almost five inches in two years. She's five seven now. It's quite likely she's at the end of this growth spurt. Skeletally, she's just about mature."

"And we're trying new things," Mom said. "We're working with nutrition and vitamins and yoga and a little, um, faith healing—"

He didn't hear the last words, exactly. Perhaps he was embarrassed by them. It was an indiscretion to speak of such things.

"Exercise can help. Nothing wrong with yoga. As for vitamins—well"—he shrugged—"do they hurt? I truly doubt it. In these cases, sometimes there's really no choice but to resort to surgery, but here it might be premature. I think we could consider giving the brace a little more time. Four, six months, maybe."

"We can wait?" my father said. "You think the brace—"

"Give it a little more time before making the final judgment. Monitor her carefully, an X-ray every two months, as you've been doing. If it begins to go south, we'll reconsider."

It was a measured endorsement, but an endorsement nonetheless. We were willing to take it and make it our own.

This is what Dr. Lyon looked like: He was a very handsome man. This is what he looked like: wise, all-knowing—a provocative, forward-thinking sort of person. His dark curls tumbled over a brain the size of Cleveland. He was muscular—strong in spirit, body, and mind. He smiled. We smiled. It was time to go see a sea anemone.

We got lost, as usual, but no one got mad. Boston was quite beautiful. We were on a one-way street in the wrong direction, but look at these brick buildings! The doors were decorated with lovely wreaths, and up the front steps came lovely happy people in peacoats, carrying baguettes and cheese. The place radiated glorious intelligence and civilized living. It seemed obvious that, as a nation, we were becoming smarter and braver about all sorts of things.

We walked around the aquarium as if we were underwater ourselves, observing the small barracudas, the schools of tiny brilliant fish like streaks of iridescent ink, flitting frantically from one side to the other of their ersatz world. Unfortunately, the dolphin show was canceled for the day owing to a chemical imbalance in the tank. But we gazed down at the sea otters, dark shadows in shallow water, and we saw, of course, the sea anemone. We'd been given just a small outlet, a short reprieve, and I savored everything about that day: the three of us sitting in the bright sun in the cold, squinting ahead at the harbor, Mom and Dad washing down any doubts they might have had with five-dollar cups of celebration beer.

"Do you think Grandma would like some tea or something?" I asked Mom in the kitchen the afternoon of Christmas Eve.

"She just had some goddamn tea," Mom whispered. "She's going to float away if she has more tea."

I went back to the living room. Grandma was in her favorite chair, which turned out also to be my favorite chair, so I sat on the couch. She was all in black, as usual, a black frock with some black socks and boots and a black scarf, hand knit, and she was bent over a nest of pale green yarn and the stumpy beginning of something.

"What are you knitting?" I shouted. Turned out she was pretty deaf.

No response.

"What are you knitting?" I shouted again.

"Thank you, dear," she said, suddenly looking up at me and smiling, then looking back down at her project.

I smiled back at her. I turned to look at the Christmas tree. I couldn't see my little blue bird from this angle, but I knew it was there. When I turned on the lamp to do some reading, Grandma looked up and smiled again, quite a dazzling, I Don't Live on a Boulevard of Broken Dreams After All smile. Her eyes were crazy blue, and when she was staring at me, it was like she was trying to light a blue fire.

"It's good to see you, dear. You're turning into a beautiful girl."

"Thank you," I said. Then: "What are you knitting?"

"Booties, love. For my neighbor's son. The baby hasn't been born yet, but they say it will be a boy. They know these things in advance now. That's tempting fate, if you ask me. Well, tell me, do you people even wear booties anymore?"

"Well, I don't wear booties, but—"

She started laughing, cackling quite earnestly, then she went back to her task.

I chewed a cracker and watched her knit. Her hands were crawling over the yarn like a spider. She addressed me again at loud volume: "Do you like Christmas, dear? I hated it back when I was your age. Didn't have too much in our day, you know. 'Twas lucky if we got coal in our stocking. Damn neighbor girls always getting pretty petticoats or floral umbrellas."

"Was this back in Ireland, Grandma?" I shouted.

"Eh?"

I repeated the question.

"Oh yes, oh yes. 'Course, they say Dublin's different now. Hard to believe it, but that's what they say."

"I'm doing a report at school. It's called Of Many Nations, into Jubilant Unity."

"What?"

"*Of Many Nations, into Jubilant Unity.* It's about settlers and immigrants and—that kind of thing."

"Well, there you have it. Isn't that America, though?"

"My friend and I are making a book, like a secret lost history of a girl who lived back in the olden days."

"If it's secret histories you're after, just have a look at your own ancestors. A bunch of pirates and roustabouts, I can tell you."

"Pirates?"

"The good ones were pirates. Most couldn't find their boats, they were so blinded by drink. Rowed away on the pub stools, those ones did."

Grandma's silver needles snapped and clacked like kitchen shears, and that conversational topic was over.

I decided to go for a short ride before dinner.

When I got back, Dad was in the living room jamming newspaper balls under logs in the fireplace. Grandma had moved into the kitchen, where she was slowly chopping the ends off beans. My mother was clattering around in the cabinet. I had the distinct impression she was going to break something.

"Can I help with anything?" I asked—on holiday behavior.

"Your grandmother has kindly offered to do the beans," Mom said, as if she'd just announced that Christmas vacation had been canceled permanently and it was going to rain for three hundred days straight. "If you'd like, you could set the table."

Grandma *did* seem to be having trouble with the beans. She would drop the knife from on high and roll it back and forth, back and forth, until she got all the little strands cut, and then she would do the other side. And then she would drop that one bean into the bowl. It looked like she had done about ten so far.

We all sat down together at seven. Dad opened wine, and we had Christmas music playing, and we had our Love's Labour's Lost beans, and the bondage beef, and some mashed potatoes. There we all were. Me. Dad and his mom. Mom and his mom. Could she hear the whispers from the past, could she hear their complaints about her?

"Merry Christmas, everyone," my father said, raising his glass. "Mom, especially, it's good to have you here. Allie. Clare."

We all murmured, "Merry Christmas," and even I, with a quarter glass of wine, drank to the night.

"Lovely meat, Clare," Grandma said after sawing off her first bite.

"Thank you, Katherine," Mom said. "And these beans are lovely."

It wasn't entirely clear if she heard that comment. No one said anything again for a bit.

"'Course, there were no green vegetables back when I was young," Grandma said all of a sudden—so maybe she *had* heard. "Not where we lived, anyway. Oh no, 'twas the lucky day if there was some mold on the potato for a vitamin."

"Yes, Mom," my father said—also on holiday behavior.

Grandma was so little, her head hardly reached above the table, and Dad kept looking over as if he were about to leap up and cut the meat for her. Whenever she reached for her wine-glass, which she did more frequently than you'd expect from a little old lady, the white tablecloth trembled in fear.

In the morning, my stocking was stuffed with presents and Grandma was still sitting in my chair, knitting—the pale green bootie puffed up to the size of a melon.

"Merry Christmas, Grandma."

"Merry Christmas, Alison, love," she said, looking up. She was in her alternate black outfit: a black dress with black stockings and black slippers.

Dad was buttering toast in the kitchen.

"There she is. Want some toast?" he said when I came in.

"No thanks." We never had toast, except when Grandma was there.

Mom and Dad both wished me Merry Christmas. I took a hunk of coffee cake and wished them Merry Christmas, too.

Things weren't so terrible.

When we sat together in the living room to open presents, the lights on the tree twinkled in a mellow kind of way. Grandma seemed to like the present I'd given her—a book of photographs of the Irish countryside—and Dad liked his fancy pen-and-paper holder, and Mom liked her glittery scarf from Raja of India.

We were alone again in the living room later, and I was just starting the Tom Robbins book I'd gotten, when Grandma looked up at me with wet angel eyes.

"I lost my first child on Christmas morning. Always comes back. Even forty-eight years later."

"What?"

"Named him in advance, I had. I knew it was a boy—didn't need any fancy goddamned machines to tell me that. His name was Chris, too—not your father, of course. He was the second Chris in my life."

She smiled at me then and went back to her knitting.

I smiled back at her, even though she wasn't looking at me anymore. I stayed for a while, keeping her company. I didn't think to ask her everything, all the stories she held in her lap like that knitting. One lost child was enough for me.

Sarah composed a letter to her parents, though they had long ago passed on to another plane of existence, and she penned it with her quill and she put a seal on it with wax made from bees native to the region (the Apis mellifera*), and she kissed its ivory folds and placed it against the candle on the table where she had been eating potatoes she'd clawed out of the ground. She did not have much in the way of victuals but for the stray unfound tuber from last year. She had to, if not find justice, find food.*

Would she stay here with the Town Fathers and the girls in their mobcaps, the girls breathing shallowly in stays of whalebone? Would she plead, would she beg for her livelihood, here in town?

Before the sun had come up over the hillock, Sarah Beckingworth left her childhood shack. She would ride away. She would make a way for herself in the world.

Chapter Thirteen

"HERE IT is, ladies and gentlemen, the day of reckoning!"

Mr. Bostitch had his hands in his pockets, and he was rooting around in them as if one last penny were eluding him. As usual he stood straight and tall, so straight and so tall that he almost bent backward.

"Grading will be strict, swift, and without recourse. Exceptions? None—except the mercy that can be found in eternal penance or, of course, work's own small reward!"

He stared at us for a while, allowing us to feel our pain, and then he gestured to Tony and Samantha, the first two sacrifices of the day.

Tony was a quiet kid; I didn't know much about him. He wasn't in the inner circle of jocks, though he was in the general jock category. One of the problems with his coolness quotient was that his jeans were always pressed. Samantha was a "brain." Not as powerful as jocks, by any means, but tolerated by them as a necessary part of the machinery of their reign.

Samantha and Tony stumbled up from opposite sides of the classroom, both clutching small caches of index cards. (Eight to ten cards, each with a main point on top and three examples, if they had done what Mr. Bostitch had instructed.)

Looking anything but happy, they stared at each other for a blank moment.

"Well?" said Mr. Bostitch. "Time's a-running."

"Yes," said Tony, and cleared his throat. He looked behind him at the long table and then leaned against it in a casual-scholar sort of way. "We would like to talk to you today about the Revolutionary War in America," he began with something resembling confidence. "In the Revolutionary War, many men were lost."

Samantha, with shoulder-length hair pulled back in a barrette, said, "Four thousand four hundred and thirty-five soldiers and sailors were killed, and six thousand one hundred and eighty-eight were wounded."

"Men were lost," said Tony. "But, class, this is what I want to tell you today: Just as many men were *made*."

"Men who were nothing—farmers and stuff—became heroes for the cause," Samantha asserted.

"Have you ever heard the phrase *you've got to lose some to win some*? Well, that's the situation. These men were brave, even as they bled to death on the lawns of Weston, Connecticut."

"Whoa," said someone. "Gross."

"Blood and guts and glory," said Tony, and shrugged knowledgeably.

Fact girl said, "At that time, we were a parish, not a town.

Only about a thousand people lived here. Of the two hundred thousand soldiers enlisted in the Revolutionary forces between 1775 and 1783, some were our founding fathers, fighting as patriots for our country."

"Yes, it's true. Our ancestors had to fight to build a country."

"Lieutenant Ebenezer Coley's company alone sent fifty-six men into battle."

Tony concluded, a conclusion being a restatement of the thesis: "We owe it to ourselves to thank the good men who lost their lives and the other men who began them. Long live America!"

Mr. Bostitch clapped energetically when they were done, and the class joined in. Horrible but true, it was our turn.

Kate was lost in a hooded sweatshirt of Mick's. I was wearing overalls with a fancy striped blouse underneath, a combination I felt had a kind of "dress outside the boundaries" appeal. I'd also tied a ribbon in my hair.

"Well," said Kate, and looked around. "Hello, everyone. We're here today, as you probably already know, to talk about the history of this town."

"Yes," I said, plunging in. "The thing is, Weston, Connecticut, has some big problems. When we arrived, you see, people already lived here. It was someone else's home."

"In the 1600s, we basically stole this land from the Indians. We made these tricky deals with the Norwalk Indians and the Pequonnocks and the Paugussetts."

"Those aren't Indians, they're cars," said Bruce Johnson— the Englishman.

"Not *Peugeots,* dummy," said Kate.

I continued: "The Indians didn't even know what money was, they didn't know how much the land was worth like that. So when the settlers offered them a few pieces of wampum, along with 'six coats, ten hatchets, ten hoes, ten knives, ten scissors, ten Jew's harps, ten fathom of tobacco, three kettles, and three mirrors,' they took it."

"What's a *Jew's harp*?" sneered Paul Knapp.

"It's a musical instrument," Kate said with glorious condescension.

"So these people ended up with some cigarettes and coats, and we had all this land. They lost their home."

"Maybe they went to the Stamford Mall," said Priscilla, causing a fierce snit of laughter among her closest peers.

Kate flipped to the next card. "But the Indians weren't the only group we didn't care much about. When Abraham Lincoln was running for president and wanted to abolish slavery, we didn't vote for him."

"There were twenty-one slaves in Weston in 1800," I said. "Think about it."

"Twenty-one? Big deal, that's nothing," said Jeff Neely.

"Well, like, there weren't very many *other* people here, either, Jeff," Kate said.

"Even if there's only one, it's still wrong," I said—feeling extraordinarily confrontational and a little dizzy all of a sudden.

Jeff Neely gave me a look of clean disgust.

"So, in conclusion," Kate said, "as a famous person once said, we should remember our crimes, so we do not repeat them."

"That's right, because history matters, right, Mr. Bostitch?" I said quite saucily.

He had a hindered sort of look.

"Fight the power!" Kate shouted, raising her fist in the air.

Mr. Bostitch squinted at her and then said, "Thank you, girls. Next?"

Kate picked up her note cards with a flourish and walked back to her desk. I smiled serenely and floated back to my seat, too.

When class was over and everyone was making their way out to the hall, Brian Nordstrom came up to us and hissed, "You ought to be ashamed. *Ashamed!* We're talking about the red, white, and blue, people. Wake up and smell the roses— this is America!"

"Yeah, you freaky hippies," concurred Jeff Neely.

"Yes, it *is* America—that's the point," Kate remarked acidly.

I stood there, trying to look dignified.

"Damn communists," Brian continued, leaning toward us, then slamming his notebook on a desktop and heading to the door.

The last guy to leave was Clyde Whist, who was either poor or a drug dealer. He had on a tattered black T-shirt and weird pants. He put a dirty, tense thumb up in the air, near Kate's face. "Down with the government, man!" he shouted, and lurched out of the room.

"Thanks, Clyde," Kate said slowly. She looked at me and whispered, "Cigarette break?"

"Just a minute, girls," Mr. Bostitch said as we made for the door. "A short word, please."

We approached his desk. He was sitting on top of it, one leg crossed, so we got a good look at his stunning white sneaker. He folded his hands together.

"Girls, your oral report had some fine elements. It certainly did. I like your spirit."

"Thank you, Mr. Bostitch."

"Now Kate, Alison." Mr. Bostitch's leg began to slip off his knee, and he pulled it back up with his hand. "I have to admit I'm worried. Kate, you look like you haven't been sleeping. You look spaced-out. I know, I know. Everything looks strange to an old fart like me. But the fact is, you're a smart girl and you look—it's just that you look tired, Kate. Are you getting enough sleep?"

"Sure I'm getting enough sleep," said Kate, sounding a little offended.

"Well, all right. Make sure you take care of yourself. Now, Alison, I can't help but be concerned about you, too. I can't help but notice that you really don't interact with your peers. Now, Kate, she's been here for a while. She knows these people from kindergarten—"

"Fifth grade."

"But you've just come in this year, and it's wonderful that you two have found each other. But really, do you think you could expand your social circle? It might help. You could help yourself academically—and socially. You're a fine young lady, Alison."

He floated out the last bit doubtfully, the way you'd say this if someone was not.

I guess we both just stared at him then, because he did a

pencil-tap, teacher move on his knee and pulled up his bent leg again. "Another thing, ladies. You do realize, don't you, that this history business is quite serious. History—and the history of our town in particular—means quite a lot, if I may say so, to many of us. Consider, if you would, treating the subject with respect." He knit his eyebrows together and continued after a false start, a hitch in the back of his throat. "There's very little we can rely on in this world, Kate and Alison, and so we must give deference to that we do know. So therefore, facts come into play. You must not dally with the facts. This does not help your cause. For instance, we didn't *steal* the land from the Paugussetts, we *bought* it. There is a difference."

"Yeah, but for like a mirror and some spoons?" asked Kate.

Mr. Bostitch regarded her and then turned to look out the dusty window, out to the playing field and the frosty bare trees in the distance. I wondered if he was thinking about his son. Was his son's death the fact that trumped all other facts, the American Revolution, entirely?

"Kate, Alison . . . you must think about the consequences of your words and actions. Do not break the hearts of your parents; do not overturn the chalice that is your grandparents." His eyes were small now. "You may go, girls. I've kept you long enough."

Kate stared at herself in the bathroom mirror, holding a cigarette in one hand. "Do I have bags under my eyes? Is that the problem?"

"Look, at least you 'interact with your peers.' Me? He makes me sound like some kind of social leper."

"Let's face it, Allie, you *are* a social leper. But it's the only way to live. Social lepers definitely have the best parties."

"Yeah, sure . . . but, I guess I've just been wondering, um, how many social lepers does it take to screw in a light bulb? Do you know? If one social leper jumps off a cliff, do all the other social lepers join in?"

"Yes, exactly. Like penguins," she said, and did a little penguin walk there in the bathroom.

Adults—who could really understand them? They needed to be told that someone had already let the dogs out. All the screens were open and the house was filled with bees.

Everything was wrapped in plastic and labeled with large silver stickers that read THE SILVER SPOON.

"What *is* this stuff?" I asked Kate. "It looks like seaweed."

"I think that's supposed to be the mushroom pâté," she said. We were going to make fifty dollars each serving it at her parents' party, whatever it was.

"Isn't pâté made from goose livers or something?"

"Vegetarians like pâté, too, Alison. Where've you been?"

"Here are some little wieners for the nonvegetarians," I said, peeking under plastic.

"So are we supposed to put these sauces on stuff, or are they for dipping, or what? Where are the instructions?"

"There are no instructions. Are we supposed to heat some of it up?"

"I have no idea."

"All right, well, the pâté probably gets served cold," I said doubtfully.

"Yeah, I'd think so."

"What about these?"

"Couldn't hurt to heat those up a little. Here, I'll preheat the oven. What do you think—four hundred?"

"I don't know. Sure, whatever. Cigarette break?"

"Yeah."

We passed Mick and Shana in the hall. They were arguing about Mick's stereo—Shana was saying he couldn't have it on during the party. Both mother and son were standing in their underwear.

The whole time I'd been there, Tut had been in his study talking on the phone. Smoke wafted around his head as he spoke and puffed on a pipe. Through the glass doors he looked like a shaman specimen, perhaps a sarcophagus.

We settled into our usual places on Kate's bed.

"You look pretty tonight," Kate said.

"Thanks." I was wearing a black silk blouse I'd borrowed from my mom. It was loose, and hid my brace pretty well, all except the chunky silver pole, the plastic neck flap, and the metal and leather lumps at the back of my head. Other than that: attractive. "So do you. That's a pretty sweater on you."

Kate thanked me, then said, "Man, I hope none of these older guys makes the moves on us."

"They wouldn't do that—we're thirteen."

"Yeah, like *that* makes a difference."

She did look pretty; she looked beautiful. In a way, this

made me uneasy. Kate had finally told me what happened the night of the Evergreen, what she remembered, anyway. She and Bo did a bunch of this kind of shot called snowflakes—vodka and peppermint schnapps—and she got shit-faced and he started putting his hands all over her body. What she remembered after that got a little hazy but involved his car and running on somebody's lawn and laughing and being mad and making up and kissing, and in the morning her gown was torn and she hurt in strange places. Then there I was, all superconcerned and freaked out, to tell her about the phone call she'd made to me. "I should never drink like that again," she said. "That's just asking for it. Especially with a boy like Bo Riley."

I said yes, that was crazy. We were at the mansion when she told me all this, standing in the little tunnel with the wispy lemon tree. She was hopping from foot to foot with the cold, and the hand that wasn't holding the cigarette was jammed in her down vest pocket. "One part's true, though. I do love you. You're my best friend, Allie."

I told her I loved her, too. Best friends. Horse Training Company. We were both hopping up and down, it was just freezing that day, and then we started laughing, and that's when she noticed the open door. Someone had wedged open the screen that led to a small room off the kitchen. We squeezed ourselves through the opening and looked around. Above the shelves, the walls were covered in old-fashioned wallpaper—trowels, rakes, and bundles of wheat, multiplied in reassuring rows. It was warm in there, and you could make up stories like anything.

The first huddle of guests was in the kitchen when we came back out from Kate's bedroom. They were smoking a quick joint before the middlebrow ones showed up. Mr. Hamilton had emerged from his study and stood resplendent in his white silk tunic and silk pants and loafers, and he had his arms outstretched like a priest.

"No, I'm totally, a hundred percent right about this. You already know I love women, so that's not it at all. I love them, I'm crazy for them. You know what I'm talking about. I wish it was Valentine's Day every day. I wish women could run the world. I wish we had a female president of the United States. But first there's just this tiny little issue. This tiny little— *molecular-level*—problem you've got to address. Women are lustful as fucking hell. They are! You can't deny it. And so if you want them at the helm of a ship—I mean a man, when he wants, when he needs, how do you say this—" He broke off to glance at Kate and me. "When he needs *satisfaction,* all right? He goes and gets the job done, one way or the other. Mano a mano, mano a womano, mano a hando—and so the thing is, women have to get in touch with this basic human need. It's there for them, okay? More than men, is what I'm saying. But they're all about denying it and getting all fusty and messed-up with ideas—shopping—and, what else? Toenails or some such thing. No, this is where I'm a hundred percent *with* the women's movement. Finally someone's got to stand up and call a spade a spade. And I'll tell you what. Women and their husbands would be a lot—I mean *a lot*—happier if this was the case."

The folks making up his audience looked at one another. Maybe someone was gearing up to tell a joke in return; most of them were just enjoying the deluge. Mrs. Hamilton, however, seemed to be in a toenail reverie of her own. Svelte in black leather pants and high-heeled boots and a tight red turtleneck, she had her eyes closed and she was smiling, rubbing her hands through her hair, first in one direction and then the other. She did a slow swirl with her body and then came back to center.

Tut continued, "Look, it's all in the book. It's all there. You've got to be true to your inner *calling*. The way we get fucked up is when we deny who we are. You can see that. You know what I'm talking about." Here he paused to take a toke before handing on the joint.

One of the guests, a young guy in a nice jacket, exerted himself. "We read the damn *book*, Tut. The question is, where's the next one, man?"

Tut turned. A mistake had been made. "You wouldn't know what it takes to write a book, now would you, Robert?"

Robert put up his hands. "No, man. You're the writer around here."

"You wouldn't know because what you do is *litigate*. What you do is live off *my* fucking back."

"Couldn't have said it better myself, Tut."

Everyone was silent, waiting. Tut took Robert's head in his arm and gave his hair a good tousle, and Robert smiled like he was still friends with the Great Man, and the party went on, no hard feelings.

A man passed Kate the joint. She took a hit and handed it

to me, fingers serving as pincers, as if she were showing me an insect she'd found. I realized that she'd done this before—it was obvious. Then I felt like an idiot. Of course she'd smoked pot before. Shana had probably handed her a first joint in the cradle.

I tried it myself, resisted coughing, held the smoke until my eyes watered.

Tut was addressing Robert now, something about a man being taken to the cleaners by his ex. He interrupted himself mid-rant, patting his wife's bottom. "Baby, do you have the cigarettes?"

Shana had her eyes open now, yet she still seemed to be giving the music, or some inner vision, her complete attention. She must have been listening to the conversation to some extent, because at this prompting she drew a pack out of her boots and started working on getting one out of the little hole.

"I smell something funny in here!" we heard from the front hall.

It was Renee, arm in arm with none other than the magnificent Ricky. Yes, Kate and I both watched carefully as he sauntered toward us in a *black velvet* three-piece suit, a white satin button-down shirt, and very tall tan platform boots. Platform boots on a man: I'd only seen this on an album cover.

"Here comes trouble," Tut said with an approving look at his secretary.

"Here he is, ladies and gentlemen, the sex machine of the century!" Renee announced as they got closer to us. She herself looked extra blond and frizzy tonight, and like she'd applied a healthy new coat to her everlasting mascara.

Ricky didn't seem as embarrassed as I thought someone might after this introduction. Maybe he *was* the sex machine of the century. He inclined his head, and his black, mussed hair fell over his eyes in an Elvis sort of fluff. He rested his weight on a single foot, one sex-machine hip inclined north.

"Want a beer, babe?" Renee said, moving toward the refrigerator. She gave Tut a hug on her way and murmured something like "Darling boss man." She got the beers, handed Ricky one, and then leaned into him, pressing her body against his black velvet back. He reached behind and gave her a squeeze, took a slug from the bottle, and smirked.

Renee told Shana she looked like a "sexy mama," and Shana murmured, "You too, Runaround Renee."

Upon the arrival of each new person, some of the dogs rose and looked around halfheartedly, then settled down again, nosing their way under tables made precarious with lit candles. This was quite a feeble showing for them. They'd all been sedated, I found out later: a dozen sleepy Egyptian gods and goddesses.

The adults went out on the deck—maybe it was a seventies thing, a deck party in winter—and we put the first round of hors d'oeuvres into the oven.

"Do you feel it—the marijuana?" I asked.

"The marijuana?" Kate echoed, elongating the word so it sounded like I was a dill-weed schoolteacher. "Yes, the cannabis is having the desired effect."

"I don't feel anything."

"So then let's have a beer," she said, and hopped off her stool. She opened one for each of us and placed mine before me. "Cheers, young revolutionary. To you, me, and Mr. Bostitch's grandparents."

Ricky returned for another beer. "You girls having fun?"

"Loads," said Kate.

He took a moment from his perusal of the refrigerator to regard her, and then he grinned.

"There's also a cooler outside, by the way. If you want more," I said—ever helpful.

"I will want more," he said. "But only if you two drink them with me, huh?"

He didn't wait for our reply, which was probably good because we might have flubbed our tentatively established savoir faire.

"Um . . . do you smell something burning?" I asked Kate.

"Shit!"

We jumped off our stools: hors d'oeuvres platter number one was history.

We had to get the people something, so we unwrapped a tray of stuffed mushroom caps and went out to the deck—mushrooms were good cold, right? Screechy jazz blared from speakers, and unruly torches, apparently providing heat, lit up the deck's corners. We held our trays daintily and presented the wealthy with stone-cold fungus.

Two beers and one hit of pot can make you feel quite relaxed and make the night seem warm and long and soft around the edges, like anything is possible, I was thinking as Kate and I sat on the front porch while a second batch of kelp crudités heated up in the incendiary oven. Cars lined the driveway and both sides of the street.

We heard a bit of rumbling in the bushes. Then someone said, "Hey."

"Hey," Kate said to the dark.

"Got an extra cigarette?"

"Ghosts don't smoke, and we don't talk to people we can't see."

"Uh," came from behind the shrubbery. A moment passed. There was more rumbling and thrashing, and then in front of us stood Ricky, his black velvet suit looking a bit undone, his satin shirt hanging.

"What are you doing in the bushes?" Kate asked.

"Nothing much. Hanging out," he said. "I'll take a couple of those."

"Going to smoke two at once?" Kate queried.

"Got a friend," Ricky said suavely.

"A chipmunk?"

"More like a fox," he said, and *heh-heh*ed.

The disco king closed his fist around two of our Winstons and dove back into the hedge.

We went inside so we could laugh hysterically. Then we heard Renee, walking toward us and calling for Ricky, and we ran into the bathroom and stayed there until we couldn't hear her anymore. By the time we made it back to the kitchen, smoke was billowing from the oven: another platter of hors d'oeuvres destroyed by circumstance.

Our next round out on the deck, this one guy went at the food like he was starving to death. He was a businessman with cuff links and a gray suit, and he looked up at me warily as he gobbled miniquiche after miniquiche, as if I might make off with the tray.

Tut called us over. He was surrounded by a group of adoring fans—he always seemed to be the tallest and most luminous in the crowd. Now he put an arm around Kate's shoulder and pulled her toward him. "Now, friends, this is what I'm talking about. Look at this girl. Isn't she gorgeous? Don't you think they're making them a little too damn beautiful at too damn early an age? And smart! She's got a mouth on her. Oh yes, she's got her opinions—don't you now?" Kate just gave a closed-lip smile. "I'd like to keep her in a convent from now until she turns eighteen." Now he looked over at me. "C'mere, honey," he said. "C'mere," he said again when I hesitated. He locked me, too, in an embrace. "You know the future of our country relies on these little gorgeous types. You've got to train them early, is what I think. Train them to lead, to take control of their lives. Don't fucking capitulate. Too many people are way too easy on their kids these days. You've got to respect them enough to rough them up a little. Right?" he asked, and gave us both a little shake. I guess I might have been smiling politely in response, but no one could tell: My body was tilted into his, my face smashed up between his arm and chest, rubbing the white silk of his tunic, slightly suffocating in a heap of Egyptian laundry.

Back inside, we firebombed another platter of food. Shana

floated in, laughing and attempting to put on some lipstick as she walked.

"Mom, what are these bread lumps?"

"Oh God," she said, peering into the bag Kate held. "I just have not a clue in the world. Use your best judgment, honey. *Fuck!*"

She leaned over to pick up her lipstick, scrutinized the red mark on the tile floor, then drifted back out the sliding glass door.

We made a decision to set out the remaining food buffet style and see what was going on with Mick. In his room, six young men were draped around his bed and windowsills, each holding a brown bottle of beer like a motto of self.

"What are you guys up to?" Kate asked.

"Hanging out."

"Going to a kegger."

"Wanna come?" said one of the leering fellows. They all looked as if they'd taken the same tranquilizers as the dogs.

Maybe it was the pot, maybe it was the beer, but I held their gazes more bravely than usual this time, even the guy Phil, with his long eyelashes.

"Only if you bring us some plates of food first, and also we need cigarettes," Mick said, not willing to let a moment of sibling extortion go unrealized.

"A couple of menthols would do me," said one guy, leaning on the wall.

"Regulars for everyone but the total fucking faggots," Mick said, and mayhem ensued, with shouts, pillows, and spilled beer.

When Kate told her we were leaving, Shana was sitting on the floor in the living room, gently stroking Nut's black ear. She looked up in our general direction and said, "Be careful, girls, it's a jungle out there!"

I slipped into Kate's room and took off my brace, put it on her bed. In the darkened room, it looked like the shell of an elegant turtle.

The keg was jammed in a silver trough, like the one we had in the paddock for Jazz's water. Mick and his friends had separated out from us, embarrassing youngsters, as soon as we'd gotten there. Now Kate and I were surrounded by guys in Weston letter jackets emblazoned with their graduation year.

When it was our turn, a burly guy leaned over the keg and barked, "You girls have ID?" We both started fumbling for an answer, and then another burly guy put his arm across the first burly guy's chest and pushed him back.

"Leave those girls alone, Schmidt. Little girls like them don't need trouble from boys like you."

"Argh, matie, I'll put your lights out any day," said the first burly guy—mocking pirates and gangsters simultaneously (clever).

"Hi, Bo," Kate said to our defender.

I froze.

"How's it goin', darlin'?"

Bo had what you might call bedroom eyes, heavily lidded that night in the sultry atmosphere of the three-kegger.

"Okay. How're you doing?"

"Sure is a beautiful night," said Bo—staring up at the sky. As if he could actually *see* the stars from here, in the circle of porch light. Maybe I could knock his *argh, matie* block off.

"Here, let me help," he said. He took Kate's plastic cup and pumped the handle behind the spigot three times, pulled the lever, let the beer flow. I hesitated, but then I gave him my cup, too, and he filled it until foam spilled over.

"You girls stay out of trouble now," he said, handing me the wet cup. "I'll catch up with you, all right?"

He winked at Kate and then went and started wrestling with the other pirate. They tumbled into the pine trees on top of a small hill. I could see their forms in the dark, like overstuffed scarecrows, then they careened down the other side and out of sight.

Music change. Whirr of the turntable, the needle dropping down. A couple of overamplified scratching sounds and then the first glorious bars of Boston's "More Than a Feeling." (People really *did* like Boston back then, their music a kind of earnest screaming that had to do with love, or beer drinking.)

"You want to go inside?" Kate said in her diffident way, eyebrows arched.

"Why don't we just leave? We could hitchhike."

"Why would we leave?"

I leaned toward her. "Because of Bo, obviously."

"He's no big deal," Kate said. "He can be kind of fun."

He can be kind of *fun*? But she didn't even remember what happened at the end of their night together, the dragon's tail of the prom. She was left only with a torn gown and the impression that when he was angry, he changed. *How, Kate? I don't know how, I can only remember that it felt like he changed, like he took off a costume.*

I took a sip of my beer. "All right," I said. Everything was tilted sideways. Maybe it was the earth that had changed.

Here's what was happening in the living room: A trio of girls sat on the couch, the one in the middle looking frightened. A group of guys in flannel shirts were gathered around a lava lamp, staring at it intently. They put their arms around one another and began singing a kind of dirge, and then they started laughing until beer spewed from their mouths. Mick and his friend Phil were over in the corner, talking to two girls. Next a swell of football players charged through the crowd, holding one gangly guy over their shoulders. *"Drink! Drink! Drink!"* they shouted, and flung him down on the couch (sending scurrying off the three girls). The gangly guy was protesting, waving his arms, but then they jammed a bottle in his mouth. After that I couldn't see his face, just a bit of his leg and sneaker, scrambling to gain traction on the rug. We moved to the hall.

"Let's down these and get another round," Kate suggested. So we drank steadily, standing in front of the family gallery, a lineup of photographs on the white wall. Who were these people? Where were they? We began to make up names and histories for them, Goofy and Tyrannograndmasaurus and Hot Cheeks and Fawn. I thought of what Warren Lipp had said: Even if they aren't there in person, somehow the parents are always there in the background.

"I've been looking for you everywhere," said Bo, coming up behind us and putting his arm around Kate's shoulder.

She looked up at him and smiled. What happened next

went too fast for me to describe—or for me to prevent, if I'd had the ability to plan, or to be a heroine.

He scooped her off her feet, and she screamed and laughed as he flung her over his shoulder. He said, "We're going upstairs."

I was standing in the hall alone then.

I don't remember everything about what happened after that, though I think I went back to the beer line more than once, and I know I ran into Lisa, Lynn, and Priscilla, all in pastels, like an Easter nuclear war. They asked me where Kate was, assuming, I imagined, that I wouldn't have come without her. I must have told them something interesting, because I have the image in my head of their eyes getting wide and concerned. I remember two guys throwing peanuts at a couple making out in the living room, and I remember explaining something to them: maybe manners. I remember looking for Mick, looking for Mick, looking for Mick, and then finding not him but his friend, long-lashed Phil, and I remember Phil putting his arm around me. He seemed really nice; he was a nice presence. But then I felt like throwing up and I think I made it to the bathroom—and when I wasn't looking for Mick, I was looking for Kate, of course, and Phil and I had gone upstairs and checked all the rooms, but two doors were locked and when we knocked no one answered.

Later, those same two rooms weren't locked anymore, they were empty, and there were more lights and fewer people, and Mick and Phil were explaining something to me, Kate was gone, Kate had gone somewhere with Bo, it was time to go home.

I woke up in the morning in my own house, without my brace. I opened my eyes to my room, the blue-and-white floral wallpaper, the peacock feather in a wine bottle, the Vonnegut novels, and the Cher album. My mouth tasted like vomit and cigarettes. The house was dead silent, and it felt as if the snake that was my spine were alive, squirming, curling; I was soft and ruined and had no borders, no restraint.

I wondered where Kate was in the world.

The journey was long and the nights were hard, and Sarah Beckingworth passed many a Cruel Sight. She passed a circle of ten abandoned tepees, Indian camping gear flung about. She passed the bodies of white men felled in anonymous combat, bones unnaturally bent, pocket watches forever silent. She rode and she toiled and she thirsted, and when she stopped to rest at the public house, the men spoke of fathoms or battalions and gave her strange, furtive looks. From then on she slept on the hard ground.

Though she didn't know, quite, where she was going, the lost heroine felt confident that she would recognize her destination when she came to it, and so she journeyed on.

Then one day she came upon a fort, a British outpost of some kind. Outside the walls, children wandered around, starveling and with no good footwear. "Look here," she said, as if to a companion, "these young children are starving." She rummaged around in her uncured leather rucksack; she gave them all her leftover gruel and persimmon seeds.

Sarah Beckingworth thought she was safe, even strong, but from the fort, Englishmen, churlish and resentful, had spotted the lost heroine.

Chapter Fourteen

THE WEEKEND my mother went to Tut's playshop, my father bought a blue 1957 Thunderbird. Blue room, blue car?

"What car's this?" I said, standing on the porch in my socks, having spied him and it from my window upstairs. This was quite a novelty, even though he *had* been on the tumultuous side lately. His face had been too red, too readable, starting with the morning he'd driven over to the Hamiltons' and picked up my brace and brought it back to me the morning after the bad party. I'd taken it from him at the door of my bedroom, then I'd asked if Kate was okay.

"She's *fine,* for God's sake. Think about yourself for a change," he'd answered, and turned away.

Now he was circling this Jetsons car, scrutinizing it inch by inch, brushing away dust and shadows with his hand.

"What do you think, Allie?"

"Neat, but whose is it?"

"It's mine. Pretty goddamned cool, wouldn't you say? I've passed it for a month on the Post Road, then I just decided to make the call. You've got to live, right?"

"Right," I said. My dad? Buying a car? But he wasn't a car guy. He liked to live in the ethereal. Or if my mother had it right, the guilt-drenched Irish entropy inherited from his mother. Anyway, "you've got to live" wasn't in the lexicon lately, not since I'd been grounded for drinking. Nor did he seem especially thrilled that my mother also "had to live" by going to this playshop in Schenectady.

"Want to take a ride? Come on—go get your coat. I'll take you out for dinner."

The steering wheel was oversize and seemed wobbly, as if Dad were holding on to a bicycle tire. I sat on the cracked leather seat and admired the dashboard, vast and empty and clean. A couple of on/off switches and a tachometer: fewer decisions per mile.

Dad giggled in a scary way as we motored down the road. I wouldn't say the car actually drove smoothly.

We went to a diner up the Post Road, almost in Fairfield. The menu had about a million kinds of sandwiches, Greek and Italian dishes, and the special of the day: quiche, at the time considered froufrou cuisine, best accompanied by a white wine spritzer. We sat at a booth in the corner. I had a chocolate milk shake and a cheeseburger; Dad had an Italian grinder and a beer.

The engine hadn't actually *stopped* when he turned off the ignition, so he'd had to go under the hood and pull some plug or wire. When we got in the restaurant, Dad had gone first to the restroom to wash oil off his hands. He was pissed about the car, I thought, or anyway he was pissed about something— but then back at the booth I found him acting, if anything, pretty pleased.

"I haven't gotten out this way in a while," he said.

"Neither have I."

"Maybe we can take more drives, just you and me. My old pal Creeley, the one who owns the glass factory in Litchfield? We could go up and see him sometime."

I said that sounded kind of fun.

"Glassmaking is truly astonishing, Alison. You'd be amazed."

I'm sure I *would* be amazed, but I just didn't feel that much amazement potential at the moment. The car was enough—that and the concept of my mother with Tut Hamilton learning the ten Egyptian secrets to success were enough to fulfill my amazement quotient for the week.

Dad was gung ho on amazement, though; he was alert to life. "Here's the other thing, Alison. Remember what Dr. Lyon said about swimming? Well, I just read in the *Forum* that the high school opens up the pool for lap swimming on weekends. I think we should consider going there tomorrow. I'd be happy to take you."

"Supplement the weird stuff?"

"Sure," he said, and here his amiability did seem a little forced. He took a sip of beer and looked out at his fabulous new half-broken Thunderbird. "We're trying everything we can, right?"

"Yeah. Even pretending to be trees."

"Swimming could be all right, though, see? It's time honored. Just look at the froth the fish make. Always excited about the prospect of a good long swim."

"But swimming in winter—that sounds too cold for me."

"I'm sure they heat the pool," he said, shrugging.

Our booth was filled with variously sized white plates—the sandwiches, the coleslaw, the French fries, the salads, the mayonnaise. A solar system of food choices.

Out of the blue, he started to talk about Kate. "So is she happy at home, do you think, Allie? Does she have a halfway decent home environment?"

Happy at home? What did that mean, exactly? It was a good home in some ways, in that you could smoke cigarettes and pot and drink. There was always Häagen-Dazs ice cream and often leftover filet mignon (what the dogs didn't get). There was the potential inconvenience of a sprawled-out mother figure having a woozy conversation with an Egyptian hound, or there was the possibility that the father might decide to knock you to the floor.

Maybe I had a funny look on my face. Dad said, "Look, I'm just asking. Do the parents—Tut and Shana—provide stability? Are they in any possible way at all *normal people?*"

"No, they're not normal at all. They've got like fifty dogs. And he's a shaman—*that's* a little weird."

He was nodding and scowling, a kind of scholarly look. "So would you say then that Kate is *thriving?* And what about her brother, Mack?"

"Mick."

"Mick. What about Mick? I've never even met this kid."

"He's on the honor roll, I think. We don't talk much." That would be an understatement.

"The honor roll? Well, that's good."

"*Thriving* is a weird word," I said. "It's like one of those guidance-counselor words."

"Oh, so you don't like the *word,* Alison?" he said, immediately hot under the collar (I knew he was mad about something). "You think it's a little much for your parents to care whether you have a productive and healthy life?"

"I didn't say that, Dad."

He squinted at me and went back to his grinder. We didn't say much until after he'd paid the check.

"Allie, listen," Dad said, sounding newly defeated. In one hand he held his balled-up napkin, splotched with ketchup. "I guess I just want to say that, your mother and I . . . well. You know we want you to be happy."

"To thrive?"

"Yes, to thrive," he said testily. Then: "That's probably what we want more than anything."

Later I told him I *would* go swimming. Not that I really wanted to, but like I said, his face had been an open book recently, and on the way home, after we'd jump-started the car in the diner parking lot, he seemed sad, so sad, as if even his beard had disappeared to reveal the quintessential sadness underneath.

Mom came back on Sunday afternoon, as energized an Egyptian empress as you would want to find in Weston. Oh, it had been a good weekend. It had been Transformative! It had been Mind-expanding! Thrilling! Willy-Nilly Good Crazy Energy Needed by Everyone! There was, it seemed clear now, Beneficence in the Universe! There was, absolutely, an Unparalleled Generosity in Taking!

She told us about it at dinner. She told me again on the way

to the Furthertons', Monday afternoon. And she told the Furthertons, too. We were standing around, all set to lay on some
hands and get going on the faith healing. Wearing what
looked like a child's plaid jumper, Mae sat cross-legged in the
corner, gathering herself up for her job; she didn't seem to be
listening. But the rugged Scandinavian milkmaid, Emma,
shook the ends of her braids and looked skeptically at my
mother. "But they didn't have shamans in Egypt, Clare—what
is he thinking?"

"No, of course they didn't—but Tut just goes ahead and
takes what he wants from different cultures and then provides
his own interpretation." Mom folded her arms against her
chest and beamed. Her earrings tinkled whenever she moved.
They were made of brilliant beads and tiny faultless mirrors.

"And this is a good thing?"

"Emma, if you saw this man, you'd understand."

"Yeah, he's bald," I said. I didn't know why that came out
of my mouth; maybe it was a coded message for Mom, or for
Emma. Obviously, I did not like my mother's rapture over
Tut Hamilton.

"Oh yes, well, the bald shamans will get you every time,"
said Emma, and she pulled me toward her and squeezed me
against her jolly mountaineer breasts and then let me go
again.

"The thing is," Mom continued, and I could tell she was
getting concerned, "he understands that you've got to love
yourself first, and it is from that space that you can best love
others—love the rest of mankind. That's what we're doing
here, too. Alison is learning to love herself; that's where the
healing comes in."

Emma smiled, and now she gave my mother a hug. "You're right about one thing, Clare. We do have to love ourselves, true. But we also have to know when we're wrong."

"Well, yes, sure," said Mom, agreeing to be polite, but of course she'd agree with this statement—who wouldn't? Well, Grandpa for one.

"Okay," Emma said, and clapped. "I think Mae's ready—right, darling?"

Mae looked over at us, her eyes as clear as an infant's. How could love of this kind, energy of this kind—coming out of an oversize baby doll, a Raggedy Ann—make any difference in this world? Wasn't real power grown up and verifiable and sharp, like a brace or a hospital or a protractor? Bones themselves are rigorous, stone-faced, hard.

I lay down on the brown carpeting, my arms straight against my body, my head turned to the right. Mae came over and sat by me, and I thought I could *smell* something childlike about her, too, blackberry lip gloss or baby powder or bubble gum, and she placed her warm hands on the base of my spine.

A dark feeling like sleep, the softening of dusk or dawn.

My parents were clueless, of course, and I was the keeper of a secret. I knew what Tut was really like; I knew what went on at the Hamiltons' and also everywhere else in postcolonial America. It wasn't just the drugs and alcohol, who cared about that? It was that you really could feel everything slipping off the edge of the world.

The morning after the bad party, I'd gone downstairs and they were sitting together on the couch, waiting, just like I knew they would be. Dad was studying the orange carpet—

surely there was something in it, some pattern he could recognize. Mom stared at me as if she'd never seen me before, and I couldn't tell if the glittery look in her eyes came from tears. At first I thought nothing was happening, that the world had stopped; then the screaming began.

It was awful, mostly because they were so surprised. As far as they knew, I was still just a Montessori kid, but now I'd gone and gotten drunk, stayed out late, left my brace by the wayside. When I'd slunk into the room and sat down, Dad got up, like he'd been stung by a bee, and began to pace. He kept looking over at me and then away again: the sight of me too problematic, too hot a place to gaze. Mom sounded as if she were confronting something for the first time. "Are you not happy, Alison? Is that it? Can that really be it? With all the good things here for us? Why aren't you happy? Tell me why you're not happy!"

When I tried to explain myself, say something about this being the first time, Dad turned toward me and abruptly shouted, "Don't lie to us, Alison! Do not let a lie leave your mouth," and inside I froze.

Their anger was breathtaking, and at one point I realized, Here I am, in a movie featuring teenage tomfoolery. But as they took turns accusing and demanding and lamenting, I began to see their anger was no longer about me. They were arguing about something else entirely.

This made it all even worse. I'd become invisible in the scene.

Afterward I went outside and stood at the side of the paddock, the January sun brilliant and mean, and I watched Jazz stomping at the white and the black, the snow and the mud. Four and a half more years—it wasn't such a long time. I could handle that. I could handle that, and when I was out of school I was getting on an airplane with Kate and we were getting out of here, we were doing something, going someplace.

The Alison and Kate Horse Training Company.

For a minute there, I fancied I didn't need the brace after all. I could handle eighth grade, I could handle any fear known to man.

Maybe Jazz felt a storm coming up, somewhere behind all the blue sky. He lowered his head and twisted his neck around, reared up with his back legs, and then kicked up his front. He galloped up to the fence by the road, whinnied, turned around. Came up to me with a snort, his breath milky white in the cold.

I petted his nose. Something about this touch, the warmth of it, the animal roughness of it, made me finally cry.

Other than cigarettes, ice-cream sandwiches at the school cafeteria, and Twizzlers at Kate's (Shana was mad for them), I *did* undertake to live more healthfully, under the watchful eye of the Furtherton sisters. Something about them—Emma and the way she'd said, "Take heart—we'll be able to throw that brace away," and winked, and Mae with her limpid eyes and bubble-gum breath—fixed me with a sense of personal challenge. And so I endured the kelp and the Green Spaghetti and the soy products.

Both parents had begun to view me as if I were very, very

bright—a bright star in their midst. They'd gaze at me at dinner, or if I was reading in the living room, and squint at the brightness of my light. Sometimes they would simply shield their eyes. Sometimes they'd shake their heads, as if stars weren't meant to be so bright—so incomprehensible; things weren't meant to go so wrong in the skies over Weston, Connecticut.

But as time passed, after the playshop and the blue car (which was returned, for it was discovered to be simply a shell over a mess of rubber bands and paper clips), no one looked at me like a star anymore. My first documented transgression became less important, and they simply went about their business. I could stand outside my mother's studio door, *Artist at Work,* and watch the wood pattern if I wanted, or I could imagine my father hunched in a tweed jacket at the university, working late.

Dressed in obligatory white, Tut Hamilton sat in the middle of the couch, his head resting back. Shana was flinging her hands back and forth, drying her nail polish. The familiar odor of pistachio shells and pot and tobacco and dog was laced with the smell of the polish, a sharp chemical bite. A white ribbon of smoke trailed upward from a cigarette in the ashtray by her side. Kate was reading a horse magazine; Mick was reading *Mein Kampf.*

It was my first time over there since the Schenectady playshop.

I think the dogs were stoned. Mut II, Nut, and Hapi had flopped together on their sheepskin bed in Romanesque decadence, and Osiris was slowly, rapturously, licking a piece of rawhide near Mr. Hamilton's feet.

"Hi, Allie, join the happy family," Kate said.

Mr. Hamilton looked up. "Lookee who's here. Little Alison. Hey, babe, how are you doing, sweetheart?"

"Hi," I said. "I'm fine. So, what's on?"

"The Poseidon Adventure," said Kate. "It's amazingly dumb."

Mrs. Hamilton lifted her eyes from her orange nails to give me a pleading look. "Oh, Allie, maybe you can get Kate out of this mood of hers. She won't even *speak* to us tonight."

Tut reached for his pipe. He peered into it, then tipped it over above the ashtray. "Don't kowtow to Kate, Shana. She's thirteen and you're thirty-six at last count."

"I am not doing—that!" Shana cried. She made an *up* or *uf* noise.

"It figures, though. These kids don't know what's good for them." Tut inserted two fingers into the opening of his purple leather tobacco pouch. "Surrounded by riches and lazy as a monkey's ass, the both of them."

Kate and Mick remained focused on their magazine and book, two studious readers in an airport.

Tut pressed the tobacco into his pipe with his thumb, held a lighter over it, and inhaled, gasped, inhaled again. He didn't seem to care if his children responded to his comment. He emitted a sigh of pleasure, resting his bright bald head back on the couch.

Shana picked up the bottle of nail polish and began to apply a second coat. She complained about her friend, who was supposed to be coming over with an ounce of sinsemilla.

"I think she said she was going to the movies, Mom," said Mick.

"But the seven o'clock show—it would be over by now, wouldn't it?"

"So your papa is a poet, is that it, Alison?" said Tut, his eyes closed.

"Well—yes."

"Can I ask you something? That poem he read at the fundraiser, what the hell was that about, anyway? Boots? Footwear? Don't real poets write about valor—or war? Injustice? What was that fucking poem they were always shoving down our throats in school—the road not taken?"

"Yeah, I think that's—"

"Whine, whine, whine. But aren't they always whining about taking the wrong fucking road? The road to nowhere. Why don't they just look at the street signs, that's what I want to know." He looked up abruptly. "Why not, little Alison?"

"I don't know." My T-shirt had rolled up from underneath the leather girdle, and I was sweating underneath.

"Ah well," he said. "Poets—what are you going to do with them? Everyone likes poetry, right? *Hey, Alison Glass, I like your mama's ass.*"

"Asshole!" said Shana, knocking her husband's shoulder with the back of her hand, wet fingernails still separated out into a claw. "Leave poor Alison alone. She just wants to watch a little TV, honey nut."

"Hey, I'm trying to get some insight here, Shana—into the *humanities.* The *intellect.*"

"Man, I can hardly hear the TV with all this talk," Mick

said now, not looking up from his book—that *was* Hitler, wasn't it?

"Oh yeah? You can't hear?" Tut delivered these new lines, too, with his eyes closed, as if he were basking at the beach or embodying the Delphic oracle. "Well, take the fingers out of your ears, buddy boy."

"Got no fingers in my ears, Pa."

"What did you say?" Tut had sat up now and was leaning on his white knees.

"I simply said—"

"What?"

"I said—"

"I don't like the tone."

"Right."

"Right?"

"Okay already."

"Yes, Dad, *sir,* to you—Mick." He made his son's name sound like a swear word.

From underneath his too long bangs, Mick looked levelly and darkly back. "Yes, Dad, *sir.*"

Satisfied, Tut settled back on the couch.

A ship was sinking on TV, but it didn't matter to anyone. Shana had dropped her emery board and was now leaning over the couch and cursing and beating back the dogs to fetch it.

Kate put down her magazine. "Want to go to my room?"

We left silently, on cat's feet.

At least we, or I, *thought* Tut Hamilton had been satisfied with Mick's acquiescence, but pretty soon we heard a tremendous fight. It seemed like they were going from room to room and arguing in each one, as if they were testing acoustics, and then there was the sound of a heavy object hitting a wall, a series of things falling, and then a kind of scrambling and more shouts, one being shrill—shrill, from Mick, who wasn't normally shrill about anything.

Soon after that, Mick was at Kate's door, and then he was in the room.

He was a blur. There was something wrong with his face, his expression. He careened around the small bedroom, leaning and reeling, and then he veered toward the bed and curled himself into a ball. He wrapped his arms around his head.

Up until then Kate and I had been two frozen people, our cigarette ashes growing long. She snapped out of it first. "Mick?" she said, leaning over him, putting her face down near his. She whispered his name again.

Her Mick, our Mick—he just pulled his knees in farther, holding his face in his hands. We'd been talking about Sarah Beckingworth and her adventures with the Indian—should they end in love or scalping? And then a real-life adventure came in.

"Mick," Kate repeated. "Are you okay under there?" She gently lifted a lock of his hair.

Mick didn't want to get up and he didn't want to talk, so Kate gave him a blanket, and she put a pillow under his head. Down the hall, we could hear someone arrive: Maybe it was the moviegoing marijuana connection. We heard Tut's voice and laughter and Shana saying something indignant on the way to the kitchen. People out there were moving, laughing, talking, but Mick remained as still and silent as a sleeping child.

Kate and I smoked a second round of cigarettes in her bright room, Neil Young playing on the stereo. In ten minutes, Mick bolted upright, as if woken by an alarm. His cheek was swollen by then. Without a word, he left the room.

"Welp, *he's* going to have a shiner," said Kate. Her voice was too calm.

We heard the front door open and shut again.

A person is made of her words and her body. And what she does. If you lay bricks, you are a bricklayer. If you ride horses, you are a horse rider.

I try to tell you about Kate, and I tell you about her words, a little bit about her body—how it was straight compared with mine, and how other than that we were twins. I try to tell you about Kate, but I'm not telling you about her, I'm telling you about me, about the way I remember the two of us together.

It snowed a couple of times that winter, but really the snow didn't stay on the ground long. Most winter days were spent waiting for the next white reprieve or watching the last one fade away. Still, when I think of snow I think of Kate. And in my memory, in my imagination, the snow is soft and deep, and when you shout, no one can hear. All is fluff and beautiful.

She started smoking pot more often, with Mick and sometimes with her parents, or sometimes, though not as much, with me. She met this girl, a classmate of Mick's, who did a lot of speed and gave her these little tablets marked with white crosses. Kate liked the way they made her feel: "zingy," was how she put it.

"Zingy?" I said. "You don't seem zingy; you seem far away."

"Oh, Alison—don't go all needy on me."

She started hanging out at the high school during lunch. I didn't go over there with her. Why? Was it because I was a Goody Two-shoes? No, it was because she didn't ask me to. And then there was the story I told myself, the story that was, in its own way, comforting: I could still make myself over. If I got my brace off before freshman year, maybe everyone would forget that I was the girl in the brace, and I could make my entrance like that, without history.

The girl's name was Vicki. Sometimes the three of us hung out together, but she was different—she didn't read books, for one thing, and she didn't ride horses. The only things she did were drive (she was sixteen), date boys, and do drugs—and she was, in that way, an Adventurer.

I supposed maybe Bostitch was right, saying I should expand out, not put all my eggs in one basket—find other friends, too. Maybe even Dave Darbis had a point. The day before Christmas vacation he'd stuck a note in my locker, a tip sheet: "Hey, brace girl, yellow clogs are for freaks. Don't wear light bulbs on your feet. Don't make that stupid-sounding laugh. Don't follow Kate around like a puppy dog lesbo woof woof hee hee."

Kate was different when Vicki was around. She acted cooler. She smoked more cigarettes. She did not giggle as readily with me.

One cold night, Dad dropped the two of us off at Cobb's Mill Inn so we could skate on the river. We made our way down the stones and the icy patches to the bank, our skates over our shoulders, the laces tied together. They'd spilled water all over one wide patch of the river, making the ice smooth and clear. The moon was sharp that night, like a searchlight. The Hamiltons had just come back from a ski trip in Vail. Kate's face was tan, and her teeth gleamed in the dark.

"I saw your mother with my dad at the Center," she said while we were putting on our skates.

"You did?"

"They were sitting in Dad's car."

"Probably talking about *Pyramid Love* stuff, huh?"

"Yeah. I guess," said Kate.

The cold came right through the rocks and crusted snow, through my jeans.

"I'm fucking freezing," Kate said, not looking in my direction, and then she staggered up on her skates and turned around. She pulled me onto the ice, and we were gone—all of Weston went dark and asleep, and we didn't know anything, didn't need anyone—skating across the night in jagged circles, short bursts of speed, halts, and turns.

When I got home later, I put on a tape Kate had made for me: Patti Smith, *Horses*. And of course it can't be true, but in my memory this is what we were listening to on that black river one night in late winter:

> *There she is, walking up my steps.*
> *There she is, walking through my door.*
> *Gloria. G-l-o-r-i-a.*

Sarah was riding away from the fort, her load lightened, when she was ambushed by the British soldiers: Loyalists they were called back then. They tied her up with leather straps and flung her into a courtyard. They cut her hair and made her wear a tannish sack dress. They put her in a stockade and made her recite verses from the New Testament, and then after that they were going to tar and feather her as well—just like, as one foot soldier informed her, her father had tarred and feathered one of theirs.

Her father? Tar and feather? And that is when the lost heroine remembered the chuckling and the sideward glances, that night the men and her father were talking about his future as governor.

In the name of her parents, she endured the ridicule of the British crowd. She endured the unpleasant outfit. She endured the drone of the priest who seemed not to recall any kindness in Jesus.

The lost heroine prepared herself to experience hot tar spread across her entire body. And the foot soldier said they were going to hang her after that.

Chapter Fifteen

THEY SAY scoliosis is hereditary—not exclusively, but that the children of those with scoliosis are more likely to develop the condition. No one knows why girls and women are affected by it most of all. The first doctor, my pediatrician, had asked my mother if she'd had scoliosis, and she'd said no, a bit pissed, as if he'd just asked if she had lice in her hair. And with a note of terror in her voice. That night I saw her and my father in their bedroom. She was wearing pants and a bra, and she was leaning over—like I had leaned over—and he was running his hand up her back. "I don't know, Clare," my dad was saying. "It could be, I'm just not sure."

I never even remotely blamed my mother for my scoliosis, though. Never could blame bones, blood—what I couldn't see. Something in the DNA, in my genes? I liked to imagine that God could solve a situation like that, or in any case it was to my advantage to imagine my problem, resistant to the brace, could be solved through invisible energy, invisible currents, invisible prayer. If I couldn't see why I had scoliosis and I couldn't see God, then it seemed logical that these concepts were in the same realm together.

Was I praying to nothing, or to DNA, or to God? Was anyone listening? Was it all about hope, my hope, my dreams, my imagination?

As an adult, I've read odd articles over the years: No one understands scoliosis yet. They still use the Milwaukee brace, though in some cases they're able to use braces that are less visible, less severe. And the surgery has gotten a little better. It's still a kind of exquisite horror, but the insertion of a rod, the fusion of the vertebrae, is performed with more finesse than in my time. Recovery time is marked in weeks, not years.

I think of the girls with me in the examination room in New York—ten girls in braces like ruined circus giraffes. That's part of history now, but there are other girls, new girls, to remember.

In addition to keeping our appointments with the Furthertons, Mom and I still went to yoga every Saturday all winter and spring, and even though it was cosmically annoying to be there with all the ladies in purple leotards, receiving gentle smiles and empathy, Energy Lady herself turned out to be okay.

One day before class, she put her arm around my shoulder and steered me into the hall. She said, "Listen, kid. Smoking isn't the greatest thing for you right now." I asked how she knew I smoked—as if I'd been unjustly accused. "You smell like a chimney, for one thing. And matches fell out of your sweatshirt last week. Listen, don't give me that look—I'm not going to rat you out. But, honey, beautiful: This is your body.

This is your life. You can't just go through the motions here. You've got to think about *continuity*. Be real with yourself. Does that make any sense at all, Allie?"

What made sense was the way Emma Furtherton never seemed swayed. She maintained that things were getting better, even though a day or two after every session with her and her sister, when I reached back to feel my spine, it seemed as curved as ever, the muscles hard on one side and weak on the other, and I both dreaded and had hopes for the next appointment with my orthopedist in May. What made sense was doing everything you could, waiting if you had to—if we'd taken the first doctor's advice, I'd have been in traction at this point. It would have been me, like I knew myself, only add a footlong rod, some screws, and some wire: Frankenstein, or a portable hardware store.

After Energy Lady gave me that little talk about cigarettes, we went back and did the Downward Dog and the Stork and the Platypus and the Gazelle and all the other creatures of the forest, desert, and prairie, and so finally I got to thinking: What if God could understand the value of hypocrisy, the balance that comes from living in two diametrically opposed ways? What if he could understand not just the Sweet Little Kid with a Bum Back Hauled Around on the Road to Health, but me?

I tried experimenting with the language I used to pray. *Listen, God, I hate having this hanging over me. I hate feeling like my body is an alien from outer space.*

At the end of class, after the Lebanese chanting, after she told us all to have a beautiful day, Energy Lady winked at me.

It seemed, mysteriously, that she knew the truth but she liked me anyway.

Problems arose at the Hamilton household. It started when Shana discovered that Tut was having an affair, and then it escalated when Shana had to go to the mental hospital (just for a week), and then it caught a wave when Mick disappeared.

One Saturday, Dad drove me to the Hamiltons' on his way to the garden center. He'd decided to take on gardening with a vengeance, and it was tomatoes in particular that had caught his fancy. He'd rented a Rototiller, dug up the ground, and fertilized it. In our garage, trays of tomato seedlings were nestled under grow lights. It was all very active for a poet and a meditator. Suspicious in that way.

In the car he kept muttering things like "The tomatoes will be up and down, short life span, just like everything," and "Never know about bugs—could kill it all, every last remnant of green. Invisible bugs. Or invisible poisons."

I had no idea what he was talking about. Forsythia and dogwood blasted color into the pale green landscape. If you squinted, it was like a painting.

"And tomatoes are like the heart, permeable and soft, prone to rotting, softening from the inside, soft as slugs, soft as—"

When we got to Kate's, he left off briefly from his muttering. "Bye, Allie, be good, would you? Soft and red and rotten, soft as love."

Dad drove off in his tomato madness, and I opened the front door. A small black nose nudged through. "Go away," I growled. Isis growled back at me.

"Like you don't know who I am," I muttered. I was arguing with a dog. (Maybe that marked the beginning of my career as a vet; sometimes that's what illness seems like, anyway: a wrestling match between me, the animal's body, and an uninvited third party.)

I tapped on Kate's door and opened it. She was folding laundry. On the bed were three neat piles—socks, pants, and shirts.

"What happened to your eyebrows?"

"What?"

"You plucked them? Where did they go?"

"Yeah, well, I gave it a try," she said, folding a sleeve in toward the center of the shirt. "Think I went a little overboard. I take it you agree?"

"They're not too bad," I lied. "Really."

"I wasn't even going to do it except for these little stray hairs, you know, down here? But when I was in the bathroom I saw the craziest thing."

She put the folded shirt on top of the pile, a rectangle of perfection.

"Mom was throwing clothes out her bedroom window. *That* was a little distracting."

"Oh yeah?" I said. "What, she didn't feel like doing laundry?"

"I just started plucking away."

"And away she did pluck."

"The thing is, they had a big fight." Kate smoothed her hand over a second shirt's collar. "I guess Dad's having an affair, actually."

An affair? I had two simultaneous images. The first was a

frothy dustup, a kind of *Love, American Style* set piece with two naked people under burgundy sheets, smoking cigarettes and sporting bad haircuts. The other was darker. Very, very, suddenly murky.

"Mut Two found a pair of lace panties in their bedroom. The dog trotted out with these damn panties in her mouth while we were all watching TV."

I laughed at that, but then said I was sorry. She was giving me a strange look. We might have gone further with it right there, but then we heard something down the hall.

"Shit." Kate jumped up and went over to the door.

Someone was coming—Shana. Shana was knocking and rattling at her daughter's door.

"Go back to bed, Mom."

"Let me in, c'mon now. Let me in, Katherine Anne Hamilton," Shana said, but then she must have moved back, away, and she screamed, and then she started screaming one word over and over.

We could hear her running toward the living room, the entire entourage of basenjis in her wake.

Kate opened the door and stepped out.

The word ripped through the house again: *Angel.* There was no sense to it, no context. It didn't fit in here, anywhere.

I jumped off the bed and followed Kate down the hall.

Mrs. Hamilton was crouched behind a recliner in Tut's study. Her hands were clutching the side of the chair, and she was sinking to the floor. She was wearing only her bra and panties, and her long legs were sprawled like a foal's. Kate squatted next to her.

"Angel," Mrs. Hamilton said again, this time softly, as if she'd temporarily resolved matters. "But he cheats on me anyway. I'm the mother of his children. I've been his wife for eighteen years."

"You need to get control of yourself now, Mom," said Kate. "C'mon, please?"

They sat there looking at each other, like a sculpture of a mother and child, half abstract, so the viewer didn't quite know where one began and the other left off.

"Do you have anything you can take?"

"I took one thing," her mother said vaguely.

"Maybe you could take something else," Kate suggested, gentle nurse of the pharmacy.

Shana suddenly noticed me. "What's *she* doing here?" she screamed.

"Mom, Mom—"

"Your mother is a fucking whore! A whore!"

"Mom, stop it."

"He thinks *her* mother is so smart and pretty. Maybe it was her—Clare!"

"I highly doubt that. Please," said Kate.

"But I don't have any clothes on," Shana wailed. "Don't *look* at me!"

I was already backing away. I knocked into an aluminum dog bowl and spilled water on the floor.

Then Mrs. Hamilton went back to a normal voice, and that sudden shift was worse than anything. She said, calm as could be, that she needed to go to town and do some errands. She had some clothes to pick up at the dry cleaners.

Kate got her to stand up again. She led her mother, an unsteady skyscraper, down the darkness of the hall.

The dogs in the kitchen scrambled up to me, as if I could save them from all shouting and strange human behavior. I squatted and rubbed heads, first one, then another.

My mother? No, it couldn't be. For one thing, she didn't wear *lace panties*. She wore plain, maternal, old, off-white underwear.

Kate got back to her bedroom and said, "C'mon, let's go to Westport."

"How will we get there?"

"Hitchhike," she said, and she'd already picked up her purse from the end of her bed and was out the door. I hurried after her. She was across the driveway and down the street, moving as fast as I'd ever seen. She was Superwoman, she was the Masked Avenger. She was running now, running, running—but I would catch up to her.

My parents had their unhappiness under control, like two brooding wizards stirring up a stew of lizards and toads. *Angel* like thunder in the house or lightning—no. We were quieter all around. My father, meditating, and my mother, painting: These things hardly made a sound.

I went riding by myself the next morning, and I cleaned Jazz's stall thoroughly. I scrubbed his water bucket, plunging my hand into the cold water and swirling around the brush until my fingers went numb. Then I went inside to come up with Sarah Beckingworth adventures and waste my time on math homework.

"Your dad and I are having pasta with capers," my mother called up to my room at lunchtime. "Want some?"

This cheered me up a little. You wouldn't make pasta with capers for your husband if you were having an affair.

Mae Furtherton leaned over me and whispered in my ear, black raspberry bubble-gum words: "Relax, sweetheart. Let God take over."

My cheek was smashed into the carpet, and the carpet was rough and hard, and the floor was cold, cold with a vengeance, from the bottom of the earth cold. From this angle I could see two pairs of Birkenstocks and a pair of brown boots (my mother). I could see the legs of four or five chairs, a stalky metal forest, the set of some acerbic drama. No, I didn't want to let God take over. That was the truth of it. God was a drunken sea captain, as far as I was concerned. What was he doing? Lurching around singing pirate songs. Beer was spilling out of his huge gold stein stolen from a pyramid in South America. I'd asked for just one thing—one thing—and that wasn't happening, and instead he was just stomping around, not even noticing what was underneath his black thigh-high boots, his spurs, his pointy-toed patent-leather pimp shoes.

I closed my eyes, though, and I said the words back to myself. *Let God take over.* And I didn't, and I wasn't going to. I kept my eyes squeezed shut, and I could feel my eyelids flickering. My head was filled with pressure, an effervescence.

That was it. As far as I'd go. Couldn't get me to go further with all the bubble gum in the world, with a waterfall of flowers.

When Shana Hamilton called my father from the insane asylum—it wasn't really that, but some kind of facility, a quiet little place with a watercolor ad in *The New Yorker*—and detailed my mother's relationship with Tut, every misgiving and doubt I'd had lined up in a row like strongmen. If you resist insanity, it seems problematic, but if you go with it, everything starts to make sense again; there's a new, inspired logic at hand. I happened to be home when Dad got the call, and I heard everything—his politeness, his anxiety, his anger. My mother, spurred on by a sixth sense or an artist's intuition, came out of her studio and watched his back as he stood in the center of the kitchen.

When he got off the phone, turned, and looked at her, she said, "No," a *no* with a *yes* hidden in it. She cried. She was crying in the hall.

My parents seemed like puppets to me then, awful puppets. They stood frozen on both ends of the split-level staircase, haggard expressions on their faces. Then there was an explosion of movement, like someone had shouted, "Go."

That night, Kate and I talked on the phone. The house was still, like a small, tidy museum of suburban life in the seventies. Here is the orange carpet, here is the unused living room, here is the kitchen with memories in each cabinet. Dad had left in the car, and my mother was in her bedroom: quiet, even when I put my ear up to the door. I sat in the studio and whispered to Kate. We thought it was, certainly, disgusting. Distasteful. We laughed about that. But as I sat perched on my mother's stool, an almost full moon blasting light and shadows across my legs and hands, we discovered we were talking around something. A silence bloomed between us.

Things like that happen: parental strife, divisions, incurable moments. But then you still go to school in the morning. And the Women of History still show up in your driveway when you get home.

I'd decided not to take the bus, but to walk home—it wasn't that far, only a mile, and it gave me time to be nowhere. Mrs. Hollbrook passed me at two miles an hour in her green Volvo when I was just about at the driveway. She waved frantically, and when she parked, it sounded more like she'd stalled out than turned off the ignition. I stood and waited for her.

For about a million years after parking, Mrs. Hollbrook rummaged around in the front seat of her car—*what* was she looking for? I thought about my grandmother and grandfather, so remote and fragile in their black clothes. They could never withstand this news about an *affair*. I was assaulted by the image of my mother that morning, all messed up looking, and her unnatural and silent hug, and then what she whispered. I was glad for the brace then: a fence. Didn't she know anything? Wasn't she, in any remote way, a good judge of character?

Finally, Mrs. Hollbrook staggered out of the car. A baseball cap was perched on top of her fluffy nest of white hair, *1776* stitched in sequins across the visor.

"Now, Alison, here it is springtime and you *still* haven't talked to me about the project you're doing for Albert's class. *What,* my darling, are you waiting for?"

For hell to freeze over, I wanted to answer—not that this was true, but it was one of Kate's snappy sayings; it seemed to get somewhere. "Hi, Mrs. Hollbrook. I really do want to talk to you about it, but, you see, Kate and I haven't had a chance to—"

"Kate, shmate. You just come along anytime. I'll try out my new iced-tea recipe on you—do you know you can brew tea outdoors? It's called sun tea, dear. Isn't that something?" She put her parchment hand on my arm. "Now, have you seen the new booklet put out by the Historical Society on the women settlers of Connecticut? No? Well, you need to read that, obviously. Oh, just thinking of all the things you have to learn makes me giddy as a schoolgirl!"

Her patriot eyes glittered, but her arm seemed to be trembling under the weight of her purse.

"Thank you," I said. "Um, do you want me to carry that in for you?"

She ignored the question. "I'd better get inside now, dear. I'm about to be late. Yes, and I do not like the direction things are headed—not at all. Too much keeping up with the Joneses and not enough of the *true past* respected here." She was shuffling forward, but then she turned to look back at me. "But not *your* mother, Alison. *She's* got her heart in the right place."

I watched her for what seemed like a long moment, letting her get a head start to the house. In my heart the idea took hold. The power of the affair, the recklessness of it, like a bullet in a closet, *ping ping ping.* It might have been then when I first realized that my family and my home were in real danger.

I followed Mrs. Hollbrook, taking tiny steps back to the front door.

"Welp, we've lost Mick," Kate said on the phone a half hour later.

"What do you mean, you've lost Mick?"

The wall by my mother's side of the bed was filled with pictures I'd made, some even from only the year before. One was a pretend photo album I'd drawn. Mom, Dad, and me on an airplane. Mom, Dad, and me having a picnic. Mom, Dad, and me swinging at the park. It was midafternoon, so the bed was made up again, no longer exhibiting the anomalous smoothness of the bedspread on my father's side.

"He ran away. Then there were two."

"Where do you think he went—do you have any idea?"

"I don't know. We tried Phil's house, but there was no answer. He left us a note, too. He wrote, 'So long, suckers,' in spray paint on the bathroom mirror."

"Well, he does have a way with words." He was a young man of talent, a smart kid. Handsome, good grades. Quick on the uptake.

"He's probably doing just fine somewhere—probably doing bongs in someone's damn basement. Meanwhile, Dad's in the kitchen snorting coke and shouting at people on the phone. I don't even want to go in there. Can you come over?"

Of course I could. I could take on her father.

"Well, if it isn't Alison Glass. Spitting image of your mother," said Tut. He was standing in the living room when I got there. He looked wet around the edges, a bright, clean, middle-aged man with a simple and successful plan involving pyramid power.

Him—with my *mother*? An *affair*?

"Hello," I said. I'd been so pumped up getting over there—and now I suddenly wondered what I was going to do exactly. In the battle of Tut Hamilton versus Alison Glass, who would be the winner?

I brought my hand up to the chin rest on my brace and pulled, a nervous habit, a tug against the armor.

"What are you looking at? What do you see, Alison? I see you looking, like you can't get enough of me," he said, coming closer.

I realized he hadn't just gotten out of the shower, as I'd first thought. As he approached, I saw he was damp with sweat. His head was glossy, and his white tunic seemed stuck onto his chest and shoulders.

When he grabbed hold of my upper arms with his hands, I jumped. I could tell from this extremely close distance that he was shaking in some way, a trembling mountain, and that his eyes were squinty. The smell of his breath and sweat made me turn my head away. "I need to talk to you, little girl," he said. "C'mon, let's go have a drink."

Probably, very likely, I would have said, *No, thank you, maybe some other day,* but he kept hold of my left arm and started leading me—away from Kate's room, which was where I'd been headed—to his own lair. The place most recently where Shana had splayed herself like a foal just born to the world.

Should I yell for Kate—let her know I was here? *Hey, Kate, just having a drink with your crazy dad. You know, the guy having an affair with my mom.* But had she not seen me coming anyway? Jazz was outside, stomping away on the other side of the fence from Peach. The note I'd left for my mother—while she discussed bunting options with the rich ladies—had said we were going riding. "Love, Alison," I'd written at the bottom (feeling a little tricky).

"Scotch? Bourbon?" he said. "Or are you more of a sherry type?"

"Oh, nothing. I'm fine—thanks."

Mr. Hamilton had released my arm, and I stood just inside the door of his study as he loped over to the liquor cabinet and splashed something from a decanter into a cut-glass tumbler. "Then bollocks to you," he said. He raised his glass at me, drank, then sat at his desk. "You look a mite scared, Alison Glass."

"I'm not scared."

He laughed. "The situation is, Alison Glass, most people do not get it. They don't get *living your strength*. Even my little wife, Shana, sometimes gets overwhelmed. And the kids. Well, what are you going to do? A man has to take responsibility for his children, for his family. I don't give in to them and their fucking bullshit agenda. Do you get good grades in school?"

"They're—okay."

"Good grades don't mean shit. You've got to get out there and experience things. And you know the first thing you need to experience? Solid, pure, paternal authority. I stay strong for *them,* goddamn motherfuckers, not that they understand. I take care of them. I'm privy to their needs. I'm privy to their desires. I know when they're down and out, when they could use a little something—a lifting of the spirits. I'm getting Shana a new puppy. I'm getting it today. And they're all about as grateful as fuck. Look what I've given them! What God giveth God can taketh away, little sweethearts. Care for a line? Have you ever inhaled cocaine, Alison Glass?"

"I came over because Mick ran away—because Kate and I are friends," I said, sort of a non sequitur. "And so I think I'll go see what she's doing now."

"She can wait. I've got a question for you." Tut had taken a packet out of his drawer and spilled its contents on his glass desktop, and he was now fingering a rolled-up bill. Then he leaned over and snorted up the lines on the glass.

It seemed logical that the best thing to do here would be to exit, to get away—still, there lingered in me, like stomach sickness, the idea of Saving the Day. Frozen in place, I found myself saying, "Well, I've got some questions for you, too, Mr. Hamilton." *Why do you act like you're the only one in the room? Why don't you ever listen to me or to anyone but yourself? Do you think you're like a real Egyptian? They didn't even have shamans back then, they had priests and pharaohs, Tut Hamilton. Do you think a real emperor would do what you do? Real emperors don't have to do anything, and all you do is stuff. All you do is stuff that hurts your family, and me.* "Have you called the police about Mick? Kate and I are going to go riding around—do you have any leads?"

Tut Hamilton, however, didn't notice that I'd spoken. He was holding his head up and sniffing up the last little sniffs of whatever he was doing. He was coughing a wet mongrel cough and then reaching for his drink. "Your mother and I have had to bid each other adieu, Alison. Adieu, adieu. Indeed. Our friendship, while so rich, so satisfying, had to come to its conclusion. So do tell me how Clare is faring. Is she finding satisfaction these days? Does she speak of me?" He stretched out the word *satisfaction* in a way that made it a soiled thing.

My vision and determination clouded. "Mr. Hamilton, I—"

I stopped midsentence, because Tut had just then polished off his drink and tossed his glass, like a softball, at the wall. It seemed to bounce off the plaster before shattering against the floor. The dog on the leather couch scrambled off and out of the room.

"It's good to be alive, isn't it, Kate?" But my name wasn't Kate. Now he was sitting deep in his chair, a contented look on his face.

"Give my love to the family," he said as I backed away.

The trees were exploding into a tender lace of baby leaves. It was spring: Promise was everywhere. Kate and I rode our horses in silence—we went to the Center, to the high school, to the parking lot, in back by the loading docks, over to the mansion. Everywhere we went, there was a remarkable lack of a brother.

By the time I'd gotten into Kate's room, after my tête-à-tête with her father, I felt light as air, really as light as you can imagine. It took about fifteen minutes for me to feel scared.

We ended up behind Cobb's Mill, the river loud as it crashed forward. The horses got nervous there, ready to run. When we let them go they hammered, as always, as before, down the frozen road, gaining speed steadily as if they'd been hurled down a ravine. I'd told her about my little talk with her dad, sure—she'd come out of the room by then, and I met her in the living room. But it seemed that something had been left unsaid, and it was Mick, of course, but really more than that, and there was no magic to the race that afternoon.

After they ran, the horses drank, long sucking swallows at the water's edge, front hooves submerged in mud. Kate laid her head down on Peach's neck and closed her eyes. The horse bore the weight of her body. Kate's face was quiet, like that of someone sleeping on the moon, and her hair tumbled in with the horse's mane. It looked like she really might fall asleep, warm and rescued. The mare would bring her where she wanted to go, and they'd get there sometime at night, lit by stars, and the horse would wait patiently for her to wake.

I was thinking about her father, and about Kate herself and how long days and weeks were, and hoping that her mother (however stupid she was, however nuts, she still provided some kind of barrier, some kind of diversion) would hurry up and come back. But Kate was thinking about Mick, the guy in the roller-coaster picture on her shelf, the other kid in the raft, the big brother, the kind-of friend when it really came down to it.

"He wouldn't do anything stupid, do you think?" Kate said, opening her eyes again.

What was stupid in this case, staying away or coming back?

"No, he wouldn't," I said. A sentry, a guard. Not knowing much.

I found a poem in my father's wastebasket when I was doing my chores (empty trash Wednesday and on the weekends, dust the living room, clean the upstairs bathroom). It wasn't

crumpled, simply folded in half, a small aerodynamic structure. It had nothing to do with tomatoes at all.

LEGACY

Now, after all this time, he comes, and every single inch of
  my renunciation, my promises upon promises, my conviction,
  ruined—

Now, after all this time, he comes—but not him this time
  laughing about nothing and no one; no, not him, hungry
  in the darkness of imagination, the imagined life of his son—

After all this time, he comes, now, and I am hobbled.
  The way out of here? Merely trample through this
  little field of kittens; all will be quiet and remarkable, a fever

of all that I've ever loved, ever wanted. Might I, after all this
  time, understand the trigger, the trick; find
  a marriage of desire and action; live even half

of what I'd imagined—oh, but it's looking more like a shamble,
  an ointment. Father, give me what you have taken.
  My house is empty; a thief stole even his own hands.

Looking at my father's poem, I was suddenly a most astute
critic of literature. I was taking note of each word. I was a
close reader, a very close reader, and a sad reader and an un-
comprehending reader, and then I set down the piece of trash,
the poem, again, and backed out of the room. Not just one
thief around here.

*L*uckily Paul Revere showed up. He was on his way through, delivering secret messages and stolen letters, when he noticed a stoic maiden on a gallows perch, all tarred up. Paul Revere plotted. Paul Revere anguished. So many Brits and only one of him. Then he saw an Indian, probably a Paugussett, standing at the edge of the forest.

"Indian brave," said Paul Revere, "what say you we rescue together yon maiden?"

And the Indian was the last and lone Indian, and he was in love with Sarah Beckingworth.

Chapter Sixteen

THEY WERE terrible at telling me, just terrible. If they'd been a medical team and this was a gangrenous leg, they'd have been taking coffee breaks between swipes with the saw. *All right already,* I felt like saying, long before they let me out of the room and out the door to the barn. *So you're getting separated, but no, that doesn't mean, absolutely, that you will get a divorce. So you need time apart. So you both need time to think. So Dad's got a little apartment now, in Westport. A guest room for me—yes. Everyone still loves me—yes, yes, yes.*

I must have tried to call Kate that night, though now I'm not so sure. She had her own problems, the quiet house providing ample time for fireside chats between father and daughter. Shana was due home the next day, and Mick's friend Phil had called. He'd gotten a call from Mick, and he'd said Mick was on some kind of vision quest of his own, a bender. So Kate had a lot on her mind, and maybe I didn't want to bother her with this—my life. Or maybe I didn't want to talk to her about it over the phone. Or maybe part of me didn't trust her. Maybe I wanted to keep it to myself for a while, my own private misfortune, and cuddle it like a teddy bear.

I do remember getting out the door early the next morning, wearing my yellow clogs and my cool jean shirt—I'd embroidered a butterfly over the breast pocket to distract from the protrusion of the metal bar underneath. Slipping out of the house into the quiet white morning.

Kate was talking to Vicki in the high school parking lot when I caught up with her. It was quarter of eight, and I'd never hung out in "The Lot" before, but everyone knew it was a fine place to go before school, at lunch, in the afternoon: brief flurries of freedom outside the regimen. Time for a cigarette, certainly, and perhaps to smoke a bowl—making the angles in geometry, the metaphors in English, all the more clear. Later I'd find out that one side was designated for greasers and the other for freaks (the jocks hung out elsewhere—locker rooms? sports stores?). At the moment, I was on the freak side. Here were parked a VW van, an old BMW, a Sirocco with a coke spoon and a few feathers hanging from the rearview mirror.

So about Vicki, who was leaning on the van. First of all, she had on those jeans with stitching on the pockets in the shape of a swirl. (Designer jeans were a new concept, with Calvin Klein, Guess?, and Gloria Vanderbilt blazing the trail that year.) She also wore a short-sleeved, sparkling sweater that tied at the neck in a little kitten collar, and she held a thin girly cigarette. Kate was looking around—maybe she thought Mick might show up—but then I walked over.

"Whoa, look who's hitting the parking lot," Kate said.

"Hey," I said. I glanced over at Vicki. "What's up?"

"Not much," said Vicki. She had brown, really kind of frizzy hair, and she was wearing sunglasses. She took a drag, looked toward the school, and exhaled. Her expression was arranged to indicate how much she had on her mind, how large and adult her troubles were. I believe I gave her a sort of smirk.

"I've got some news," I said.

"Really? What?"

"Not about Mick—nothing new, huh?"

Kate took a last drag of her cigarette and then shot it, from between finger and thumb, off into the distance. "The boy's probably gone off to become a male prostitute in New York City by now. He's probably joined the Rockettes."

Vicki laughed knowingly at this.

I pulled a cigarette out of my purse and proceeded to light it. I used the don't-pull-the-match-out-all-the-way-just-bend-it-back-and-rub-it-hard-against-the-striker method.

"So what's the news, then, Alison?" Kate was stretching now, a spontaneous moment for calisthenics.

"I found out last night my parents are getting separated."

"Bummer," said Vicki. She regarded me from behind her mirrored sunglasses. In her world, this news was a kind of credit. Health concerns (other than VD or pregnancy) had no cachet, so the saga of my back and brace was simply a useless unpleasantry; but parent problems were different. Universal, classic. I knew this. I was showing off.

Kate kept doing her side bends. "Jeez," she said. "I guess that was bound to happen, huh?"

"No, it wasn't." Actually, it was all a mistake. It shouldn't be happening. I wanted the other way back.

It seemed a little irritating that she was doing calisthenics.

In the distance, the eight o'clock bell struck.

"Look, when we get to Westport, there's this person I need to visit—okay? He lives out by Compo, and he owes me something."

We were standing on Route 57, thumbs to the wind. She'd convinced me to skip school after lunch.

"What person?"

"He's a friend of Mick's. He might know how to get in touch with him, plus . . . well, just come on, don't be a wimp."

"I am not a wimp. At the moment, I'm a tragic orphan—it's different."

The faux/true proclamation finally got her attention. She'd been eyeing a passing station wagon, but then she gave up.

"Allie, it is sad. Are you sad?"

"Of course I'm sad. My parents—my little family—have been dashed on the rocks."

"You sound like the lost heroine now: 'And then, out of mishap, came redemption. For young Sarah Beckingworth would not be daunted.'"

"Oh, shut up."

"Look," she said, and took my arm and started marching me down the road, "Chris and Clare will be happier, I'm sure of it. Your dad looks like an owl all the time, like he's going to die if he eats another Frau Fritter with seaweed sauce, and your mother is obviously ready to do a little stepping out. Best if she stays away from my father, but other than that—"

"Don't talk about my mother "stepping out." It makes me sick to my stomach."

"And you're going to have the perfect situation—divide

and conquer, that's the ticket with parents. You'll be able to play them off each other. It'll work out great."

"You're insane!" I said, but Kate had started jogging ahead. A car had pulled off to the side of the road.

"Mick's friend" had a tan, but it was a glossy tan, as though he'd spilled creosote on his skin, and his shirt was unbuttoned to the navel. When he saw us on his doorstep, he turned back to whoever was in the other room and shouted, "Check it out, boys, got us some afternoon entertainment."

"Yeah, right, Harry," said Kate, taking the high road, and strolled by him.

"*Whoa-ho-ho,* what's wrong with this girl?" he said, apparently registering my brace, or me, for the first time.

"I had reconstructive surgery after I fell out of a rocket ship."

He grinned as I passed, and his teeth were brownish.

The shades were drawn in the living room, and bright slashes of light broke out of rips in the plastic. Four shapes that were male sat around watching TV. The room smelled slightly chemical, slightly old.

"You haven't seen Mick, have you, Harry?"

"Mick-o called for product a couple of days ago, but then he never showed up."

"Really? No shit," said Kate. She had her arms folded, and she seemed to be wavering between her own personality and another one. "Where'd he call from, do you know?"

"Hell if I do—hey, you missing a big strong brother? Might be something I can do for you." Harry threw his arm around

Kate and started honking at his friends. Now I was beginning to see them better—they were definitely high school or older. I didn't recognize anyone. Their knees pushed out from where they sat, waiting, sunk into the furniture.

Kate ducked from underneath Harry's arm, but then she met his eyes again. "What I need is what everyone needs, Harry."

He gave her an awful smile. "I'm your daddy. I'm your whole family, baby. Come."

Outside you could hear cars pass, Beemers filled with folks longing to put their boat in the water. Porsches on the way to the grocery store.

He repeated, "C'mon with me."

Kate pulled a lock of hair to her mouth, stared over it. "No," she said, but that was not the kind of no I was expecting at all. It was a no invitation, plain as anything. But he had brown teeth. But the room reeked of bong water.

Harry held out his hand, and I could smell Kate's new perfume—Rive Gauche—as she passed me and followed him out of the room.

"Don't use her up," said one of the guys, and they all started to laugh slow.

Without Kate, I felt the other guys looking at me. I imagined the silver bars of my brace gleaming like stars in the dark room.

"Is this a soap opera?" I asked, glancing away from the soundless television. No one answered. Eventually they started talking to one another, something about cars.

When Kate came back twenty minutes later, she said, "I've got to go somewhere with Harry. Want to come? It's in Bridgeport."

"Bridgeport?" Bridgeport was the hardest-core town around, poorer even than my old town of Norwalk.

"Yeah," she answered, poker-faced.

Harry had trouble finding the ignition, but Kate didn't seem to notice. She was chatting away in the front seat— scandalized, it seemed, by some kid's phone call, a kid and a phone call I hadn't heard about before. When Harry succeeded in starting the car, he screamed with happiness and gunned it in reverse down the driveway, craning his neck to look past me and into the void of his life.

We hit 95 and shimmied along toward Bridgeport. It felt as though the car could slide off the road at any moment, and I laid my head back, half on the seat, half into my brace, and inhaled the exhaust streaming in from Harry's window. Oh well, I said to myself. All right.

Two cars honked as they passed us, the people pointing and shouting—about what I didn't know. Kate smoked and talked and smiled in the front seat like some kind of doll.

When we got there they both looked back at me, and then Harry said to "hang tight, catch some z's," and that they'd be right back. He and Kate went into the dumpy little house, and I waited in the car for ten or fifteen minutes, long enough for the black dust that was circulating through the car's interior to settle on my lap and hands. I waited and waited, and they kept not coming back. Finally I went up to the front door and knocked. Nothing. I knocked again. I tried the doorknob. Weird, how unconcerned I felt about just walking in.

I went down a hallway and into the living room, painted bright blue-green, like the inside of a swimming pool. A car seat served as a couch, and a cigarette burned in one of the ashtrays. I said hello a couple of times, my voice unnaturally thick. I wandered into the kitchen. I was looking at the back door, wondering vaguely if Kate and Harry might be in the yard, when I heard a woman's voice behind me: "What the fuck are you doing?"

I spun around. A man and a woman stood in the entry, both in black leather vests. Oh, great, drug dealers.

I started to explain about Kate and Harry, but it seemed they didn't actually *want* an explanation, so I edged past them and down the hall. The woman was right at my neck, screaming about Harry and Greenwich and prep school fuckheads and how I'd better just disappear. I was fine with that, seemed like a good idea, really, and then I was out of the house and walking past the car, away, away, on the street, out into the neighborhood.

It was what you'd call a bad block. Chain-link fences, dogs, garbage, an ominous silence, and black windows all around. Which way should I go? I felt preternaturally calm and simultaneously on the verge of a mental breakdown. Why, I'd just try one direction, and if that didn't work, I'd turn and go the other way. No problem.

Two blocks away, I saw Harry and Kate at a phone booth in front of a gas station. Kate saw me, too, and started jumping up and down and waving.

"What the hell happened to you two?" I said when I got to their side of the street—my tamped-down anxiety turned now into anger.

"Thank God you're here," Kate said, gripping my arm. Her face was flushed, and she was obviously thrilled with the excitement of it all. "We were just about to sneak back and get you. They kicked us out. They took his car keys—as *collateral!*"

Harry got off the phone and rubbed his hands together. "Good news, ladies. Our chariot doth approach." His grin was that of an amnesiac.

I got home at the normal time and washed my hands and face in the upstairs bathroom, then I helped my mother set the table. It would be one of our last family meals together. *How was school? Fine.* The afternoon cluttered up in my chest, wouldn't go away even after dinner.

What is history? When does it begin? Surely it begins yesterday. But can that yesterday be really *yesterday,* not yester*year,* not back in the olden days when they wore lederhosen and said "ye" this, "ye" that, and smoked corncob pipes? And if yesterday can really *be* just yesterday, a day in the life of a thirteen-year-old girl, then what matters most—is it all about numbers? True enough, they had only twenty-one slaves in Weston, but there were—as Kate pointed out—only a thousand people total. If there are two people and one of them is miserable, or exploited, or destined to failure, or breathlessly excited, or beautiful, doesn't that still matter—statistically, I mean?

One out of one daughters at 12 Ramble Lane now knew that her parents' imminent separation was going to work well as a party favor, a kind of sorrow to trot out to establish depth of character. At the same time, one out of one daughters at 12 Ramble Lane felt superstitious, like maybe parents' unhappiness was not only their own individual unhappiness but destined her—in the blood—to a kind of unhappiness, too. Unhappiness in love in particular. One out of one daughters at 12 Ramble Lane felt, beneath any bravado, heartbroken at the core.

And where, exactly, was Kate? Sometimes when I looked at her, I didn't see her anymore.

I was out by the barn on Saturday when Dad came up to say good-bye. All morning he'd been walking to and from the garage with his things: a typewriter, a poster, a suitcase, some albums, some books. Between each box stretched an inordinately long interval, as if he and my mother were discussing each item. I figured this wasn't true, though I kept hoping it was. Maybe in contemplation of a lamp or a flashlight or an album they'd listened to together or a book of poetry he'd read to her, they'd realize this was a mistake after all. Did an affair have to be like this, a closed door, a final answer? Mom had told me it wasn't really an affair, just a brief and stupid idea. Other than the one time, the Threeway Talk, Dad hadn't talked about this aspect of their separation. This was so Grandpa-like—avoid all mention of the central idea—that I suddenly had the notion that maybe now, after all this time, Dad was becoming more like Mom's father—and maybe this could help matters!

But this was a desperate concept, and I was confused, and no matter what I hoped, the wind kept opening the front door in stray rough gusts, and each time, another part of my dad's life moved into the back of the car.

Jazz stood in his paddock, nibbling around in an invisible

maze, a map of curlicues and figure eights and secret destinations. I was sitting on the grass, transcribing my entries and Kate's entries into this cool brown suede journal I'd gotten at the art store. Kate and I were going to pick out the lost heroine's journal together in Westport the afternoon we skipped class, but instead we'd hit Bridgeport with Harry. I'd gone to the art store with my mom. Besides the journal, she bought me a special calligraphy pen, the nib fat on one side and thin on the other.

I heard the hatchback shut. I stared at Sarah Beckingworth's latest adventure.

"Hi," Dad said, like I was wildlife and he didn't want to startle me.

"Hi," I said back. He tugged at his beard, then put his hands in his pockets and came closer. He took his hands back out of his pockets again.

"Working on your project?" he asked.

"Yeah."

He bent down and pulled at a piece of grass. "Well, it's a pretty neat project, from what you've told me. I'm looking forward to reading it."

I didn't say anything. There probably were some right things to say in this circumstance, Dad on his way out. Maybe they were written down somewhere in a kind of handbook.

I put the top on the pen. I had to concentrate or something bad might happen.

When he spoke again, his voice was messed up—the tiny breath of a lifetime smoker mouse. "I'll see you soon, all right?"

And then I felt my father's arms around me, and his knee pushed awkwardly on my arm, and his nose went in my ear.

He stood back up. He went to the garage.

The sound of the engine was poison in the air, the stupid, slow Tercel.

Then it was gone, the low rumbling of our second-best car.

*P*aul Revere rushed into the middle of the courtyard, waving his letters and laughing like an insane Pioneer. All the angry British stopped what they were doing and jumped upon their (stolen!) horses and chased Paul Revere; meanwhile, the Last Indian swept in behind them and cut Sarah Beckingworth down!

Chapter Seventeen

SHANA NAMED her new puppy Tommy, which in and of itself shouldn't have been such a big deal, though it did break with the time-honored tradition of naming every new conscript after an Egyptian god. The assumption was she'd found her Self, found her Strength, at the treatment center.

Still, this particular self was a bit restless. Kate said that after the first couple of days at home, Shana quit with the pajamas and the herbal tea, lit up a cigarette, and began shopping compulsively in Westport—perhaps making up for all the clothes she'd thrown out the window earlier. She bought two fur coats (spring sales) and a new set of silverware.

The day she came back—maybe he'd been lurking in the bushes, like the Italian sex machine earlier—Mick returned as well. He wouldn't talk about his week, except to tell his sister, in a voice somewhat slurred by a fascinating new substance mix, that "it's a wild and woolly world out there, and a young person had best be well prepared." By prepared, he meant something to do with fortifying yourself with music and ingestibles, as well as the alignment of your face into a near glacial placidity—the look he attempted when he endured Tut's welcome home party: a cocaine-inspired rant with little physical violence at all.

For me, Mick's homecoming meant the return, mostly, of his music. I smiled, glad to hear *John Barleycorn Must Die* emanating at top volume from his closed door.

It was the first afternoon I'd seen Shana since her breakdown. She was sitting on the red couch, melancholically massaging the belly and hind legs of the new puppy, when I got there. When she looked up at me, her face betrayed no feeling.

Kate and I were in the kitchen making Pop-Tarts when she decided to join us, letting us in on her maternal wisdom, as it were.

"You girls are lucky," she said. "Here you are, in the lap of luxury. Everything you want, everything you need. In my day, things were different. Don't you want to know why?"

Neither of us said anything.

"For one thing, men weren't having affairs with their fucking neighbors," she said, and now she did give me a look of the venomous viper. "My father never did that. But my mother— my mother, you see . . ." She pushed her hands between her velour sweat-suit knees. "She just didn't pay attention to me."

"Poor you," said Kate, but I don't think Shana heard her.

"But you and me, we're friends, we're like sisters." She smiled at her daughter, a smile like a plea. The kitchen was quiet except for the hum of the refrigerator.

"Sure, Mom."

"She was a *bitch,*" Shana went on. "Tiny little heart, the size of a damn pea. I always said I'd never be like her. Never. Anyway, I know I'm not perfect, far from it. But I try—that's what matters."

"Yes, it does, Mom. Can I bum a cig?" Kate said, narrowing her eyes.

My own mother and I continued our self-improvement scheme, as if no separation had ever occurred. Indeed, she seemed more determined than ever. One week Energy Lady went to Bali on vacation, and Mom decided to pick up the slack at home. Why not? I could think of a lot of reasons, but that didn't matter. We lay side by side on the orange carpet in our living room, and she played "Abbey Road"—not all that close to Lebanese chanting, but it would have to do. "Breathe in, breathe out," she murmured, and, "Your vertebrae are lining up like a ladder." She was trying for a mellow, UFO-landing type of voice, as if she could hypnotize me into getting better. She had her eyes closed and rolled her separated-middle-aged-cheating-heartbroken-regretful-forgetful body around, and I lay still, eyes on the walls.

Mom moved on to the Sun Salutation, and when she turned over and stretched up on her arms, I did, too, so in her sight it looked as though I were participating. But everything felt heavy, earthbound. Marriages fall apart, backs sag—gravity was heavier than it had ever been before.

Meanwhile, Dad had taken to bringing me swimming. We'd gone twice. Not at the Weston High pool after all, but at the YMCA near his new place. I did laps and he read the paper or graded student assignments, or maybe he wrote poems. "Girl swims / water stays still / outside it is raining." Plunging into the cold water was like skipping school. I swam up and down the length of the pool, pretending to swim far, get somewhere, but always coming to the wall, turning, going the other direction again. I guess I had no idea I'd need my swimming skills, and so soon, too. I just liked the feel of it: Vixen Glass, Speed Racer.

But sometimes fear would overtake me there in the pool, and I'd stop at the end of a lane, pant, and push out of my mind the inevitability of my next doctor's visit, the still very real chance of surgery, despite swimming, kelp, and Mae Furtherton's warm hands.

Kate's idea was to take the horses out overnight. In that we hadn't gotten caught skipping school—the forged notes had helped, plus my mother's preoccupation with the fall of her marriage and the possible onset of dementia in her father (she'd gotten a call from the property manager: some concerns about two flooded bathtub incidents, one midnight pajama stroll)—I still had a free ticket for mischief, for "tomfoolery" as the elders called it. And weren't the children of broken homes almost required to misbehave? It was something you had to do, a rite of passage, a walkabout.

We used the old switcheroo system: Her parents thought she was spending the night at my house with Peach in *our* barn, and my mother thought I was spending the night at her house with Jazz in *her* barn. (Holed up in Westport, Dad didn't know where we were.)

In my book bag, I packed sweet feed for Jazz, peanut-butter sandwiches, and two cans of Black Label beer. When I took off my brace and put it in the closet, I was practicing a kind of faith of my own—or was it a lack of faith? Sometimes it's hard to tell the difference. My mind felt clean, that's all I knew, like I could smash the figurine that was the stupid doctors, smash the figurine that was the two stupid years in the brace, smash the appointment next week, all in one smooth gesture.

Jazz was suspicious and reluctant, which was the first indication that this whole plan was a bad idea. He took each step down Ramble Lane and then Steephill tightly, fighting me, ducking and rolling his head against the bridle.

It was dusk when I got to the mansion. We trotted up to the lemon tree portal and looked through to the other side, and I didn't see Kate anywhere. The sky was a throttled purple against the edges of the trees and a brighter blue higher up. Watched by the black windows of the abandoned house, I shivered, alone in the glorious seclusion of crime, or what felt like crime to me.

Jazz heard Peach first. He pulled up his head and pricked his ears, nickered with hope that he'd have the consolation of company in this cockeyed scheme.

We rode single file down the road, practicing being invisible when a car passed. Every set of headlights took with it a part of the day, leaving us in greater darkness. I heard the horses' tails swish, their hooves knock on the pavement. It was only when we stepped into the woods surrounding the reservoir that the night seemed to lighten up again. The trail was a glimmer of gray, a silvery stream through the forest. Bright scraps of sky illuminated a tree, a patch of nothingness. A solitary bird called out.

"That sounded like an echo," Kate said. "Didn't it?"

"Yeah."

"Maybe we're close to the lake already."

A rushing sound came from the bushes, and Peach scrambled, skating sideways. Her rump slammed into my leg, and then Jazz was backpedaling, too. He caught a rein on a branch and reared up, flinging his head high.

"All right, all right," Kate said when it was quiet again.

We walked on, and the woods suddenly let go. We were on the edge of a vast, mirroring lake.

"Nice," said Kate.

I agreed.

"Well," she said after a minute. "See any flat places? I'll get my flashlight."

We set up camp under a tree about fifteen feet from the shore. An inch of dead pine needles all but covered the hump-backs of roots. We unsaddled and unbridled the horses, tied them to a tree with their halters and rope. Kate sat next to me.

I held my back straight, straighter than ever, tightening the muscles around my ribs and my shoulders. Looking out at the wide, soft lake, I had this thought: Maybe I could be my own brace.

"So this is what it's all about," she said.

"Seems like it."

We drank the warm, awful beer.

"I like it," she said. "No one but us."

"I like it, too."

I did like it. It seemed as though we were on a new planet—we weren't so many miles away from home, but to be here at night, in secret, made everything different.

"Although it does kind of suck," Kate said after a while. "I mean—this beer sucks, and it's cold out here. Who knew there wouldn't be any electricity?"

"I know. And no damn bathroom, either."

"Oh, for chrissakes."

"Camping just isn't what it used to be."

"What time is it now?"

"Eight-thirty," I said.

"Oh my God. Only twelve hours to go."

"You want to go back?"

"Go back? No way! I'm ready for a swim."

"No."

"Not *no*. Yes." Kate jumped up and was scrambling down to the lake.

"But we don't have towels or anything!" I protested, standing up, too. She was already taking off her boots.

"So what? Like the Indians had towels."

"The Indians? What Indians?"

"The damn Paugussetts," she said, throwing a boot toward the blanket.

"This is really stupid. I don't want to do this."

"So don't, you wuss." She stepped out of her jeans. Now she was wading in and yelping with each step.

"I think I'll just . . ." she said, spreading out her arms and letting herself fall back on the water. "Lovely. Lovely. Just like the beach."

"It's too cold!"

"What are you talking about?" Kate shouted back at me. She splashed back with her arms and then turned around and started swimming out toward the middle of the lake.

I stood there for a moment, and then I pulled off my clothes and jumped in myself.

"Don't go too far," I yelled, swimming toward her. Yes, it was fucking freezing in the lake. Kate was far away already, just a little disturbance on the surface.

I swam, and I was a pretty good swimmer—but I couldn't catch up. The more I swam, the more she swam: The distance didn't get any less. For some reason (it really doesn't make any sense when you think about it: Did I think she was going to just keep swimming forever? Did I think she wasn't going to come back?), I began to panic. I put my head down and started swimming like a crazy person. The water sound was rough in my ears. My breathing was loud as gunfire.

When I looked back up, she was right in front of me. I'd gotten to her. She was looking at me curiously, treading water. We were far into the lake, black on all sides.

"Kate."

Her hair was smooth and dark around her face. "Look how big it is," she said.

"Let's go back."

"Why? What's the point?"

"*What's the point?* C'mon, Kate." My legs bicycled underneath me like wild bent wheels, and with my arms I smoothed black sheets.

"Well, don't be in such a rush."

She tipped her head back and let her body rise. She was staring at the sky.

"I'm not in a rush," I protested, the words seeming wrong somehow.

Her face was lit by the moon. She was made of shadows and light and that was all. I paddled around aimlessly, a futile warrior. Finally she lifted her head back up and looked at me. "Okay, we can go back."

I swam behind her, watching her slow, resigned strokes—as if she didn't really want to get back, as if she were leaving the place she preferred after all. And it's too bad that I started thinking about myself then, instead of her. I began to think, Wow, I'm not much of an adventure girl. I began to think, Wow, I know how to ruin a party in a lake.

I wasn't listening: That's what I thought later.

We were both trembling when we got out of the water. We got into our clothes and unzipped the one sleeping bag and sat under the tree, holding the sleeping bag around our shoulders. After a while, we lit cigarettes and had the other beer and joked about some people at school and about the Furtherton sisters and then about the lost heroine. Sarah Beckingworth, we decided, could never really be much of a swimmer. She'd drown in all her pilgrim gear.

Kate fell asleep first, hard, like she hadn't slept in days, years. All kind of gnarly insects were probably making their way around the blanket and our sleeping bag. The insides of my socks were gritty with pine needles and sand, and the moon was bone white that night, big and flat.

Our horses stood next to each other, a double image, a horse and his shadow, and patiently waited out the night.

In the morning, birds cartwheeled over the lake and it all felt like a dream, except that we were there, together, and my body was bruised from the roots and rocks underneath us.

When I got home, my mother was sitting in the living room. She was a bit pissed, a bit worried. A dream, a mother's intuition, had woken her up early (so maybe dreams really did come true, at last) and she needed to find out where I was immediately, no fooling. What she did is she called over to the Hamiltons and talked to Tut—and if *she* was pissed, he was still worse.

After I'd been yelled at and released, after I'd received word of my punishment, I went upstairs and took a shower and put on my undershirt and my brace and jeans and a T-shirt. I put on Patti Smith, low, and then lay on my bed. The peacock feather in the bottle moved slightly in the breeze from my window. The wallpaper strips kept peeling away from each other, slow as who knew what slow thing—understanding, history, love. The second hand on my little green desk clock, which I'd had since I was small, clicked around steady as always.

Why did they have to break up, anyway? They were meant for each other, as mismatched and perfect as Sonny and Cher. They were—we were, despite the artistic leanings—the quintessential normal, or had been. We were the normal of family photos in the album, the normal of Christmas dinners, the normal of getting lost on the highway on the way to anywhere.

She'd called Dad, too. Now that I was home, I was supposed to call him back.

In April, in Connecticut, rocks turn up in the soil like a harvest, a hard revelation of what's been underneath the earth all winter long. Under the lawn, they just press up in suffocated little bumps. But in the paddock it's an Easter egg hunt, an easy one. Besides being grounded, my punishment for staying out all night was to clear the paddock of rocks. "Down to the size of avarice," my father said over the phone, getting a little carried away with himself.

I drove the wheelbarrow into the soft, swelling mud and looked around. More rocks than you could possibly imagine. To pick them all up would take a million years.

Jazz stood in the doorway of his stall, chewing innocently on some hay, as if he hadn't been involved in any of it.

I picked up a rock and tossed it into the wheelbarrow, and it clanked and rolled to a stop.

One.

I picked up another, threw it in, *clank*.

Before I knew it, I'd done 7 percent of the paddock.

At last his curiosity got the better of him, and Jazz roused himself from his meditation at the stall's entrance and lopped toward me. About ten feet away, he stopped, sniffed a rock, and then looked at me, ears up. I threw the next one in the wheelbarrow gently, but he still lurched back. Then he peered forward again. Took a couple of steps toward the wheelbarrow. I tossed one. He reeled back again and waited for the next affront.

The way my mother came up the path was unusual. She was still in her robe, for one thing, and there was a kind of leaning, disorganized aspect to her walk. She grabbed on to the fence as if it were the end of a pool, as if she were holding on to it for help. "Allie," she said—sobbed. "Kate's on the phone. You've got to come."

If parents don't talk to grandparents and kids don't talk to parents, then who's left to talk to anyone? I hadn't told my parents about the Hamiltons—not about the drugs or any of those other little sordid details parents are likely to be curious about. I had my own world, they had theirs, and it certainly had been disconcerting when my mother stepped over the line to have her little fling with Kate's father, but I assumed the fallout from that was already over. And if there were any implications in my own silences—what I knew, what I saw—this was something I'd chosen more or less to ignore.

One obvious reason for what happened that morning was that Tut thought his wife had been fucking around the night before, at the bars. Shana had gone out with a friend. Turned out she'd planned to nettle him, and she managed to do that, and who knows what kind of splash she made with her husband at two in the morning when she finally came home, and they argued and argued, and then she went into the bedroom to pass out and Tut was left alone to brood—brood and do coke until Kate came home. I suppose it was really one of those horrible chances, bad luck, "a confluence of conduits," as Tut might have said. Maybe neither thing would have been enough in itself. Maybe if the guy in Katonah hadn't come through with double the regular order.

He didn't even know she was gone, not until Clare Glass's call around six in the morning. But oh, he *did* get angry after that call. None of his ducks was staying in a row.

What did Shana have to do with Peach—what did Peach, really, have to do with any of them? There was also the fact that the last playshop hadn't netted as much cash as usual, and that Renee had quit without notice, and that Kate and Mick were good-for-nothing kids who needed to finally, *finally,* learn a lesson about respect. Or maybe it was simply the dark side of the morning. Whatever it was, Tut took it upon himself to fetch his gun from the dresser drawer, load it, bring it out to the barn, and shoot Kate's horse once in the temple, killing her.

Kate had tried, at the door, to hold him.

I've seen dead horses since then, but Kate had just turned fourteen, and she had not had the experience of seeing a dead horse before. Certainly not one shot in the head, her body still hot with life by the time Kate leaned over her, stretched her arms out around her. Peach was still bleeding, a pool of blood widening under her neck, like shifty life, even after her heart had gone quiet.

"And he was angry at *her.* But I'm not my mother," Kate said over the phone in a voice I could hardly hear, and again: *"I am not my mother."*

I got off the phone and ran out to the barn, saddled up Jazz. Mom was screaming for me to stay, that she'd call the police on them, that I had to stay away from that house. Finally she followed me in the car.

The road was slow under Jazz's feet, sticky like mud, all the way there. No cars in the driveway. I threw his reins over the fence post and went inside to find her. She was alone, sitting on her bed.

I got her Kleenex. I straightened out the pillow behind her back. I got her a glass of water. I wanted to get to her, *get her* somehow, take her—as unlikely as grabbing hold of your reflection on the other side of the mirror. *Hey, buddy. Hold on, I'm here.* But when I hugged Kate, her arms hung loose on both sides of her body. Her hands were loose, and her fingers—it was as if all the tendons had been cut, and she couldn't make a fist anymore.

*A great early spring squall struck the Narragansett val-
ley, and Paul Revere, the Last Indian, and Sarah Beckingworth took cover under a canopy of trees. The rain turned
to snow, and one of the trees (a deciduous tree; a maple)
broke under the weight of the copious spring snow, and a
large branch struck Paul Revere in the head. He was felled
(for the time being).*

*The Last Indian and Sarah Beckingworth looked at
each other. What should we do? it was as if they said, for
they suddenly realized they were in this together. And this
is when the Last Indian said to Sarah, "Sarah, I, too, need
to bury my parents." Sarah looked at the Last Indian and
then looked back at Paul Revere. And the Last Indian said
to her, "I am, as it were, just starting out in life. I merely
want to make something of myself. Why don't you just call
me Sam?"*

*Sarah Beckingworth peered into the dark, glittering
eyes of the man before her, nearly naked in the snowy
dawn.*

Chapter Eighteen

"CLASS, CLASS, class. . . . *Class, class, class,*" said Mr. Bostitch, hands clasped behind him, pacing between his desk and the door.

"One week from today, we shall witness the culmination of the Of Many Nations, into Jubilant Unity project. Think of it. All the work, all the planning. And what, may I ask, was it all for?"

"Party time, friends and countrymen!" said Bruce Johnson.

"Let's try this again. Two hundred years, one nation. Does anyone get it? *Does anyone get what I'm talking about?*"

Mr. Bostitch looked hopeful, eager.

Priscilla said, "Get what?"

He sighed. In a quieter voice, he said, "What has been the *cost*—and what has been the benefit?"

I glanced over at Kate. Would she say something smart, something snappy? She was wearing a white short-sleeved shirt with two Chanel C's interlocking on the front. She gazed ahead, quiet. It had been two weeks since Peach had been shot.

Mr. Bostitch rubbed his forehead. "We have an obligation to the past, you see, but it, too, can tell us things. It's a relationship, a give-and-take, alive like anything else. Does that make any sense?"

He sat on his desk and peered around the room. *Did* any of us know what he was talking about? We wanted to rescue him from his sadness but could not.

"I understand," said someone.

Mr. Bostitch turned his head toward her, gentle student. Did she mean it? Could we possibly understand? No, it couldn't quite be true, after all. He gave us a wan smile. Class was over.

"Kate," I said, catching up to her. She'd started down the hall without me.

"Yeah?"

"I thought you might want to come over this afternoon to work on the cover. We could use my mom's fancy watercolors and—"

"I can't."

"Okay, well, maybe tomorrow, then? If we get it to him by Thursday, that would still probably be all right."

"I can't do it tomorrow, either, Alison. Why don't you just do it? You're the better artist anyway."

She was there, in front of me, but I was missing her—missing something. She wasn't listening to me, or she was pretending that she didn't understand. And I consoled myself later for not grabbing her and making her come my way—come have a Winston, come create lost heroines—by imagining that I was respecting her privacy, her sadness.

Kate turned her skeptical gray eyes down to the floor, scuffed from a stampede of children, and hesitated for about a millisecond. Then she turned and began to walk away. Her white T-shirt fit close, and it made her body look thin and small. Her hair was pulled back into a long ponytail, last summer's blond still bright at the ends.

"Kate?"

"What?"

"I'll do it, and then I'll show it to you before I hand it in, okay?"

"Okay," she said, her voice a singsong, a small clear bell on a spring day.

Mom had ended up calling the police the day Peach was shot, and they'd told her that since the horse was Mr. Hamilton's property, he could, under certain circumstances, do anything he wanted with it. Of course, *cruelty* was always an issue, a misdemeanor or sometimes worse. But apparently (because the police did come by, finally; in Weston there's not a heck of a lot to do on any given day) the horse hadn't particularly *suffered,* she'd merely died. Tut told the police that Peach had been sick, incurable, and that he'd wanted to spare his daughter the agony of seeing her decline in health. I suppose an enterprising law enforcement officer would have asked for a veterinarian's verification of this. I have a vision of Tut patting the cop on the back, handing him a little something—but of course I'm not the shaman around here. I can't see through walls or down long suburban streets or into the past.

The morning it happened, I could hold her. I could help

Kate in this small way. But then I went home and she stayed. It was her family, after all. Her father.

For a while I avoided Jazz completely. I didn't ride. I didn't hang out at the fence. When I fed him, I kept my eyes down, letting the water stream in the bucket, listening to that sound and the crunch and grind as he ate his sweet feed. He ate as if nothing were wrong. But I held my breath, as though I were preparing for a long swim. I tensed up the muscles in my body, the way you do to theoretically stay warm.

Sometimes it hit me, what Tut had done, and it was as if some kind of vortex opened up in my vision. Most of the time I didn't believe it, didn't believe the eight-hundred-pound corpse I'd seen with my own eyes, even though you'd think a physical thing like that, a reality, is something you'd have to believe in.

In the last two weeks, Kate had become remarkably well groomed. She'd begun to put a lot of effort into wearing the right makeup and jewelry. And her father had given her a new Louis Vuitton purse and wallet. His way of saying he was sorry, perhaps. *Sorry I shot your horse!*

She was still with me, still open to the consolation of friendship, two days after it happened, when we walked together to the mansion after school. We knelt in the courtyard, past the fountain with the broken Cupid in it. She took out an envelope with a lock of Peach's mane—one cut piece, long as a beautiful girl's—and we placed it at the base of a mulberry bush and said a prayer together, first her soft voice and then mine. The strands of the gray-black mane were curled loosely together into a kind of braid, a soft curl, and the hair looked strong, out of place, tremulous, lying on the cool, moist earth. We'd pushed away the leaves to give it a place, a small grave with no stone and almost no witnesses—but two witnesses just the same.

Eventually I did ride again. At first I rode alone in my paddock, circling and circling and circling back around.

All through childhood and even later, home from college, I loved to linger by my mother's jewelry box—picking up things, mauling them, messing up her systems of organization, making the collection of gnarled, broken, fantastic, mysterious, blackened, repaired, glinting objects my own.

Some of the rings and chains had belonged to my grandmother. I imagined they'd been sent to Mom by her father after his wife's death, that black hole, that stiff safety pin pinching his grief to her own. He *did* like to send things. This might have been the one trait he and my father's mother had in common: the U.S. Postal Service was there for a reason. Bar none, best method of communication.

We'd all have forgiven Grandpa if it was true that he, by some strange jerk of the hand, had nicked the lining of his wife's gallbladder in surgery, had somehow let in the foul world. But we didn't talk about it, so there was never that chance to move on with things. Now he was beginning to put his slippers in the toaster. It wasn't too late to reach him yet, but it would be soon.

On the other hand, Mom wasn't in a "reaching out" mood. I'll never know quite how fucked-up my parents felt in the spring of 1976, but I do know that my mother seemed to take the loss of Peach about as hard as anyone.

She'd taken to lying in her bed, under the pink coverlet, and staring up at the ceiling.

"What are you doing, Mom?" I'd ask.

"Nothing. Just thinking."

"What are you thinking about, then?"

She'd just gotten separated, her father's mental health was in jeopardy, and the man she'd had a love affair with—a pivotal, marriage-destroying affair—was capable, in a drugged and rageful fugue, of shooting his daughter's horse. With luck, her mind was a blank.

"Oh, nothing."

I was standing by her dresser, by the jewelry box—fingering things. Affair or not, we were still linked. It was in the blood.

"Can I borrow this necklace?"

"What necklace?"

"The one with the lady on it."

She lifted her head to look. "Okay. Just don't lose it."

I held the cameo in my palm, tilting it to one side, watching the design change. "Was this Gram's?"

"Yes."

"But you never wear it."

She remained still, eyes up to the ceiling. Finally she said, "It just isn't my style, Alison."

"Well, you should wear it. To remember her and everything."

She curled into herself then. "I feel ill. Maybe I'm going to have a nervous breakdown."

"Don't, okay?" I said crisply, like a nurse in a war zone.

This is what she mumbled into her pillow: "The life of an artist was never an easy one."

I shrugged. I laid the pendant down.

Many years later, I remembered Peach. Neal and I were meeting at a bar in the Foothills after work, and it was the night he'd propose to me for the first time. I had a dead horse on my hands—not so unusual, but that day I couldn't get rid of the smell, even after five frantic Lady Macbeth minutes at the sink. I could smell him in the open air. I could smell him at the bar.

He was an eight-year-old gelding, no good reason to die. Except he had acute laminitis and would waste away in a gruesome fashion if we didn't do what we call "the right thing." This time the mother had brought the girl—his rightful owner. Panda stood with his head down, like America had just been lost, our little version of "The End of the Trail." America *had* been lost, that was the thing. The mother was far away, as if she were in a suitcase. I explained the prognosis: The damage had been done. Her daughter was in the waiting room. It was time to tell her.

The kid was wearing a little jean jacket with appliquéd red roses and vines. She clutched a bottle of Absorbine hoof treatment—she'd have a chance to use it if I helped her horse get better.

I stood there and lost all my nerve. Even as I approached her, wading across the linoleum, ten miles to go, all I could think of was Kate—of course, Kate—and the fact that here was another horse I couldn't save, here was another girl lost in the landscape.

The girl turned to me. "Hello, Dr. Glass?" she said as professionally as possible. Her eyes were little steely knits of pain. She knew what I was going to say.

At the bar that night, Neal stared at the menu. "Thirty dollars for a shot?" he was saying. "If I was having a thirty-dollar shot of tequila, I'd do it in Mexico."

People stick around for a cat's euthanasia, but not always so with a horse. I'd just as soon spare them the experience anyway, the loss of a brilliant friend. But that day, the girl stayed and watched it all.

"A hoity-toity place like this, though, do you know how little of that thirty bucks goes back to the Mexican workers? Harvesting the agave? Not that we care so much on a Friday."

I put my face in my hands.

"It's okay, the workers probably get a little something, Alison," Neal said then. He knew about the horse; I'd told him over the phone. He put his hand on my arm. "Hey, listen."

"I know."

"You did all you could, Alison. You couldn't save him."

I went to the bathroom to wash my face, again. When I got back, sixty dollars' worth of booze was lined up on the bar, two shots.

"We'll toast the girl," Neal said. "We'll toast the horse and the girl."

Tequila has a smell to it, like a shooting star.

My dad drove me to my doctor's appointment in Boston. "Don't lose this," Mom had told me, again, pressing the manila folder into my hands that morning. In the new division of labor system, it was Dad's turn to drive me to see Dr. Lyon. The folder was filled with handouts, scrawled useless directions to two doctors and one brace maker, and a worn-out sheet of paper with the dates of all the X-rays I'd ever had and the degrees of the curves.

I was still not used to my father sitting in his car in the driveway, rumbling away, only a slice of his body visible from the window. He seemed too much like a deliveryman at the wrong address or some kind of evangelical stranger with many a door slam to his name.

The only time he'd actually come in the house since the separation was the day Peach was shot. I don't even know how he found out—Mom must have called him—but all of a sudden there he was, at the door of my bedroom.

He'd given consoling me a fair shot, but I could tell by the look in his eyes that he didn't know what he was saying. He was just as blown away as I was by the event. Later, my parents talked furtively and for a long time down on the front step. The shooting of a horse rubbed both poets and artists the wrong way, it seemed, even if they had rubbed each other the wrong way in the first place.

On the way to Boston, I slept for the first half of the trip, but for the last bit I was awake. I read the map. We didn't get lost this time! The first miracle of the day.

We stood in front of the receptionist in the orthopedics department and stared at her as she shuffled papers. This person, that person. Broken bones, twisting spines, feet that looked like hammers. When it was time to get the X-ray, she handed us a yellow slip and I put on my hospital frock and shuffled down the hall. Stood in front of the cold plate. Smiled.

We went to the exam room to wait. I sat on the table. My

brace was on the chair, and my dad stood next to the window and stared out at the trapped world.

After a while the door rattled and there he was, the man with the answers. He had quite an amazing tan.

"Ladies and gentlemen," Dr. Lyon said, and shook our hands. He snapped the X-ray into the light box and took the measurements. He was whistling. He seemed to be in an especially good mood. Why? Had he had a good breakfast? Had he won the lottery? Was he just back from a beach vacation?

"Hm," the doctor said.

"What?" my father said, suspicious.

"Well, this looks promising."

Dad bought me an absurd purple bear in the hospital gift shop. He laughed a bit maniacally, as he had the day he'd composed, on the fly, his tomato poem. (All his tomato plants had died in the wake of his departure, though we had watered them for a time.) He ran his fingers through his hair and pawed at his beard as if it were a Halloween getup, itching his skin. He laughed again, in the car, and that was when I saw he wasn't actually laughing. I'd never seen him cry before then.

For me, it didn't really kick in until the next morning. I undid the screw behind my neck, slipped open the strap holding the leather-and-plastic girdle in place, and lifted the brace from my body.

The degrees of my curves had, for the first time since the onset of the scoliosis, actually *improved,* however slightly, in the past two months.

For some reason—whether it was circumstance (the end of my growth spurt, the mercurial nature of the human organism), determination (dogged, irritating, but perhaps helpful yoga; swimming), a last-ditch victory for structures made of steel and leather, or a gift coming by way of the Furtherton sisters, the manifestation of wishing, good luck, and prayer— the course of my scoliosis had, at least temporarily, reversed. We'd have to keep an eye on it in the next few months, Dr. Lyon had said, but we might well be out of the woods, no hunchback situation having occurred just yet. No danger to my internal organs. There was a strong possibility—a *probability,* he'd called it—that I'd stabilized. While he did not expect my back to become straight per se, there was no reason that I couldn't live this way, with a curved back, in peace— like any imperfect but plausible thing, a tree growing around a telephone wire.

I had to come back for another X-ray in the fall, but for now I could take off the brace for eight hours a day.

That first morning afterward, I wore jeans and the tightest T-shirt I could find in my dresser. When I walked in the front door to school, I thought: This is it, just like in "Cinderella."

At first nobody seemed to notice the sea change. Dave Darbis passed me with the same look of hollow hostility as usual. But then I did notice Lisa, Lynn, and Priscilla arch their eyebrows, and I could see appraisal in their expressions: a new, more thorough scrutiny. Mr. Bostitch said, "Well, Miss Glass, don't you look especially, um, pretty this morning."

Still, it was different from what I'd imagined, this dream day. I could feel the clothes against my body, tickling me. I moved slowly, almost on tiptoe. Was this how I'd always feel, so small and weightless, almost as if I could fly? I'm normal, I said to myself, walking down the hall, not sure even if regular gravity applied to me. I tried out other words: I've got a curved spine, and I'm beautiful.

No one heard me, but that was okay.

"Sam," she said to the Last Indian, "what's that on the horizon?"

"Sarah, darling, I believe that is smoke."

Sarah and Sam stopped short at the edge of the clearing. It was the shack, her childhood home, engulfed in the most horrible flames.

And oddly enough, it was the Town Fathers in their white wigs standing by the fire, flinging papers in, and alongside them were some Indian henchmen (Sam's other-side-of-the-tracks second cousins) and also that pesky British foot soldier. Using her pocket telescope, Sarah Beckingworth noted that the papers were those of her father and that they bespoke such things as Liberty, Independence, and the Rebel Cause. Oh, what did she know—what had she known—about the chancy lives of the adults in Wistin? Apparently her father had been a Rebel of the first order, and now even his papers were being cast to the flame by the Town Fathers, Loyalists all.

Sarah felt strange misgivings. She remembered the dream she'd had the night before, the dream of Sam. While she was sleeping, Sam had gathered up the small beautiful flowers of spring. He'd laid the garland at her feet, and when she woke he asked if she would marry him. She said yes, and then she wept. For she felt, after all, that she was to blame for her parents' death. Why didn't she warn them from behind the curtain?

Even now she can remember standing next to her mother in the field. Compared to the Paleozoic rock, they were virtually the same age. The fact is, there were many things she'd exchange, if it meant they could be together one more time.

The mica under Sarah's feet felt real enough as she stood before the burning building. The heat seemed to melt away all hope, all consolation.

———⌒———

Chapter Nineteen

IT WAS a beautiful day for a jubilee—May 29, 1976. Twenty-three days after Kate's fourteenth birthday, sixteen days before my fourteenth birthday, and approximately two hundred years after "Wistin" became a township. Back in the old days it was a heathen wilderness, and then it was a territory, and then a little kingly outpost, but here we were in 1976, flush with progress, and it was our town now.

On the way to the jubilee, I watched the side of the road, squinting my eyes and waiting for the orange. It was the beginning of tiger lily season, and they grew in patches all over, little outposts of gangly green stalks, violent orange. The car rushed by. Fence, mailbox, dirt, grass—then the profusion of color, and then again it was gone. Sometimes just a few, sometimes a great wild garden.

My mother, driving, was not wearing her standard Women of History clothing: She had on her bohemian wear. Had she forgotten which costume matched the occasion, or was this a conscious decision to be a more unified person? Whichever, she had recovered, or so it seemed, from her interlude beneath the pink coverlet. When I'd come home from the doctor's appointment and told her the news, she'd sat right up, and the amazing thing about it was that she really didn't make much of it at all—her role, the fact that if she hadn't followed every cockamamie wacko scheme that came down the pike we might never have even met the Furthertons, I wouldn't have done any yoga, and it was more than likely we would have simply followed the traditional medical route, yielding finally to the surgeon. I don't know if she was a totally bona fide New Ager or if she was simply scared witless of the knife that had killed her mother—just like I'll never know what my back would have done without faith healing, or without a brace, for that matter. I do know that Mom hugged me that day, and seemed quietly happy, and began to get out of bed more.

Was my back really getting better, had healing occurred? When we'd gone to our next appointment with the Furthertons, Emma had winked at me and said, "See? Told ya," and pulled her Scandi-design braids in an exuberant, We Shall Overcome gesture. Mae only smiled at the rug. I felt strangely guilty that time, accepting the warm, light touch of her small hands. I didn't believe, not wholeheartedly, before.

Would this be the right time to mention what happened to them, the women who bought us time, supported our perseverance in the face of a threatening doctor, a daunting medical condition? Would it be the right time to mention that these women—apparently renegades, with nothing to gain from their work except the satisfaction that they were, as Emma had put it, doing what God had told them to do—later joined a very rigid, very conservative Christian ministry and decried all their earlier work? Does knowing this, the zigzag nature of their interpretation of God, alter the value of what they gave us back then, faith, at least—and maybe more, maybe even a physical demonstration of the power of love?

I was still practicing a new normal/beautiful walk whenever I went down the school hall. But normal/beautiful was getting normal already, and in the car on the way to the jubilee, I didn't feel the pleasure of the soft clothes on my skin, didn't feel the car seat. Something else was wrong.

That morning, Shana had called. Kate was missing. Apparently, she'd been out all night. They had no idea where she was.

It was like the situation with Mick, only different.

Different because I was having trouble breathing. I was overreacting in my brain. She and Vicki had probably been out partying, I thought. They'd probably gone off to Harry's House of Morons in Westport. It wasn't the first time Kate had stayed out all night—of course, this time she didn't have a horse, so it wasn't a camping adventure, and she didn't have me with her, so whatever she was doing couldn't be all that great, couldn't be all that much fun. So I told myself, shivering in the new midriff-exposing blouse I'd bought at the Selective Eye.

Cars were lined up along the road long before we got to the Grange. I was scheduled to roll cotton candy from two to four. Before then, I was free to sample apple butter, get my handwriting analyzed, look at watercolors of native plants, track the military maneuverings of the Revolutionary War in Connecticut (dioramas put together by a retired World War II admiral who lived on Kettle Creek), get a copy of *Pyramid Love* signed by the man who would be there, after all, despite my mother's frenzied calls to Grete—betrayal of her Egyptian.

When we arrived, Mrs. Feneta came running down the driveway and seized my mother's arm. "Clare, darling, the Porta Pottis. We've got to decorate them."

"Decorate the Porta Pottis?" Mom still looked a little fragile, then.

"Can you help? We've got sprays of meadow grass and asters from Sally's garden—"

My mother looked at me. "Alison, can you hold these? I'll meet you later by the concessions."

When she passed me the pile of flyers, her hands were shaking. Had she ever shaken like this before? I didn't remember ever seeing any such thing. She turned and followed Mrs. Feneta, who kept going topsy-turvy in her cream-colored heels on the gravel drive.

I walked over to the Of Many Nations, into Jubilant Unity tent.

Brian Nordstrom and Jeff Neely's diorama of the 1777 British invasion of Compo Beach, little plastic green men landed on a sandpaper shore, was the central exhibit. Our classmate Shannon's Declaration of Independence, the photocopied version, had been attached to poster board, and all around it she'd glued magazine cutouts of things American: toasters, Cadillacs, golden retriever puppies, flags, bottles of Coke. Someone else had made a time line showing her family's origins in Germany, with a little bottle marked *XXX* depicting a schnapps factory, and then a tiny toy boat for arrival at Ellis Island, and then a black clump of something—plastic? a Brillo pad?—to symbolize her father's job as a salesman of machine parts. Some boy I didn't even know was apparently a kind of architectural engineering genius, based on his elaborate model battleship. His father had come here from Italy at fourteen, then lied about his age to enlist.

It wasn't as flashy as some of the others, our brown journal tied with baling string, though I had glued a small piece of cardboard on the front for the title and drawn flourishes on the first and last letters of each word.

The Chronicle of the Lost Heroine

∽ By Anonymous ∾

Circa 1776

"Here it is," said my father, putting his arm around my shoulder.

I looked up. "Oh, hi, Dad. Thanks for coming."

"I'd never miss this, Allie. You should know that."

The jubilee seemed as good a place as any to wait for Kate, to expect her to show up. She knew it was taking place. Of course she did. It was the birth of the lost heroine, her entrée into polite society, her opening night. Even if Kate had left most of the final touches to me in the last couple of weeks—extenuating circumstances, anyone could understand that—we'd done it together, a little of this story, a little of that, and it had weaved in and out of our friendship from the start.

"May I look?" said Dad.

I said yes, and he picked up our book and opened it to the first page, written by Kate.

Once upon a time there was a girl who lived in a small shack made from oak and maple trees, quite plentiful in Connecticut.

I held my hands tightly behind my back as Dad read about horses, vague countrymen. He turned the page. On the draft, Mr. Bostitch had written, "Which Indians? Specify tribe." Well, the Paugussetts, of course, but if I kept forgetting who they were—if all I had was a name—could they be made real like that? It almost seemed worse to use the name with nothing underneath, like a patch. Dad got to the death of Sarah Beckingworth's parents—I'd been a little worried about this part. Mr. Bostitch had written on the margin here, too. The murder was overkill: Might the villains simply *wound* the parents? My father kept reading, flipped forward to the end.

Even now she can remember standing next to her mother in the field. Compared to the Paleozoic rock, they were virtually the same age. The fact is, there were many things she'd exchange, if it meant they could be together one more time.

Dad stopped here. He kept looking down, but I could tell he wasn't reading. His nose started twitching. He put down the book and blew into a handkerchief, then he picked it up again.

"This is good stuff, Alison."

"Thanks, Dad."

"Your grandmother would like to see this," he said, looking down at me from above his reading glasses, and it was then I realized there was alcohol on his breath—mouthwash or jubilee gin?

"Really?"

"Yes."

I looked over his shoulder doubtfully. I'd thought the book was incendiary, revolutionary, certainly too much for a grandmother-type person.

Out of the corner of my eye, I saw something: a crow, a black umbrella. It was Warren Lipp, the photographer. He was squatting in his black trench coat, taking a picture of us.

"Oh," I said. "It's Warren Lipp."

"Is your project here, Alison Glass?" Warren looked at me, then my father.

"Yes—we're looking at it."

My father was clutching *The Chronicle of the Lost Heroine* to his chest, as if he were not going to let go in his lifetime. "And you are . . . ?"

"Dad, this is Warren Lipp. He takes pictures for the *Weston Forum*."

"That's my name, that's my game."

"How do you know my daughter?"

Warren looked at me and gave a slow, Grinch-like smile. "Well, Mr., Mr. Glass? We met on the rocks, by a river."

I thought my father was going to have a panic attack. I could sense, as all daughters can, that his rage button had been pushed.

I tried to explain. "Yes, we met at Devil's Glen when I went there with Kate once—"

"Can I see the book, Mr. Glass?"

"No, you can't," my father snapped.

"Right. Okay, then. Well, nice to meet you, Mr. Glass. Nice to see you again, Alison Glass. But Alison, where is your friend?"

"I don't know," I said. *I just don't know, Warren.*

He walked away, heaving his tripod over his shoulder, a caught animal from technology land.

Dad turned to me. "Who the hell was that?"

"Just this guy we met."

"He's an adult, Alison. You shouldn't have adult friends."

"What's wrong with adults?"

Dad pulled out his handkerchief and blew his nose again. "What's wrong with adults? Everything."

"He just asked us some questions," I said, suddenly feeling exhausted.

"What kinds of questions?"

"We just talked about the river, and kids and their parents."

My father shook his head. "Are you hungry at all? Can I get you something to eat? Someone said the squash-and-persimmon-seed pancakes are excellent."

"No thanks. I'm going to wait for Kate."

"All right," he said, and gave me a foul look, the scowl of love.

I walked around by myself awhile after using the Porta Potti—a well-decorated one.

Where was she? The last time I'd seen her was Thursday; we'd walked home from school together. It was a warm and fragrant day, and birds were singing as we made our way across the school field and then hopped the stone wall and walked over to the mansion and through the grounds, past the courtyard with Peach's makeshift memorial. I was very much feeling that I was no longer "the girl with the brace." Now I could be of greater help to Kate—greater help to anyone! I had the currency of my own skin, my own body. I had the means to be a champion adventuring freshman the next year, to crash high school parties all summer, to forge a life for Kate and myself outside of the Egyptian empire. I would survive; we would survive together.

But Kate was quiet again that afternoon. After Peach's death, she was sometimes like that. Either quiet or supersarcastic—she could come up with the funniest meanest things you'd ever want to hear.

I suppose it can get to you, the smell of smoke and pistachios and leather, the sound of the Mercedes purring up the gravel one more time, the filet mignons in the oven, the ceaseless herd of dogs scrambling around the glossy wooden floors as if nothing had ever happened. You might find that you're feeling things by proxy—that the sound of the gunshot is everywhere. Even in the wand of your mascara. Even in your clothes folded in the drawer.

"Hey, Kate," I said when we were near the mansion, "I'm thinking about a second volume of adventures for Sarah. New York City this time."

"Good. Maybe she'll like it there. She can jump off the Empire State Building and into the sea."

"Well, the Empire State Building is inland, I believe. There are only sidewalks and hot dog vendors underneath."

"So she'll fly out. That's not so hard."

She was looking ahead. Her hair was down that day. Long brown hair on a girl—this is a classic thing. Her eyebrows had begun to come back after the terrible plucking in the wake of her mother's laundry-flinging episode. She wore Bonne Belle lip gloss, the same kind as me.

"We can call it *The Lost Heroine Grows Wings*. Maybe, what, around 1804?"

"Right," she said, but she didn't sound all that interested. "The whole thing's getting a little boring, don't you think? It's kind of a kid thing, anyway."

Now that we didn't go riding anymore, and now that I didn't really like hanging out at her house—now that I hated it there—we hadn't developed much of a routine for after school. We did go to the Center together a couple of times. We hung out at the mansion once. We went to Vicki's once.

When we reached the road, we stopped and looked at each other. Our hands were in our pockets, and the afternoon was wide with possibility.

"Welp?" she said. It was a question that seemed like an answer. We weren't seeing eye to eye.

I let her go. She hitchhiked back to her house, and I walked back to Ramble Lane, a little pissed at her.

At the jubilee, Mrs. Hollbrook was in the Grange proper, giving a slide show on flag making. She was standing on a wooden crate and holding a pointer, speaking enthusiastically about star patterns to an audience of ten or twelve. What was she going to do after this? I wondered. This had to be the pinnacle of her patriot career. Mom and Lucille Bix were handing out sheets of music from back when they used buckets and string to accompany Christmas carols, and over by the pond kids were getting pony rides. The Shetlands all looked as if they'd taken growth-stunting medicine, and their fur was dull and rough.

I walked away from them, the image of Peach's body a blank spot in the sky.

I lingered at the silent auction table, not because I was interested in bidding on the pair of prints depicting the Boston Tea Party, but because from there I could see the high schoolers doing gymnastics under a huge oak tree. They did slow, lazy cartwheels (even a cartwheel, even a decent somersault, was beyond me), and then they started on their back bends. First the girl in red shorts arched her spine back and dropped her head, her long hair falling down. She curved into a hump and started walking like this, upside down on her hands and feet. The other girl did it, too: dropped down, found her balance. Her shirt rode up, exposing her stomach and hip bones.

People kept bumping into me. The event was pretty crowded, considering there were no rides other than the midget ponies and that the inauspicious theme was history.

"Where's Kate?" said Tut Hamilton, immediately in front of me on the green, green lawn. He was wearing sunglasses, black against his white forehead. His temples were pulsing, squeezing in and out as he did something with his teeth.

"I don't know where she is, Mr. Hamilton," I said. Carefully.

"She's supposed to help me sell books. She signed on to be my marketing assistant today. But she's not here—she fucking disappeared. You know where she is, don't you, Alison? C'mon, don't be a little weasel."

He stood in front of me, large as a flag, blocking the door to the rest of the world.

Weasel. The Hamiltons always said things like that. And usually I'd freeze, a weasel in the headlights. I could imagine all the ways I was weasel-like.

"I don't want to talk to you," I said. "Go away."

"*Ho-ho!* Look who's got an attitude now," he said, and for a moment a person could have mistaken the sound in his voice as delight: *Look, an adversary.* But then Tut took off his sunglasses and looked me in the eyes. "Well, Alison, you better tell me in the very near future, because that girl's going to be in a holy hell of a lot of trouble if she doesn't show up soon."

That was when my father appeared—huge, like he'd puffed up his beard with hair spray and spread his poet's arms as far as they could reach to save the day.

"Get away from my daughter," Dad said, shoving Tut in the chest. The sham shaman stumbled back. His sunglasses fell out of his hand. My dad lunged and shoved him again, wrangling him until somehow he'd knocked the bald man down onto the Grange lawn.

"You—freak!" my father stuttered, apparently tongue-tied, unable to find the right word. "You freak—you—pony killer!"

There was a strange look on Tut's face then, confusion and then a sort of pale, expansive terror. Until that moment he'd kept his bravado, a bit of his charisma, even as he'd been toppled to the ground.

"What the hell?" Tut shouted finally. "Are you crazy?"

My father was still hovering over him, a bearded samurai. He suddenly looked uncertain.

I'd never seen my father like this in all my life—never had he beat up anybody, never had his poet's hand touched someone else in anger, that I had known.

Now Tut sprang back up and swiped dirt from his ivory sleeves. "You knocked me down! You knocked me down!"

"I did, and I'd do it again," my father countered. "You stay the hell away—from everyone. Don't you have any sense of—of fucking shame?"

Tut Hamilton was not listening. He was looking around, trapping onlookers with his eyes, looking for witnesses to the affront. "Did you see that? This crazy man knocked me over. He came up from behind and knocked me right down!" His voice was high and frightened sounding.

"C'mon, Alison," Dad said, taking me by the arm.

On Sunday I called over to the Hamiltons' in the morning. Shana answered on the first ring.

"Hello?" she said, sounding as though I'd woken her from a trance in which she was a wife and mother.

"Hi, Mrs. Hamilton. Is Kate home yet?"

"Oh, Allie, no. She hasn't called you? We haven't seen her since Friday now, and we're worried sick. I just don't understand. Is it because of the horse? Do you think that's it?" She'd started whispering. "Because I think maybe Tut overreacted on that one."

I studied the white plastic pen-and-pad holder glued by the phone.

"Okay, thanks," I said. "Just have her call me, all right? When she gets home."

It was a strange, still morning. I went out to the barn, slipped a halter on Jazz, and led him through the gate, out of the paddock. I clipped the ropes to his halter, and he stood between the barn and the tree, ears up as he tracked a squirrel's progress. I opened the lid to the tack box, pulled out the brush and currycomb.

I scrubbed softly at the dried mud patches on his withers, on his rump. I brushed his black coat, sleeker now and shedding in the warmth, holding the brush with two hands, then just one, then running my bare hand over the currents of color, invisible to almost everyone. And then I laid my head down in the soft embrace of his back.

"Sarah," said Sam.

She turned. It had been a bad day. And besides, where had Paul Revere gone? And what would happen with the Revolution?

"The men who killed your parents will be brought to justice," he said. "What say we ride, you and I, into the sunset, into another and a more glorious time?"

The lost heroine looked down at her hands and then up again, past the charred remains of the shack. She had no more gruel, no more persimmon, no more ideas of any kind.

There was only one thing to do. Put one strange black boot in front of the other, there in the Narragansett region, a place of silt and stony soil and crops of some berries but mostly corn.

Chapter Twenty

WARREN LIPP found her.

He had gone to the river. Why hadn't anyone else seen her? Maybe it had just happened. Maybe the body had slipped down, slipped into the crevice between two boulders. Then she had been lifted up with water hands, *here*.

From the look of things, it had been at least twenty-four hours, according to Shana Hamilton, who called my mother.

Mom ran from the house to the barn—again. She ran like a car careening into a ditch or a bat flying without radar. She gripped my arms, held me hard, hard as someone banging her head against the wall, and she seemed to look up at the sky first, as if she could find some shift, some answer in the fat clouds that covered half the town, and then she looked back down at me and told me that Kate had drowned.

Based on the condition of the body, they determined it had happened Friday night or early Saturday morning. The police conjectured that she had jumped off the daredevil rocks at Devil's Glen and gone too far out or maybe not far enough— maybe she'd slipped as she was jumping and hit something on the way down. Anyway, she hit her head, blacked out, and opened her mouth.

No, there had been no suicide note.

This is the place I'd like to leave white, empty, and very quiet. Mostly that mirrors my consciousness anyway. The aperture had widened so far, everything was bleached out, blank. I guess you could say I'd had a premonition, a sense that something was very wrong. But no, I didn't think it would end this way.

Can we skip over the funeral, too? A church full of eighth-graders. A new dress, a white box. *Kate isn't in there.* That's all I could think to say.

Peach kept coming back to me in a half dream. She'd be running—running beside me. Her mane long in the wind, her barrel belly full of sweet feed.

My dad moved back in with Mom temporarily. Both of them lurked in corners of the house for days, putting down their newspapers when I came in the room, smiling encouragingly. Dad put a new hook up in the bathroom for my mother. He didn't meditate, Mom didn't paint, I didn't go to school. I'd told my parents I didn't want to go, and they'd tripped over themselves saying, "Sure, okay, of course."

Someone came and brought the lost heroine journal back to me. The Women of History dropped off some cobbler left over from the jubilee.

I'd felt lighter without my brace: a light, new person at school, a person with a future. But now I was too light. I could float away into another place, but then someone would swing a machete; I felt everything, I could hardly breathe.

The worst have been the futures; I've thought of so many of them. She could have been a total pothead and lost all her ambition; she could have been a waitress; she could have been a famous poet, writing in fractured sentences *love you I* about fractured life; she could have been a mother, she could have fallen in love with someone—maybe a charlatan, a bogus man, or maybe someone different; she could have killed herself in some elegant way, later on; she could have lost herself little by little, like a bloodletting; she could have loved children, loved animals, been a veterinarian, too; she could have been a Greek tragedy; she could have been a statistic, a newspaper story, a victim. She could have been the president. She could have been anyone.

And then she started coming to me. She came to me the night I miscarried the child I might have had with the Italian waiter—late term, I'd known already what her name would be. And then she came to me the day of my wedding. It was in the yard, after the ceremony. All of a sudden there she was, out with the chollas and the saguaros and the paloverde and the mesquites. A girl—she looked older than Kate had been when she'd died, as if she'd grown up a little, maybe she was eighteen—standing out in the desert in a yellow dress, looking away from me. It was six o'clock, and I was filled with plenty of wedding champagne, because I felt good about this, I had finally let Neal love me. But now I felt as sober as a person might feel on her first birthday. It was Kate. She was looking at something out there, and then I saw what it was. Kate Hamilton saw a javelina. Now she was squatting, putting out her hand. Now she was offering the beast a little tidbit, I couldn't see what from here—tiny toast and marmalade. Then the woman in the yellow dress stood up again and looked, as if I'd called her name, toward me.

I left my house the Sunday after the funeral, holding on to the screen door so it wouldn't slam. I walked down Ramble Lane and crossed to the other side of Steep Hill. The first car stopped, and as soon as I opened the door the woman inside leaned over and started chastising me for hitchhiking. Turned out she was a teacher from the elementary school. The floor of her car was littered with loose crayons and faded-out construction-paper cutouts. She was nice enough, though. She drove me all the way.

I stood at the top of their driveway for a moment, and then I walked toward the house, the gravel crunching loudly under my feet, and there was also the thick hum of a zillion crickets, or it might have been the gypsy moths—they'd come early that year, it was all over the *Weston Forum*. One morning we'd wake up and all the leaves in Weston would be gone. It would be a town of stick figures and skeletons: happened once every seven years, the article said, with an accompanying photograph of a dead tree.

It was quiet when I opened the door—no dogs came. I smelled it all, leather and pistachios and tobacco and money, and then the smell disappeared. I walked into the living room. The cocktail table in front of the couch was clean, except for one ashtray with a couple of butts in it. I didn't know why I was there. I was sleepwalking.

Mick was in the kitchen. He looked up at me from what he was doing: nothing.

"You're here," I said.

"Yes." His hair was wet, and he was wearing a red T-shirt. I squinted at him. It felt like I hadn't seen him in twenty years.

"Where are your parents?"

"They went to church," he said hollowly.

"Church?" I said.

"Yeah."

The phone started ringing. It rang eight times, and then whoever it was hung up.

Mick had Kate's eyebrows, arched and bunched up this funny way.

"It's so quiet here," I said, sick to my stomach.

"The dogs got out."

Mick looked over to the backyard then, and so did I. There they were, a few of them anyway, rushing around, sniffing, shitting, eating worms. They were drunk on chaos, spinning out and frayed at the edges. Behind them stood the empty barn.

"Hey, I wanted to show you something," he said to me.

I followed Mick down the hall, past Kate's room and his room, to his parents' suite. He stopped at the bathroom and turned on the fake torches that served as lighting. They had two sinks, Shana and Tut did, and a Jacuzzi tub, and gold handles and gold faucets on everything. Mick opened a cabinet door. No room for calamine lotion or Band-Aids here: The shelves were lined with prescription bottles, some upright, some toppled over. This wasn't a big surprise; the Hamiltons probably had illnesses of many kinds.

He picked up a bottle and unscrewed it, then spilled green-and-yellow capsules into his hand. "Look," he said, his palm slick with perspiration. He poured those back and put the bottle on the counter and found another to open. Spilled out a litter of blue ones. He picked one out, popped it in his mouth, and put the rest back in the bottle.

"Anyway," he said, slamming the mirror shut and turning abruptly, "that's not what I wanted to show you. It's just a stash of mine."

I followed him into the bedroom, past the king-size bed and its black pillows. He rummaged around on top of a dresser until he found a small yellow box.

"So I gave this to Mom for Mother's Day, and she hasn't worn it yet. You're a girl—was it a stupid gift?"

Mick opened the box. Inside was a small watch with a yellow-and-pink flowered band.

"See, it's still in the plastic," he said, his voice fragmented.

We stared at the little daisy inside the crystal, telling time.

"It's really nice," I said at last. "Maybe she just forgot about it."

He shrugged. "Eh. I should take it back. She'll never notice."

One of the dogs ran up to the entrance of the room and then stopped, skidding on his claws. He'd found a way back in. He raised his black head and cried out. And again.

"Shut the fuck up!" shouted Mick, winging the watch at the dog.

We walked down the hall ourselves, defeated.

At the front door, I turned to him. He was seventeen—old to me then. He had pale, delicate skin. The ends of his hair curled up around his ears. I thought he was going to say nothing, or shrug, or scoff, or swear, but then he said, "Alison, I'm frightened."

Kate's eyebrows lifted, as if she'd just heard something she didn't quite understand. It was beautiful in the hall at that moment, like a cathedral. Light came through the glass bricks surrounding the front door. Light danced around the surface of the darkness.

"We'll see each other again," I said, but Mick wasn't listening.

Too loudly, he said, "So did you want to see her room? No doubt it shall soon be our guest room. Too *rife with tragedy* to keep it as it is, of course." He wasn't talking to me anymore. He was talking to an audience of many, none present.

"Right." My stomach was clay, his face unbearably like and not like hers in the dark hall. "No. Not today."

"Suit yourself," he said, and opened the door. Given the right circumstances, he might have been a gentleman one day.

I walked out of the house for the last time. The Hamiltons, what was left of them, would move away within the year, and I'd never, never, never pass this way again.

Mick shut the door behind me, and I started to walk down the driveway. Past a clutch of the last basenjis, fitful and tired of freedom, wishing to get back in, back to their home, the modernist house on Glenwood, home to many a good party.

I crossed the road, and that's when I suddenly thought of something and looked back to the house. Maybe I could see Mick's face in the window, watching me.

But when I looked back, all I saw was wobbling glass, a shadow that might have been nothing. I didn't know if he was standing in the hall or not, or how long it would be before the little blue pill kicked in, or how soon his parents would come home from their newfound church that Sunday.

A car was coming, and I started to put up my thumb: a hope, a thought, a way to be cool on a summer day. But then I dropped my hand again and let the car pass.

The water must look very, very black from above, at night. It must look so black that you think it might go on quite a while, forever, a black velvet river to someplace far away. There is probably music—the sound, the rush of things. Somewhere in that noise you can hear your own breathing. Somewhere you can feel the joints in your knees, your elbows, as you pad up to the edge, as you remember something, as you forget something.

Was it an accident? Did you mean to do it, Kate?

Because it matters, our history. That's what I wanted to say.

Acknowledgments

ELLEN AND MOLLY, thank you for believing in my work. I am grateful to the University of Arizona for a grant to research history, and to Thomas J. Farnham's *Weston: The Forging of a Connecticut Town*, among other books, for interesting context from which I took many facts and some liberties. (Some of my history and all my Westonites are imaginary.) Love to my parents, and my gratitude for showing me from an early age that art was a possibility. My darling Alexandra, thank you for your amazing spirit; thank you for teaching me. Thank you, Reed, for everything, but most of all for the illuminated present day.